Until We Die

a novel

Jockie Loomer-Kruger

© 2021 Jockie Loomer-Kruger

All rights reserved. No part of this book may be reproduced or transmitted in any form or by any means, electronic or mechanical, including photocopying, or by any information storage or retrieval system, without permission in writing from the publisher.

Cover image: Rebekah Wetmore
Editor: Andrew Wetmore

ISBN: 978-1-990187-00-1
First edition November, 2021

MOOSE HOUSE
PUBLICATIONS

2475 Perotte Road
Annapolis County, NS
B0S 1A0

moosehousepress.com
info@moosehousepress.com

Robert Frost's "The Road not Taken" first appeared in his poetry collection *Mountain Interval*, published in 1916 (Boston: Henry Holt).

We live and work in Mi'kma'ki, the ancestral and unceded territory of the Mi'kmaw people. This territory is covered by the "Treaties of Peace and Friendship" which Mi'kmaw and Wolastoqiyik (Maliseet) people first signed with the British Crown in 1725. The treaties did not deal with surrender of lands and resources but in fact recognized Mi'kmaw and Wolastoqiyik (Maliseet) title and established the rules for what was to be an ongoing relationship between nations. We are all Treaty people.

In tender memory of HBK

Praise for *Until the Day We Die*

I was quite frankly hesitant about reading yet another book about a family coping with dementia...However, Jockie's story about Jenny and her husband Rudy is different. It is simply written, but with so much heart and selflessness that I just kept turning the pages. I could so clearly feel (and remember) the anger, frustration and powerlessness Jenny felt as she had to deal with the 'professionals' who at times could not be bothered or turned the other way to avoid having to deal with a 'problem' resident. But her love for her husband Rudy and her optimism and grit rose above all the obstacles they both faced.

One last thing: *Until the Day We Die* honestly addresses the often ignored sexual needs of those with dementia, a need that remains with us until the day we die.

- Karen Henderson, Independent Planning Specialist
Aging / Long Term Care, Toronto, Ontario

The great achievement of this splendid book is its depth of understanding and compassion. Jenny's love and dedication are a model for us all and the final pages come as a benediction. *Until the Day We Die* is beautifully written and relevant for these times.

- Author Janet Baker

This intimate glimpse into a long love illuminates for readers that as our bodies and minds grow old, and we move within the painful hollow space left in our hearts by something as devastating as dementia, our love for each other remains steadfast in the memories that we hold dear.

- Tara Mondou, author of *Little Girl in the Mirror*

In its pages, we encounter the vast expanse of human emotion and physical fragility and the eternal presence of Love. I miss the characters already. A stirring and inspiring read for our times.

- Rev. Catherine Crooks, Truro, NS

Jockie Loomer-Kruger does not shy away from the harsh realities of aging and loss, and the desire to still be present in the world. With crisp writing and characters that are vivid and honest, this is a tender yet clear-eyed look at the complications of an enduring relationship.

- Pamela Mulloy, Editor, *The New Quarterly*

Until the Day We Die is a poignant story of care-giving and marriage in the face of adversity....Jockie Loomer-Kruger also reveals the troubling state of for-profit Senior Care.

- Journalist Wendy Elliott, Wolfville, NS

It is a beautiful love story, yet a realistic and sad tale of those who are caught in the death trap of the dreaded and cruel grip of dementia. It also gives one an insight into how our lives can be changed by evil people and circumstances over which we have no control. It vividly portrays the difficulty of adapting to that change.

- Hattie M Dyck, author of *Best Kept Secrets*

Not-for-the-faint-of-heart, *Until the Day We Die* is a skilfully-crafted story about marriage, romance, aging, memory loss and long-lasting love....Ultimately, this novel is a tender love story for our times.

- Author Catherine Walker

This is a work of fiction. It draws on stories lived, told, heard, and imagined. From the mix emerges a new story understood through the heart of the reader. Any resemblance to real persons, living or dead, is coincidental.

The drug Triadone, which appears in this book, does not exist. Do not implore your medical professional to provide it for you or someone you love.

The remarkable device for delivering personal music, and so helpful to people with dementia, is, sadly, no longer in production.

Contents

Part One..9
Part Two..23
Part Three...77
Part Four...148
Part Five...179
Part Six...197
Part Seven..217
Epilogue..225
Acknowledgements..231
About the author..233

Jockie Loomer-Kruger

No story has power, nor will it last, unless we feel in ourselves
that it is true and true of us.

— *John Steinbeck, <u>East of Eden</u>*

Part One

When two people meet, each one is changed
by the other so you got two new people.

—*John Steinbeck, <u>The Winter of Our Discontent</u>*

Jockie Loomer-Kruger

Spring, 1983

"*The Moon is Down* is one of Steinbeck's lesser known books," a voice said.

Jenny looked up to see a tall, broad-shouldered man in beige safari jacket and matching Tilley hat, sporting a tidy ginger-tinged moustache and a carefully trimmed goatee—more blond than ginger—standing opposite her.

She slid her book onto the counter and hopped off the stool. Patted down her short navy skirt. Caught sight of herself reflected in the glass display case that showcased an assortment of vases. At forty-five she was only a few pounds more than the slender girl she'd been at nineteen. She pushed the stubborn lock of dark hair with its few threads of grey out of the way—that annoying cowlick that habitually tumbled across her forehead and over one eye.

"Good morning. May I help you with something?"

"I see you're reading Steinbeck. He wrote that book as American war propaganda, intended to encourage the resistance movement in Europe."

"Oh, that's interesting. Mr. Duggar didn't tell me that part when I bought it."

"You know Duggar?"

She nodded. She loved popping into the second-hand bookstore next door when she had someone else helping in her shop.

"A bit eccentric," the man said, "but a fount of knowledge. In fact, he found me a first edition of that book. I collect the works of Steinbeck." He paused. "Do excuse me. My name's Rudy Hoffman." He reached across the counter to shake her hand.

The introduction surprised her. So did his easy flow of words. And there was something soft and sexy about his voice. Like promised intimacy. He seemed so unlike most of her male customers, who rarely bothered with names unless there was to be a later pick-up or a floral delivery.

She met his firm grip, "I'm Jenny Allen." She pulled her hand back, the warmth of his palm still clinging to hers.

"I teach Modern American Lit at the University...but I really didn't come in to talk about Steinbeck. I'm invited for dinner tonight, and I want to take a few flowers to my hostess."

They discussed selection. He liked carnations. And chrysanthemums. He rested one hand on the counter, "What else do you have that won't be gone in three days?"

"Alstroemeria lasts well," Jenny said.

"I don't know that one."

He followed her to the other side of the room to the cooler filled with tall aluminum containers each holding a different flower variety. "Alstroemeria is a small Peruvian lily that comes in assorted shades," she said.

It surprised her to meet a man who made his own flower choices. Generally, when men came into the shop they wanted a dozen roses. Or they quoted a dollar amount and asked her to 'fix up something pretty'. Then took themselves out of the shop as quickly as possible, as though associating with flowers somehow diminished their masculinity. But not this man. He oozed testosterone even as he admired blooms.

In the end, he decided on deep pink mini carnations, yellow tiger-striped alstroemeria, and white daisy mums. Jenny added a sprig of baby's breath and two stems of fresh green leatherleaf fern, along with a trail of ivy. Wrapped the selection in clear cellophane, and tied a maroon ribbon about it. The faint cinnamon aroma from the carnations funnelled up from the bouquet as she lay it on the counter while she finished the transaction.

"Would you like a little card to go with the flowers?" She pointed to the rack of enclosure cards.

He chose one that simply said, '*Thank You*', picked up the pen lying beside the cash register and wrote, '*for your kind hospitality, Rudy*'.

He handed the card to Jenny and she slipped it into a tiny envelope. Placed it deep inside the bouquet.

No wedding ring, she noticed as he paid with his credit card. She had taken her own wedding ring off a year ago, exactly three years from the day her husband died. *After he crashed the car into the light pole near our own driveway.*

As soon as Rudy left the shop, that day came charging back.

Peter, storming out of the house, pausing with a hand fumbling at the doorknob. 'Who the hell do you think you are? Always so goddam holier than thou. Just because you don't drink doesn't mean I can't have a glass now and then.' He was half-drunk by then, and she'd known he was on his way to the liquor store.

When Rudy came to her shop again a couple of weeks later for a similar bouquet, Jenny had a well-thumbed copy of *East of Eden* sitting next to the cash register.

"Still reading Steinbeck, I see," his smile was warm, his teeth even.

"I'm guessing you have another dinner invitation."

He laughed. "And another later this week. I could be in for more, I'm afraid."

"Popular man, you are."

"Not really." He smoothed his goatee. "Seems some of the faculty wives have gone into a match-making frenzy once my divorce became final."

He bought his flowers and, indeed, came back a few days later for yet another order for yet another hostess.

This time Jenny knew exactly what kind of bouquet to put together for him in the back workroom. When she brought his purchase out for him, he looked ill at ease, drumming his fingers on the counter.

"May I ask you a personal question?" He looked seriously at her.

What penetrating eyes he has. The colour of a clear summer sky.

"Are you single?"

"Ah...that is definitely a personal question," she said lightly.

"Oh, I'm sorry. I-I-I don't mean to be rude—to pry." He shifted from one foot to the other.

His discomfort intrigued her. There was a shyness about the man that made her think of Peter the first time he had asked her to dance. How flustered he got, as though his tongue was stuck to the roof of his mouth. When she was in grade ten and he was in grade twelve. The only high school dance they'd both attended because that summer his family moved away from the Fundy Shore of New Brunswick to the Fundy Shore of Nova Scotia.

Rudy swallowed, "I don't really know how to go about this. You see, uh, well, I noticed you seem interested in Steinbeck, and you're not wearing a wedding ring, and well, if you're free, I mean unattached, we could get together to talk about Steinbeck's writing."

She felt a flutter in her stomach, "You understand, I read Steinbeck strictly for pleasure." She hoped her voice was steady. "I'm not sure I'd be able to keep up." Then she grinned. "But to answer your first question, I am unattached. Four years a widow."

"Good. No. I don't mean good that you're a widow. I'm sorry about that." He lowered his eyes, tugged at his beard. "Oh, damn. I told you I don't really know how to go about this." Then he brightened, dropped his hand to his side, "What I'm actually asking is—may I take you to dinner Sunday evening?"

Jenny could feel a smile spreading, the corners of her eyes crinkling, her cheeks flushing. "Why, thank you. Yes. I'd like that." She felt the relaxation of his responding smile, "We could meet here, at the shop, around six, Professor Hoffman, if that would work for you."

"Wonderful! But please, forget the Professor Hoffman stuff. I'm Rudy. Just Rudy."

"Rudy," she said, and the name felt welcome on her tongue. She knew her rising colour must be showing.

"Sunday at six, then." He tipped his hat the way men used to do in the old movies, and strode toward the door.

"Rudy!" she called after him. "Your flowers! You forgot your flowers."

After he'd gone she chided herself. What did she think she was doing, accepting a date with an academic?

Would it bother him to learn that she didn't have a degree? That when Peter breezed back into her life, cocky and self-assured, she'd left university to marry him? She'd believed Peter's job as a furniture company representative was only temporary. Someday, just like he promised, he would indeed own a chain of furniture stores reaching from one end of Canada to the other.

She'd intended to complete her studies before they had a family, but the children came quickly. Now the children were grown. Dave, an IT specialist in Toronto; Pam at the same Nova Scotia university where Jenny had started out.

Achieving a degree was no longer one of Jenny's goals. She'd decided years earlier her education would come from the school of life.

Jenny brushed the self-doubt aside. The only thing that really mattered right now was that Professor Rudy Hoffman appeared interested in her. And she felt attracted to him. Very. And they were planning a scholarly dinner together.

A few days later

Rudy had arrived punctually. They strolled from her shop to a charming little Italian restaurant in the next block.

Rudy helped her off with her coat, hung it on the bentwood stand near the entrance. "You're looking lovely this evening," he said, admiring the moss green dress with a modest V-neck she'd worn. "Your dress accents your eyes."

"Thank you," she said, her cheeks warming. She liked the way he looked, too. Casual in a navy suit jacket with a pale-blue turtleneck sweater. A good match with his eyes, as well.

She tossed her head, as though to flip her bouncy hair into place, but more to centre her thoughts. It bothered her that she was feeling almost as giddy as a teenager off to her first prom. After all, she and her date were middle-aged. And they scarcely knew each other. Just out to have dinner and a discussion about a favourite author.

To hold their Steinbeck conversation, they chose a table in a far corner away from other diners. When the waiter came for their order, Rudy asked about wine. Jenny's red flags fluttered. "The house wine sounds very good," Rudy said smiling at her, "shall I order a bottle for us?"

"No. No, please. I'm a teetotaller. Just ice water with lemon."

"Water with lemon for my friend, and I'll join her with water, but no lemon, please."

Jenny could scarcely believe that he had foregone wine to share her beverage preference. She felt her red flags lower, her body relax.

When the waiter left, Rudy commented, "I don't think I've ever met a *bonafide* teetotaller before, other than my mother, who didn't drink for religious reasons. Is that what governs your choice, as well?"

"No. My husband was an alcoholic. Rather than drink along with him as often happens in such cases, I chose not to drink at all." She hadn't expected to tell him about Peter so soon. He listened intently. With empathy, she felt.

"I'm not very much of a drinker, myself," he said. "I've seen too many people make idiots of themselves under the influence. I prefer to know *what* I'm doing, even if I don't always know *why*." Rudy scanned the menu. "But I do enjoy a glass of wine with dinner sometimes. And a beer now and then in hot weather."

The waiter returned to take their orders. A bruschetta appetizer to share. Stuffed eggplant for Jenny. Chicken parmesan for Rudy.

"You may be wondering about my divorce," Rudy said when the waiter left. "I still find it hard to process. To think I missed seeing the signs. That I let Adeline—Addie—struggle so long with who she really is. My wife—my ex-wife—left our marriage to be with a woman friend she'd met years before in college."

Jenny could hear the angst in his words. But didn't know exactly what to say. Instead she reached across the table and placed her hand on top of his.

"Thank you," he whispered.

Slowly she pulled her hand back. A silence fell between them punctuated by the waiter's arrival with water and the appetizer.

Marriage history was not the information she had thought they'd be exchanging so early in the evening. Since the need for small talk seemed already past, she tiptoed into something he'd already mentioned.

"You said your mother didn't drink for religious reasons…"

"My mother was very devout. An avid evangelical Lutheran. She observed a long no-no list of sinful behaviours. Consuming alcohol was near the top. I rejected her beliefs in my teens. Well before I had my first taste of beer, by the way." He chuckled.

Jenny liked his easy laugh that made her think of a brook bubbling over rocks.

"Her religious devotion extended to her minister. She idolized him." Rudy leaned back just enough that Jenny could see the light from the centrepiece candle reflected in his eyes.

She nibbled tomato-topped bruschetta as he continued.

"To her, that man was a near-perfect human being. But I detested him. He was a lanky fellow with a grizzled beard, like a three day's growth of steel wool. He liked to draw children close to him so he could rub his stubble against their smooth innocent cheeks. I hated it when he did that to me."

The repulsive mental image screwed up Jenny's face.

"I remember one day when he came to see my mother at our house. This was in Saskatoon, when I was about seven. She had me answer the door when he knocked. He was barely inside the vestibule when he grabbed my hand and pulled me toward him, bent down and scraped his prickly beard on my face. By the time my mother had removed her apron, smoothed her hair, and come to the front room, the whisker rub was finished. I remember holding onto my cheek because it felt raw and sore.

"They immediately shunted me off to the kitchen, because he'd come to talk about what I'd done in church the day before. I stood out of sight near the door jamb and listened."

Rudy paused to eat some bruschetta. She waited until he'd also had a sip of water.

"So, what terrible thing had you done in church, Rudy?"

"I'd giggled in the middle of the sermon."

"Why?"

"Because the lady sitting in front of us had catapulted forward with a huge sneeze, and her hat, with its long black ostrich feather, fell off, right onto the shoulder of the man ahead of her."

Jenny giggled.

"I couldn't stop laughing. My mother was horrified by my behaviour. She promptly escorted me outside, boxed my ears and sent me home sobbing."

"Oh, you poor, kid. So, what did your mother and the minister say about you?

"Well, my mother complained that all I ever wanted to do was play—"

"But you were only seven. That's what seven-year-olds do."

"Not in my mother's eyes. She wanted me to be serious, super-studious, like my brother, Klaus. He's five years older than I. He was an 'A' student, and always helping. Splitting kindling, hauling water from the standpipe at the end of the street to keep the water barrels full—we didn't have running water. After school he ran deliveries for a grocery store using the basket carrier on his bike. A sled in the winter."

Fascinated by his story and his ease in storytelling, Jenny didn't interrupt.

"We were poor and on relief, so what Klaus contributed helped. You see, my father had lost his job early in the Depression. He didn't get another until I was ten. My main chore was feeding the chickens in the backyard. But there was no income from that since we didn't have extra eggs to sell. The chickens were great amusement for me, though. It made me laugh to see them bob their heads when they pecked at the grain."

The waiter set their entrees in front of them.

They sampled and then Rudy continued. "What happened, that particular day, was that my mother complained about me wanting to play all the time, and how dreadful my behaviour in church had been. The minister agreed, and then he added something that made me feel as low to the ground as a dachshund's belly. 'Klaus will succeed in life. But Rudy…Rudy will never amount to anything.'"

"So you're saying you were a disappointment to your mother?"

"I always felt I was."

"But she must have been proud of you when you became a university professor?"

"She didn't live long enough to see that happen. She died at fifty-three of a stroke, still despairing for my future. And my soul."

He paused, ate for a while, before looking up thoughtfully, and off to one side, "I find it hard to believe I'm only two years younger than she was when she died." He took a sip of water. "But what about you Jenny? Was religion a significant factor in your growing up? Is it now?"

"Although I've lived in the city for years," she said, "I still think of New Brunswick as home. At heart, I'm still a country girl. We lived on a farm in a community with only one church. Baptist. I've heard that area referred to as a Bible belt. I remember there were regular revival meetings at our church. My mother was more deeply into religion than my father."

"Do you remember anything specific about your early religious training?"

"Yes, actually, I do. I must have been about nine, and my sister, Esther, was a year and a half older. There were just the two of us in our family and we were in the same Sunday School class. Our Sunday School teacher was a high schooler, the daughter of the local grocer. On this particular Sunday she informed us that Jesus was just like Mandrake the Magician in the funny papers. Only smarter."

Jenny took a sip of water before continuing, "Esther and I were both duly impressed by this comparison. We were well acquainted with the comics character with his swishing red-lined cape, his cane and top hat. We saw his amazing feats every day in the paper in black and white, and in full colour in Saturday's edition of the *Fredericton Gleaner*. But somehow the comparison didn't quite work for us, so we asked our parents, 'Is Jesus just like Mandrake the Magician, only smarter?'"

Rudy was laughing silently.

"Our father guffawed at our question, until Mum gave him 'the look'. Then he cleared his throat loudly and tried very hard to keep a straight face. Our mother wanted to know where we got such a terrible notion. So we told her. I can still hear her outrage. 'Don't you ever say that again. Either of you. Mandrake the Magician? The very idea! Oh, the ignorance of it. The sacrilege! In a Sunday school lesson, at that!' She sputtered on and on."

Rudy tilted his head back, his laughter exploding, his even teeth gleaming.

"I also have a visiting minister story," Jenny said when he'd stopped chortling.

"I love stories. Tell me."

"The previous pastor at our church, who had a new church in Moncton or somewhere, sometimes came back to visit my parents—well, I suppose, mostly to see my mother. When Esther and I were five and six or thereabouts, he'd bring us chocolate bars each time he visited. Chocolate bars were a rare treat back then. But he didn't just hand them to us when he arrived. They had to be earned. Punishment first. Then our reward."

"That sounds ominous."

"Pastor Brown had a great rollicking laugh, and as soon as my mother excused herself to the kitchen to prepare tea for him, he'd curl his finger and beckon us over to where he was sitting. He'd show us the chocolate bars in his vest pocket, then ask, 'So, who's first today?' Usually, Esther went first."

"And?" Jenny could tell Rudy was listening with interest.

"In turn, Pastor Brown would upend us over his knee, lift our skirts and spank us. Very hard. But neither of us made a peep because we knew a chocolate bar was coming. All the while, he laughed loud enough to cover the sound of the spanking. Then he'd prop us to our feet. Dole out the candy and send us off to play."

"And your mother never knew?"

"She found out. One day she had the tea ready early, and walked into the living room carrying a plate of cookies in one hand and the teapot in the other. The minute she saw me over his knee with my exposed panties and his hand raised in the air ready to wallop me, she plunked the teapot down on a side table, then threw the cookies—plate and all—right at his head."

"Good for her!" Rudy cheered.

"The cookies hit him. But the plate missed. I remember the sound of china shattering against the edge of the fireplace. I don't remember what she said to him, only that he slid me off his knees pretty fast. My mother shooed me outside to join Esther—without a chocolate bar, I might add. Of course, Pastor Brown never visited at our house again."

She paused, "I'm sure that's why all my life I've abhorred Jersey Milk chocolate bars."

"So, have you followed in your parents' religious footsteps?"

"No, to their everlasting grief—at least to my mother's. I'm not sure why I began to question their beliefs in my teens," she said, "but I did. Maybe I thought of it as being similar to no longer believing in Santa Claus—or Mandrake the Magician."

Rudy grinned.

"I'd heard enough about human reproduction that an immaculate conception sounded like a fairy tale. And I just couldn't believe that two thousand years ago anyone was magical enough to walk on water, or turn water into wine, or feed a multitude with only a few fish and loaves of bread when no one could do that now."

"A wholesale rejection?"

"Not really. I accepted Jesus' teachings about being kind, loving, forgiving, but the rest of it—the miracles, the resurrection—I simply had too many questions. Too many doubts.

"My difficulty with Al-Anon when Peter was alive had to do with the religious component of the meetings. I couldn't bring myself to declare I was powerless, let alone submissive to a higher power. Frankly, as a woman, the concept of submission incenses me."

"As it should," Rudy said. "Women are much stronger creatures than men. I have tremendous admiration and respect for women. But that's another topic. Tell me what you've done about your religious divergence."

By her late twenties, married with a son and daughter, Jenny told him, she began searching for a place to take her skepticism. She also wanted her children to garner some understanding of many religions, their common threads, their differences, and what they've historically meant, and still mean, in the world. So, offspring beside her, she ventured to her first Unitarian service.

"I'll never forget it," she said. "The minister spoke about Doubting Thomas, and the importance of asking questions. Of being wary of easy answers."

Then Rudy surprised her, "Is that what you usually do on Sundays? Meet with the Unitarians?"

"Fairly often."

"I'd like to go with you sometime. Perhaps that's a place for me, too."

She didn't respond at once. The self-invitation surprised her. Did she want to suddenly bring a man with her to the Centre? Someone she was just getting to know? *Maybe later. If later developed.*

He sensed her hesitation. "I've read somewhere," he said, "that there are two topics to be avoided when you're just getting acquainted with someone. Religion and politics. We've covered religion. Shall we tackle politics?"

"Why not?" Jenny laughed. "You first."

By then, they were into dessert, Rudy with a sumptuous serving of tiramisu, Jenny a simple scoop of chocolate gelato.

"Growing up in Saskatchewan, I got very excited by the birth of socialism in Canada. My father joined the CCF. And Tommy Douglas became my hero," he said. "What direction are your political leanings?"

"Left," she said, "probably influenced by my father. He got pretty involved in the co-op movement. He was on the board of the first credit union in our area. Likely a natural route for him to take. He was a farmer and farming requires cooperation."

During the entire unhurried meal, they never managed to get to the writings of John Steinbeck.

After dinner they ambled back to where Rudy had parked his car beside hers, in front of her flower shop. He took her hands in his, and said, "Jenny Allen, I'd like to see you again. I admire the way your mind works."

No man had ever before complimented her on her mind. It made her feel beautiful from the inside out. They had shared but one meal, but already she liked this man a lot. Seeing him again was an appealing prospect. And oh, how she hoped that on their next date he'd also kiss her.

He did. And two years later, exactly to the date when they'd first met, they married.

Jockie Loomer-Kruger

Part Two

They's times when how you feel got to be kep' to yourself.

— John Steinbeck, <u>The Grapes of Wrath</u>

Jockie Loomer-Kruger

Wednesday, December 9, 2015, early evening

The home's minibus bounces over potholes on its return from the Christmas Light Tour. Except for the thrum of the engine, relative quiet reigns.

Across the aisle from Jenny and Rudy, Harry snores, his flopped-over Santa hat bobbing with every bump. Jenny guesses that some of the other passengers behind them have also dozed off. In the seat ahead, Cheryl, the rec director, lowers her head to tend to tasks that Jenny can't see.

Jenny holds her husband's pale hand. She likes the comfort, the long-time familiarity of their intertwined fingers. He whispers to her.

"I didn't hear that, dear. What did you say?"

"I SAID, ARE YOU GOING TO HAVE SEX WITH ME TONIGHT?" His words reverberate throughout the bus.

Cheryl's shoulders jiggle. Jenny thinks she hears a suppressed snicker. But no other audible reactions reach her ears.

"Well, are you?"

"Shh. We'll talk about it when we get back. In your room. Where it's private."

"Then you're going to stay all night so we can have sex?"

My god, where has this come from all of a sudden?

"Well?"

She lets her husband's question dangle between them. "Rudy," she points through the window, "look at the decorations on that house. See those dripping lights that look like icicles? Aren't they pretty?"

"I guess so," he mutters into his snowy beard, scarcely turning his head to look. The distraction is short lived. "Jenny, you're my wife. I'm your husband. Married people have sex."

"We'll talk about it later," she checks her watch—seven-thirty. "You'll be home again soon."

His forehead wrinkles, "Where do I live?"

"In a retirement home, sweetheart. It's called Shasta House."

"Do you live there, too?"

"No, I live in a condo just up the street."

"Why don't I live with you? We're married."

How many times in the past three years has she answered that same agonizing question? "Darling," she says, hoping he will understand, knowing he probably won't, "you need more help now than I can give you. They have nurses and other people at the home who are trained to help."

"Why? What's wrong with me?"

"Your heart, for one thing."

"Oh, yes. My heart." He sucks in a breath, "I had rheumatic fever when I was nine. It damaged my heart."

She knows what will follow. His background—born in Saskatoon. German immigrant parents. His father unable to find work. The family on welfare. His mother's sporadic house cleaning jobs. His brother Klaus delivering groceries.

The story never varies. Told in the same words he used when he first dictated it to her for his book of *Rudy Stories*. Starting always with his own desire to contribute to the family coffers.

> But there weren't any jobs for a nine-year-old. And then I got sick.
>
> My legs hurt so much that one day I couldn't walk. A kid who lived on the next street went to our house and told my mother I was lying beside a caragana bush near the school. She and Klaus carried me back home. Dr. French came. He said I had to stay in bed for three months.
>
> Just before Christmas my godmother brought me an old wallpaper sample book. I made a special card for Dr. French from one of the pages. The next time he came to see me, I gave him the card.
>
> He wore little wire-rimmed glasses, and he took a hanky out of his pocket and poked it up under his glasses. He had tears in his eyes. I couldn't figure out why he felt sad.
>
> Then he went out to the kitchen. My mother always gave him two dollars when he made a visit and then he would leave. But this time, he came back into my bedroom. He handed *me* the money she had just given *him*. 'Merry Christmas, Rudy,' he said and he patted my shoulder.
>
> As soon as he was gone I called my mother to come to my room. I gave her the money. At last, I was helping our family just

as much as everyone else.

Rudy ends his tale the way it began, "I had rheumatic fever when I was nine. It damaged my heart."

"That's likely why you had a stroke."

"I had a stroke? When did I have a stroke?"

"Oh, quite a few years ago." Shortly after he retired. After she'd sold her flower shop to join him in retirement, just before they expected to go on a major trip.

She doesn't mention his dementia. The peeling away of memory, increasing loss of judgment, confusion. Unexpected behavioural changes. Like tonight. Like asking her to sleep with him after all this time.

Rudy stares out the window. Then squeezes her hand, his voice low and intimate, "So, will you? Will you have sex with me tonight?"

She doesn't answer. She can't—just can't—tell him that, along with his cognitive losses and his long-time impotence, he's also lost all bladder control. She can't say that a foggy-headed man in a soggy diaper completely lacks the appeal of a brilliant man bulging with desire in fresh cotton briefs.

"Well...will you?"

Jenny looks straight ahead, adjusts her glasses more comfortably over the bridge of her nose.

On the yellow light the bus rolls to a stop at the intersection not far from the home. She studies the snow-capped traffic lights. *Functional Christmas décor on a post*. Green, yellow, red. At least she can distract herself even if she hasn't succeeded in redirecting her husband's focus.

The light turns green. She'll try another tactic, "Look out the window, Rudy. You're almost home."

She fastens her jacket. Tucks her stubborn cascading silver wave into the fur-trimmed hood. Then she helps Rudy put on his gloves, and zip his jacket. Out of the corner of her eye she glimpses Cheryl tug on a pink knitted hat, her long blond hair flowing halfway down her back.

A wooden sign at the edge of the lawn displays Bellis-White Corporation's daisy logo. Rudy reads the sign softly, "Shasta House Retirement Home."

Jenny hears the same smooth, mellow voice she recalls from phone conversations during his teaching days. That unintentionally seductive timbre that triggered a wish to fly through the phone into his arms. Tonight, though, it triggers something else. A pressing resolve to keep him safe.

The driver sidles the bus to a stop in front the home's long, ribbed, green canvas canopy. Jenny unclips her lap belt, then undoes Rudy's. Her husband squirms his way across the seat, and she steps back to let him out in front of her, watching carefully as he maneuvers the two steps down off the bus. Poised at the bottom, Cheryl takes his elbow and guides him safely onto the asphalt, her hair blowing onto her face like the slapping strings of a car wash.

"Wait right here, Rudy." Cheryl rubs her hand down his back, "The driver will get your walker for you."

Side by side, Jenny and Rudy take shelter under the canopy tunnel that makes Jenny think of a giant caterpillar. Its clear plastic side-flaps fend off the frenzied wind that flings erratic clouds of snow. Jenny's right hand covers Rudy's left on the handle of his walker. To match his shuffling gait, she slows her pace.

He looks at her, "I love you, Jenny."

"I love you, too."

A faster moving resident catches up to them. "*Gute Nacht*," she says and moves on by.

Rudy stares at the figure striding toward the door, "Who was that? She spoke German."

Jenny explains she's a new resident. Her name is Helga.

"Helga? I don't know her, do I?"

Jenny lets the question go unanswered. She doesn't bother telling him they were introduced the afternoon before, and he got very excited to meet someone else whose first language was German.

Jenny and Rudy are the last to step in out of the cold. In a green Bellis-White smock, Dolly welcomes them, her brown skin glowing and cheeks dimpling. She has already instructed the others to wait in front of the elevators.

In her youth, squat, middle-aged Dolly immigrated to Canada from Jamaica. She's worked in senior care since she was nineteen, she once told Jenny. There's a tenderness about her that Jenny likes, and a sense of humour. She'd heard Dolly joke when a resident commented on Dolly's vivid dyed orange hair. "I used a pumpkin for a hat, and that's what happened. So, remember, never wear a pumpkin on your head." When she'd earlier dyed her hair green she told residents that's what happens when you kiss a leprechaun.

Jenny unzips Rudy's jacket. The same faint whiff of ammonia that she smelled as he got up from his seat on the bus stings her nostrils, "I'm sorry, Dolly, but I expect he's wet."

"That's okay, I'll look after it."

Why do I always apologize for my husband's incontinence? Is she embarrassed about it, or is it because she understands the work PSWs do is often unpleasant? Their rewards limited. She mulls over what she's learned about the plight of PSWs during her three years of daily visits to see her husband. Low pay. Part-time status. Too much work for too few people. She wishes those who handle resident care were better rewarded, that it didn't take three jobs to make ends meet.

Dolly winks and grins at Rudy as she nudges his walker forward to join the others waiting at the elevators. Jenny walks along beside him.

"Did you enjoy the Christmas lights, Rudy?"

"Did we see Christmas lights?" He appeals to his wife for the answer.

"Yes, lots of them. They were lovely."

"I don't remember."

"Jenny looks tired, Rudy," Dolly says. "It's time for her to go home and get some rest. You come with me, and I'll help you into your pajamas."

"I don't need any help."

"Then I'll just make sure your bed is ready to crawl into." Jenny appreciates the way Dolly avoids contradicting Rudy, even though Dolly knows he needs dressing and undressing assistance.

As an elevator door opens and the others step in, Jenny leans forward and pecks her husband on the cheek, "Goodnight Rudy, I'll see you tomorrow."

"Goodnight *mein dollink.*" The door slides shut between them.

Jenny hurries through the giant caterpillar onto the sidewalk. Gusts of wind at her back hasten her hike up the hill.

Before turning off her bedside lamp, she writes in her journal: *Tonight, out of the blue, on the Christmas light tour, Rudy asked me to go to bed with him. Repeatedly. After all the years of sexual dysfunction, all he could talk about was, sex, sex, sex. I wonder why*?

Jockie Loomer-Kruger

Thursday, December 10, early evening

It only takes a few minutes to walk the single block from her condo down the hill, past Sonnenberg's historic Button Factory district, to the paved entrance that snakes behind Shasta House to its parking lot. Then on to the loading zone in front of the protective canopy.

Windows spill light from all seven floors of the nondescript red brick building that started out forty years earlier as a modest downtown hotel. Before Bellis-White Corporation bought it fifteen years ago. Now it's promoted as an exciting, rewarding place for lively seniors to experience the pleasures of 'carefree independent retirement living'. But Jenny knows otherwise.

She ducks in under the canopy, tugs the outer door open, and steps into the glassed-in entry. The inner door opens before she can touch the handle. It's as though Nancy, the longtime receptionist, has a sixth sense about when to press the button to admit visitors.

"Evening, Jenny. Feels like it's getting colder." Nancy hugs herself against the draft that has swept in. "I've had to wear an extra sweater since the first of November. Believe it or not, long johns under my slacks, too. Brrr, every time that door opens..."

Jenny nods. "Hard to believe we're already into December, unless you're out in the cold." She doesn't stop to chat further, instead turns toward the large bevelled mirror above the table across from the reception desk. She pulls off her gloves and stuffs them into one jacket pocket; her crimson popcorn-pattern skullcap Esther had knitted go into the other.

Since she came in, her trifocals have steamed up. She takes them off to clear, setting them down beside the attendance binder. Fluffing her short silver hair, she pushes the errant lock that tumbles forward onto her forehead back to where it belongs, but seldom stays. Without her purple-rimmed glasses she can't discern the crosshatching of her cheeks, so like her mother's had been. She now has her mother's age-sagging jowls, too. And the same gold-flecked hazel eyes. Even their smiles reflect the genetic connection. That identical minor overbite.

The difference is that when her mother got old, she didn't go anywhere without her lips glossed in brilliant red. Jenny seldom wears lipstick anymore, but earrings always. Clip-ons or screw-ons, some of them rescued from her mother's jewelry box when Esther was clearing out the family home before renovating it to suit her own tastes, right after the farmland was sold.

Tonight, Jenny's earrings are squares of jade to match what she's wearing, commonly derided as an 'ugly Christmas sweater'. But she didn't choose this picture garment of a Santa with one foot inside the chimney because it was pretty. She knows Rudy will like it; and so will the others.

Her glasses transparent again, she perches them on her short, turned-up nose. Picks up the pen anchored to the top of a binder ring by a soiled string. She notes that a fairly recent move-in has signed to go by himself to Trillium Mall. *It's been such a long time since Rudy's signed himself out to do anything on his own. Not even to walk the block to their condo. He's lost his sense of direction.*

She fills in the hour, who she's here to see, and scrawls her own name: *Jenny Hoffman*.

A few steps into the main lounge she unzips her navy jacket and hangs it on the back of a nearby wooden chair. She tries not to breathe deeply, to give herself time to get used to the smell of disinfectant and air freshener that attempts to mask lingering hints of urine.

Jenny spots Rudy at the far end of the room near the fireplace, with the regulars. He's in one of the twin turquoise wing chairs, his head lowered to focus on the newspaper he has spread in front of him. Each time she sees him with the paper, she marvels. Literature. Reading. Those were her husband's mainstays. She's so glad he can still read. So many with cognitive impairment lose that ability. *What dementia robs from one, it leaves intact in another.*

She tiptoes to the side of his chair. Leans over and plants a kiss on the top of his bald head. A remnant of the spaghetti he had for supper dries in his wavy white beard. From her slacks pocket, Jenny pulls out a facial tissue, flicks the supper sample into the tissue, scrunches it, and feeds it to her pocket.

Looking up at her, Rudy seems surprised to see her, "Jenny! You came!"

"I always come to see you, Rudy. Every day I come to see you."

He hesitates, folds up his newspaper, "I guess you do. I forget sometimes."

She drags the other wing chair next to his and greets the others. He reaches for her hand, looks at her the way she remembers when she used to tell him, 'You're looking at me with bedroom eyes, Rudy Hoffman.'

He whispers, "So, did you come to have sex with me?"

"Is that why you think I'm here?"

"I hope so. Is it?"

"Actually, I thought we could all talk about Christmases from when we were young. You always liked Christmastime. Don't you think that would be fun, Rudy?"

"I guess so." He sounds deflated. "If that's what you want."

She squeezes his hand. "We can just sit here and hold hands while we wait until everyone is ready to tell Christmas stories."

She glances at the others gathered near the fireplace. Harry, a former bank manager in his early seventies, sports the same furry Santa hat he'd worn on the bus tour. Harry seldom wears his too-loose upper dentures. His salt and pepper moustache, which curves almost into his mouth, needs trimming. Mansplayed, he slouches on one of the matching tan loveseats that flank the grey brick fireplace. The zipper on his trousers has inched down. Off-key, he warbles, "Jingle bells, jingle bells..."

Opposite, separated by an oversized square fabric-covered ottoman, Florence and Colette sit side by side. Jenny isn't close enough to know whether Florence smells strongly of body odour tonight. Florence often forgets to shower. Sometimes Jenny gently reminds her that today is a good day for a shower, and Florence always thanks her, explaining that she can't smell things anymore.

Tonight, to a non-listening audience, Florence is retelling her favourite story, her fingers absently combing through her permed white hair.

"I grew up in Nova Scotia. Right beside the Atlantic Ocean. In the winter the ice come right in on shore. And the seals was on it. Us kids, we'd go out on the ice. We liked to play with the baby seals. Then my grandfather, he'd see us out the front window, and he'd come down to the beach with his cane. He'd yell at us. Shake his cane. Tell us to leave them baby seals alone and get off the ice. And when we got back to the beach he'd sit on a big rock, tell us to line up, and he'd spank us. Every one of us. Didn't matter whose kid you was, Grandpa whoopped every one of us." She chuckles, but no one joins her laughter.

Colette, with tiny burnt umber eyes and long nose, rests her hands on the top of her stomach that bulges like an eighth-month pregnancy. She's from a small town in Quebec. Her husband's dead and she has no children. A niece, who never visits, has power of attorney.

Colette abhors the Catholic Church. Jenny remembers what Colette told her shortly after she moved in: 'Albert, my fiancé, wasn't Catholic, and we wanted to get married at city hall. But my parents said I could only get married in the church. The priest said he wouldn't marry us unless I told everyone I was pregnant. I was still a virgin. But I lied and said I was pregnant because I wanted to marry Albert. I never went to church again after the wedding. Never. Ever.'

She had shared that story a year and a half ago. Since then, Colette's cognition has plummeted. Tonight, she stares at the backs of her hands. Traces the raised blue veins with her fingers, first on one hand, then the other. Pokes at the profusion of brown age spots on her translucent skin. "Old. My hands are old," she mutters to no one in particular. "My hands are old."

The gas flames lick artificial logs. Harry's song peters out. A hush settles into the fireplace alcove.

"So how *is* everyone tonight?" Jenny asks without expecting answers. "Harry, you look all ready for Christmas." She stands. "So am I. Do you like my sweater?"

"I hope Santa doesn't get stuck in that chimney. He has a pretty big belly," Rudy says.

Harry sits up straight on the loveseat. "I like your sweater. It's lovely."

"Oh yes, it's as pretty as can be," Florence adds.

Colette turns her hands over, then back again.

As she often does, Jenny nudges the residents into recollections. "It won't be long now until Christmas. I was wondering, when you were little, did you hang up a stocking on Christmas Eve?"

Memories tumble like an overturned barrel of apples. "We didn't have a fireplace," Rudy volunteers. He tells of hanging a stocking at the end of his iron bedstead. Of his excitement in the morning when he found a tangerine in the toe of his sock.

Florence remembers hard candies. Striped humbugs and a clear red barley candy shaped like Santa Claus. And a fragile celluloid kewpie doll with pink and blue feathers, just like the ones you could win at the fair. When she saw the feathers sticking out of the top of her stocking, she thought Santa had brought her a dead bird and she sat down on the floor and bawled.

Harry got a new rolled-up scribbler that had the multiplication tables printed on the back. He liked numbers. He was good at arithmetic.

Jenny's surprised when Colette joins in.

"My father was carpenter. We had a big family. I was the youngest. He made something special for every one of us. He made me my very own little rocking chair."

Harry laughs, "You can't put a rocking chair in a stocking!"

Oblivious, Colette repeats, "My father was carpenter...." She notices her hands, "Why are my hands so old?"

Jenny spots a slim, dark-haired woman, stylish in a tailored ruby pantsuit and holding a colorful aluminum cane, standing near the coffee machine. Watching. Listening. Jenny recognizes her as the newest Shasta House resident.

"Hello Helga," Jenny calls, "would you like to join us? We're talking about Christmases when we were children."

"*Nein, nein,*" Helga says sharply, "no *Weihnachten* then."

Rudy leans forward, "That's German. '*Weihnachten*' is 'Christmas'."

Helga doesn't hear him. She has already wheeled around and strode purposefully toward the twin elevators at the other side of the room.

"Perhaps her Christmases were in Germany during the war," Jenny says to herself, as the newcomer disappears into one of the elevators.

Talk resumes. Memories of school Christmas concerts, the janitor who wore a gauze mask with a ragged cotton beard and handed out gifts from under a tree at the front of the community hall. Florence recalls desperately needing to pee when on stage, forgetting her lines, as her long beige ribbed stockings darkened with an urgent, embarrassing trickle.

A red sled with metal runners thrilled Harry one Christmas. Jenny adds memories of steamed puddings that her mother made every year, and Florence tells of sneaking into the pantry and gorging on brandy-laced sugary hard sauce. "Boys, oh boy, was I some sick!"

Even before she sees her, Jenny smells the clinging cigarette smoke as Charlene, a recently-hired personal support worker, barges into the scene. Vigorously chewing gum, Charlene flicks her mousy ponytail, and blares, "Okay you guys, gotta break up the party. Time for beddy-byes."

She cajoles the three closest to the fireplace to their feet and skedaddles them off toward the elevators.

Rudy leans forward and yawns, "I want to go to bed now, too."

Jenny caresses the edge of his beard—his full white beard, not the trim tawny goatee of teaching days. "Wait there a minute until I get your walker." She fetches it from behind the loveseat Florence and Colette have just vacated.

In his room, Jenny guides him to the bathroom. "I'll call someone to come help you get ready for bed, Rudy."

"Don't, Jenny. Please don't. You know what I look like naked. Only my wife should see my penis."

"It's okay, Rudy. Really. The women who help are only getting you out of wet underwear and into clean pants." Jenny steadies him as he steps out of his sopping protective briefs, "They're like nurses. They see lots of men with their pants off. It doesn't turn them on at all. They just want the other men, and you, to be dry and comfortable."

"Why do I wet my pants, Jenny? I don't mean to."

"It's from the drugs, Rudy. You're on a very strong diuretic. It makes you pee a lot." She wraps her arm around his waist and squeezes, "And it's truly okay. You don't need to be embarrassed. The staff understands."

With the familiarity of years together, she washes his bottom and genitals, helps him into a dry Depend and pyjamas, "Now, how about washing your face and hands and cleaning your teeth?"

He does the rest of the bedtime routine himself, and she takes his arm as he pads in bare feet to his bed, sits on the edge and waits for her to lift his legs up onto the mattress.

"You're going to stay all night, aren't you? Stay and have sex?" His tone is plaintive.

She doesn't answer, instead, she poses a distraction. "A story tonight Rudy, or a poem?"

He wants a poem. She picks his worn Robert Frost from his bookshelf. His eyes close. From his pillow, he recites each word of the first verse with her.

> Two roads diverged in a yellow wood
> And sorry I could not travel both
> And be one traveler, long I stood
> And looked down one as far as I could
> To where it bent in the undergrowth

She draws a breath before continuing.

He opens his eyes, reaches a hand toward her. "Have our roads diverged, Jenny?"

Surprised by his question, she clasps his hand. "I think we're still travelling together, Rudy."

He closes his eyes again, listening in silence to the lulling cadence of the remembered words.

> Then took the other, as just as fair…

Jockie Loomer-Kruger

By the time Jenny reads the final three lines he is asleep.

> Two roads diverged in a wood, and I—
> I took the one less traveled by,
> And that has made all the difference.

She closes the book and wonders what they'll yet find on their road less travelled. And what kind of difference will it make?

Jenny pulls the blankets up under his chin, touches the tip of his nose with her finger and whispers, "I love you, Rudy Hoffman." Then silently returns the book to its shelf.

Downstairs, she gathers her jacket, zips up, and signs herself out. Nancy is not at her desk to release the door, so Jenny pokes the code into the pad near the sign-in table. It has been a good evening.

Leisurely, she wends her way up the hill to home. At the top of the gentle incline she waits for the light to change, then crosses the intersection to the burlap-wrapped bayberry hedge that fronts her condo building.

It's eight o'clock.

Friday, December 11, early afternoon

Jenny checks Rudy's activity schedule in her datebook. Today there will be an entertainer at Shasta House. She won't attend. She finds that particular karaoke singer—a bi-weekly regular at the home—quite unenjoyable. But Rudy doesn't seem to mind being corralled with others to the lounge to listen to country and western songs, and a spiel of commentary delivered at racehorse speed. Far too fast for her, or probably any of the residents, to catch what the man is saying.

She loads the dishwasher, sadness pushing itself under her eyelids. Rudy never cared for country music, but he did like folk—Pete Seeger, Joan Baez. Mostly, though, it was classical. Live concerts by the Sonnenberg City Orchestra.

In the living room she picks up the remote, finds the baroque Stingray channel and flops into her rose-coloured recliner. She raises an imaginary glass, lifts her chin, "Here's to the music you really loved, Rudy."

Lowering her arm and her head, she sighs, "Oh, my darling Rudy, how you've changed!" The Bach organ crescendo drowns out her other words, "How I miss the man you used to be."

She remembers holding hands during concerts. It was an important part of the whole experience, to be loving each other while they loved the music together. At least that hasn't changed. He's still a hand holder. Whenever they sit together at the home; if they go for a walk. Their hands always touching, even as he pushes his walker.

She wishes he could still operate a CD player. The music the rec director chooses for the sound system in the lounge is always the same. Big band. Swing era. Elvis Presley. Loud. Cheryl never offers classical. As though that kind of music might upset someone's sensibilities. Jenny has read that quiet baroque music is recommended for people with dementia. She sighs again.

The sky has begun to darken when Jenny leaves the condo. The streetlights are already on. Each replica Victorian lantern dropping a pool of golden glow at the base of its standard.

She finds Rudy in the nearly-empty lounge. He sits in the middle of the sofa, a woman beside him.

Jenny recognizes the German lady from three nights ago. Today the new resident sports throwback black, plastic-rimmed glasses, embedded with rhinestones in the corners. She's smartly dressed in the same ruby pant suit she wore before. Her lipstick matches her outfit, and just the right amount of powder blurs the wrinkles on her cheeks. Oval earrings repeat the colour of her clothes. Against the arm of the sofa her multi-coloured metal cane forms a protruding triangle with the piece of furniture and the mottled grey-and-brown carpet.

Jenny notes the cane's an easy tripping hazard for anyone coming around the corner of the snack bar. She'll move it out of the way before someone bumps into it.

Slipping off her jacket, Jenny drapes it over the arm of the sofa. "Hi, my love. Looks like there's room for one more here." She sinks down beside her husband, brushes his cheek with a kiss, takes his hand and squeezes it.

He turns to her and smiles. "You came to see me. I like it when you come to see me, *mein dollink*."

"Every day, Rudy. I come every day to see you."

Then, to the new lady, "Oh, excuse, me. We met before, but let me introduce myself again. I'm Jenny. Rudy's wife. You'll see me around here a lot."

She's surprised when Rudy interjects, "This is Helga. She speaks German."

Interesting...he remembers <u>her</u> name. Rudy has never called anyone else here by name. Not even Florence or Colette or Harry who became his tablemates five months ago when the mealtime seating rosters changed. Nor does he remember the names of any of the others he's shared meals with since he moved in three years ago. *How very strange that he knows this woman's name.*

Rudy elaborates, "Helga is my new friend."

Over the years, Jenny had come to accept Rudy's preference for the company of women. A preference that in no way threatened their own relationship. She knew and cherished that he was a devoted and faithful husband. Just as he'd been during his first marriage.

Helga says something in German to Rudy, and as their comments continue in words Jenny doesn't recognize, she remembers how he'd long ago explained his appreciation for women. 'Men can be so arrogant. We think we know how to solve all the political and economic problems of the world. Or we want to talk about cars, or investments, or pretend to be wine connoisseurs when we only care which kind makes us tipsy. Or, what bothers me most of all, we denigrate women. I say *we* but I don't include myself. I have far too much respect for women. Unlike most men, women know, and understand, *life*.'

In the back of her head she'd wondered if those were the only reasons. Could there be a subconscious fear, dating back to when his adored brother Gerhard died when Rudy was five?

He hadn't told her about that brother until she and Rudy had been seeing each other for over a month. And when he did, she could hear the pain of the child in the voice of the man.

Gerhard was almost three years older than Rudy, but the two were inseparable. Playing catch with a sponge rubber ball, teasing the chickens, digging roads in the backyard with a stick to run their toy cars on—cars their father made from blocks of wood with empty thread spools cut in two for wheels. On winter nights in their shared bed the two brothers snuggled close to keep each other warm. They told sillies to each other and giggled in the darkness.

When Gerhard got sick and went to hospital, Rudy didn't understand his mother's long hours away from home. Or her tearful pleading prayers during after-supper devotions. He didn't understand why Klaus was always grouchy, and why he told Rudy to stop pestering him to read stories. To go out and play with the chickens. Or why his father was seldom home. Was his father going more often to scavenge at the city dump? He didn't know his father was also at Gerhard's hospital bedside.

When the tubercular meningitis raged beyond medical rescue, Gerhard died. Rudy couldn't understand why his brother, his best friend, had abandoned him.

Throughout their years together, Rudy described his family to Jenny as being just two boys, himself and Klaus. Even when she gathered Rudy's childhood stories, shortly after he moved into Shasta House, she found that what he said about Gerhard was brief.

> I had another brother. His name was Gerhard. He was almost three years older than I was. He died when I was five. I liked to play with him. We used to hold hands and run together out on the prairie. We scared the grasshoppers and they rose up into the air like a black cloud ahead of us.

Jenny wondered if the death of Rudy's closest early-teen friend in a drowning accident hadn't cemented an unacknowledged fear of loss should he form deep friendships with other men. But she let Rudy believe she accepted what he had convinced himself were his valid reasons for preferring women for friends.

She glances at Rudy and Helga, wonders if she should interrupt their conversation to include her, but decides what they're talking about is part of their getting acquainted. Important groundwork for friendship.

She stands and steps behind the sofa to the snack bar. Presses the spigot on the water dispenser and fills a glass half full. With the first sip she drifts off into the bonds that evolved between Rudy and her special women friends. Women she'd met when her children were young, or through her flower shop.

Closest, and with the longest history, were the Lavender Ladies. Three of Jenny's dearest; a teacher, nurse, and legal secretary. The four friends had nicknamed themselves when they'd all, coincidentally, appeared for a luncheon date wearing purple. Most often, in retirement, it became the Lavender Ladies plus Rudy, as the three—by then widowed or divorced—Jenny *and* Rudy celebrated birthdays together, threw impromptu potlucks at one another's homes, and shared the joys and sorrows of their lives. It was apparent early on that her friends liked and trusted Rudy. And she liked and trusted him with them.

Rudy and Helga seem unaware that she's no longer sitting with them as they continue to speak his first language. Jenny takes another swallow of water and recalls how, when Rudy first moved into Shasta House, many of her women friends came regularly to visit him. But gradually the visits dwindled, then stopped altogether when conversation floundered. When he could no longer follow their thoughts on life.

Two of the Lavender Ladies have died. Jenny wishes she had time to see Ivy, the retired legal secretary, more often. Of course, if she did they would now be the Lavender Ladies minus Rudy.

The flow of German subsides. Jenny leaves the water glass on the counter and hurries back to the couch.

"It sounds like you and Rudy have lots to talk about, Helga," she says, standing next to the newcomer's cane. "Now, I hope you don't mind if I move your cane just a little bit, so nobody trips over it."

Helga shrugs. "Move it if you want to. I don't need it. But *mein Sohn* tells me to use it."

Jenny relocates the cane close beside Helga. "A cane can be very helpful. My husband used one for a long time before he got a walker."

Helga lifts one shoulder and the corner of her mouth twists, almost like a sneer.

"I hope you'll like living here" Jenny says as she re-seats herself beside her husband.

"I hate it. I want to go home. *Mein Sohn* made me come here. I don't know why." Helga purses her red mouth, and glances sidelong at Rudy. "But *dein Mann* is very nice. I like *him*." Rudy nods and smiles slightly. "He speaks German. I speak German. *Sprechen Sie Deutsch?*"

Jenny guesses she's been asked if she also speaks German. "Only the one phrase Rudy taught me." She winks at Rudy, wraps her fingers around his. "*Ich liebe Dich*. There, did I say it right?"

"Almost," Rudy grins, "and I love you, too." He turns to look at her, their gaze arcing like cloud-to-cloud lightning.

Jenny revels in the firm pressure of their clasped hands. For a moment there is no sound.

Then she clears her throat, "You'll have to excuse us now, Helga. It's almost time for supper. Rudy and I are going up to his room to get ready."

Helga lifts her fingers from her lap in a modest farewell. "*Auf Wiedersehen*, Rudy."

After supper, Rudy issues yet another invitation to join him in bed. Offering him a magazine, Jenny is able to distract him, and leaves him sitting in his overstuffed blue power-lift chair, deeply engrossed in reading reminiscences of prairie pioneers in *Folklore*.

On her walk home, she ponders again his recurring spikes of interest in resuming a sex life with her. And deep in her gut, she wishes it was possible. She cannot deny it's a part of their life that she also misses. And has missed for a very long time.

At bedtime, she writes in her journal: *Rudy has identified Helga as his new friend—the first friend he's actually made at Shasta House. Friendships are so important to one's well-being. I hope this one enriches his altered life.*

Jockie Loomer-Kruger

Sunday, December 13, mid-afternoon

It's three o'clock when Jenny arrives at Shasta House. No resident activities are scheduled for the afternoon. Rudy is in his room, in his big chair, beside the window that looks out over the parking lot. He concentrates on the weeks-old *Maclean's* magazine he holds in front of him.

The sound of the door snapping shut shifts his focus and he glances in her direction. "Hello, *mein dollink.*"

"Hello, yourself." She smiles as she removes her coat and tosses it on the bed, pulls off her boots, and retrieves the pink slippers she keeps in his closet. "How's my best buddy today?"

"Pretty good. Much better, now that *my* best buddy's here."

She takes the few steps from the closet to his chair and kisses the top of his head.

He looks up at her. "How about a real kiss?" She bends over and kisses him softly on the mouth. His hand cups her breast. "Are you here to have sex with me?"

Gently, she pushes his hand down and steps back. *Déjà vu.*

Yesterday she readily distracted him, first with a game of Scrabble—it still amazes her that he's able to play their favourite game, albeit more slowly, and leaving all the scoring to her—then a visit to the snack bar in the lounge for coffee and a chocolate chip cookie.

Before leaving for home she had seen him settled contentedly in his preferred chair near the fireplace, with a three-day-old newspaper across his knees. She assumed he'd also spend time before supper talking with his new friend Helga, who had wandered in just before Jenny left. She'd seen Helga seat herself primly in the chair next to his.

Today's distraction, however, lies on the top shelf of the low bookcase next to his recliner. "Actually, I came to hear one of your stories." She passes him the green binder full of printed memories.

For a moment he studies the cover. *RUDY STORIES by Rudy Hoffman* above an enlarged black-and-white snapshot of a little freckle-faced boy wearing a floppy pork-pie hat, saggy sweater, woollen breeches, and laced boots. Young Rudolph sitting on the front steps of the humble Hoffman home in Saskatoon.

"That's me. I had a lot of freckles." He opens the book. "Which story do you want me to read?"

It really doesn't matter to Jenny. Having heard all of his stories so often, she knows most of them by heart. "You choose, while I get the folding chair out of the closet."

Close to his recliner, she opens the black metal chair and sits. He methodically searches through the pages for what appeals to him today.

Although he still likes to read to her, more and more often he now asks her to read to him. She laughs to herself about the first time she read one of his stories aloud to him. A tale about his father's frequent trips to the city dump, commonly known as 'the nuisance grounds.' Forays to see what Mr. Hoffman could salvage, repair, and make work for his family, including most of Rudy's few toys.

When she'd finished the story, Rudy's voice rang with amazement. "You know, that's exactly right. That's exactly the way it was."

Of course, it was, she thought, feeling pleased that she'd collected his stories when she had. *All the stories are in his very own words*.

Today he has found his cat story.

> One day, when I was about four, a kitten strayed into our backyard. I wanted it to stay, so I got pieces of kindling that my father had chopped, and I pounded the sticks into the ground with my father's hammer. I made a little round yard for the kitty. Then I lifted it inside the fence. Now it was mine. It meowed at me.
>
> I thought it must be hungry so I went into the house and looked for something to feed it. All I could find was a slice of dry bread. I thought the bread was too hard for a little kitty to eat, so I chewed it to make it soft. But when I offered it to my new pet, it wouldn't eat it. Instead it jumped over the kindling fence and ran away. I was very sad.

Rudy closes the book and hands it to Jenny to put back. "I always wanted a calico. But just before I went off to university, I developed an allergy to cats. They make my eyes itchy and my nose runny."

More talk of cats, and she takes the box of coloured felt cut-outs and flannel board from his shelf. "The cats in here don't bother you, though, do they? I wonder what kind of picture you can make today?"

She places the binder-size board on his lap, and the open box of assorted figures on the wide arm of his chair.

First, he sticks two clouds onto the top blue section of the board along with a couple of red birds in flight. Then lifts out a tree form, and centres it as though it were growing from the lower green half of the background. Next, an orange cat climbs up the trunk. Additional cats soon peer out from branches. "This one's really acrobatic," he says, hanging a tabby by its tail from a limb. Jenny laughs.

"Oh, oh, the black cat wants a mouse." Rudy grins. "He's the best mouser ever." He attaches a grey mouse near the base of the tree with the black cat close on its tail.

When all the cats in the box are situated, he pushes the board from his lap to his knees, "Done."

Jenny gathers up his game. "Would you like to go down to the lounge for a cup of coffee and a cookie now?" Rudy nods and she brings his walker to him.

As on the day before, she leaves him near the fireplace, newspaper in hand. On her way out she spies Helga, elegantly dressed in a black pleated skirt, high-necked pink blouse and black bolero jacket, stepping out of an elevator. Jenny waves, thinking as she does that Helga must have been strikingly beautiful when she was younger, for she's a most attractive older woman.

As Jenny tramps the gentle incline toward home, Helga vaporizes from her thoughts. She replays her afternoon with Rudy, the pleasure he had playing with the flannel board game, something a five-year-old child would enjoy, contrasted with the smooth way he read his story. Struck again at how remarkable it is, considering the depth of his dementia, that he's still able to read. He looks at newspapers and magazines these days, but never opens a book anymore. Not even the few thumbed Steinbeck novels in his bookcase.

Jenny remembers standing in the doorway of his study, watching him, admiring his deep concentration. Several books open on his desk, his computer screen showing additional printed material, his head down making notes for another research paper on the works of Steinbeck—the author they considered *theirs*.

Two weeks ago, when they were doing one of the simple quizzes she devises for him, she asked him to name three prairie animals, three streets in Saskatoon, three kinds of fruit. Then added a new category. Name three favourite authors.

He reeled off answers to the first categories with ease. For a moment he paused before tackling the last. With a grin he answered, "Frank Baum. He wrote *The Wizard of Oz*. My favourite book when I was young."

"Do you have any other favourite authors, Rudy?"

Silence. He looked toward the ceiling as though mentally reaching to tether a drifting-away helium balloon, then shook his head. "No. That's the only one I know."

John Steinbeck, the author they'd fallen in love over, was now the author he'd forgotten.

Jockie Loomer-Kruger

Sunday, December 13, late afternoon

Jenny unlocks her condo door. Snaps on the foyer light and takes off her outerwear. In the kitchen she turns on the electric kettle and fills a mug with boiling water. She swishes a teabag around in it, lifts the soggy bag out by its string and tosses it into the garbage can in the cupboard below the sink. As she places her steaming drink on the kitchen table and slides onto a chair, it surprises her to feel tension squeezing the back of her neck.

Why am I feeling so uptight? The afternoon, after all, went well. She had successfully distracted Rudy. Why this tightness creeping from neck to scalp?

It has to be Shasta House. Every day. Shasta House. Sometimes it's as though she lives there instead of in her own place. She knows residents and staff better than she knows the people she's lived beside in the condo for the past seven years. She has scarcely any time for friends, or to sandwich in medical appointments for herself, or even do the grocery shopping. How long since she's visited the library? Or been to the art gallery?

Sometimes she wishes she could just have her own life back. Have time to read. To paint. To take a bus into Toronto to see her grandchildren. Fly to Nova Scotia to visit her daughter. Find her way back to the old homestead in New Brunswick for time with her sister.

She sucks in her lips. "Damn you, Shasta House," she mutters as she pounds her fist on the table. Tea splashes out of her cup and she sops it up with a paper serviette. She scolds herself. How can she even think such selfish thoughts?

Freed-up time will come. Too soon.

For now, she'll follow Ellen's advice.

Two days before the bus tour, the stout, relatively-new head nurse referred to as the 'Director of Wellness' had called Jenny into her office.

"Have a seat, Mrs. Hoffman." Ellen pointed to the wooden arm chair in front of her desk as she edged around to the kneehole side and lowered herself into her high back leatherette chair, "Would you care for a chocolate?" She pushed a box of gold wrapped candies across her desk.

"No, thanks."

"Hope you don't mind if I have one. These are too good to resist."

"Is there something wrong with Rudy that I need to know about?"

Ellen pulled a tissue from the box on her desk. Wiped her lips and swallowed the last taste of the chocolate she'd so obviously relished. "No, no. The problem is that Shasta House is basically an independent living facility."

Jenny furrowed her brow. *The whole fourth floor is dedicated to residents who need major assistance.* Most of them with Alzheimer's or other forms of deepened dementia. What was Ellen getting at?

"Rudy is requiring more help than our PSWs have time for. His incontinence is extreme. He's not able to dress and undress himself. My girls are very nervous about him trying to take a shower on his own. I know you help him with showers, but sometimes he tries to do it by himself. He should be having supervised baths now. Of course, you know when staff have to handle bathing it's an extra charge. The fact is that they just don't have time to look after all his needs."

Of course they don't. The facility is so blasted understaffed. "So how can I help matters?" Jenny asked. She knew she could do something about the shower problem—maybe put his laundry basket in the end of the shower stall. Keep the plastic curtain pulled most of the way to hide the faucet and showerhead.

Ellen sifted through pages in an open file on her desk, "I see here that you have him connected with Community Care Access Centre."

Jenny nodded, "He's had a caseworker with CCAC since he was first diagnosed with dementia. The memory clinic that monitors him set things up for him. Well before he moved into Shasta House."

Ellen unwrapped another chocolate, popped it into her mouth. Her words slurred as she chewed. "I don't see that he's been placed on a waitlist for a nursing home..."

"I'm not sure why that information isn't there. I told the charge nurse that he was registered for long-term care." *That's too important not to be in his file.* "He's been on the CCAC list for sixteen months."

"Do you know what number he is now, on the list?"

"When he was first added he was number twenty-seven. The next assessment moved him up to fifteen. Last spring, he was number six."

That was when Ya Ping, his caseworker, advised Jenny to check out nursing homes in the city. She'd visited seven. And decided on five that could potentially work for Rudy, and for her. Parker Place became her first choice.

The sixty-five-person facility, only ten blocks from her condo, set back from the street, with a broad front lawn, is conveniently near to a shopping plaza she frequents for groceries. Most rooms at Parker Place are private, no four-to-a-room like she'd seen in most of the homes.

She found the three-story. family-owned-and-operated nursing home clean, odour-free, and with a vibe of true caring.

Staff interactions with residents appeared patient and understanding. She appreciated that staff were assigned to a single floor, giving residents a sense of continuity. That each floor had its own dining room. That a registered nurse supervised each floor, both day and night. That a doctor visited each patient weekly, and for emergencies, was always on call.

It pleased her greatly to know all staff at Parker Place were full time employees, with no chance of contagions being carried from another facility to this one.

Not like Shasta House with part-timers doing shifts at three Bellis-White facilities, or elsewhere. Carrying infections back and forth, so that every winter a worn cardboard sign would appear on the main door: *OUTBREAK - No Visitors until Further Notice*

Just to be sure, she visited Parker Place twice more. Each time what she saw, heard, smelled and learned from answers to her questions, assured her that this would be the best location for Rudy.

"Number six, you say? That's encouraging to hear, Mrs. Hoffman."

"His caseworker came to see him two weeks ago, but I haven't heard back from her yet. I don't know how close he is to the top now."

"Perhaps in the next little while you can find out. We like to keep his file up to date. Of course, other than the physical demands he puts on staff, he's a very easy resident. Cooperative and pleasant. He has a very agreeable temperament. The staff describe him as a true gentleman."

She paused to again wipe her lips. "Sure you won't have a chocolate, Mrs. Hoffman? They're awfully good."

Peeling the wrapper off Ellen's treat, Jenny left the office.

Now, Jenny pulls the wine cable stitch afghan her sister knitted over her lap and flips the nuisance lock of hair off her forehead. Ellen *is* right. He is getting to be too much for the retirement home to care for. But until he's moved closer to the top of the long-term care list, or he has a medical emergency that hospitalizes and debilitates him to where they won't or can't take him back at Shasta House, where else *can* he live?

She picks at a piece of lint on the afghan. Sooner or later he'll qualify

as number one for nursing home placement.
 For end-of-life care.
 I'll call Ya Ping first thing Monday morning.

Jockie Loomer-Kruger

Sunday, December 13, early evening

After a bowl of split pea soup and a kitchen clean-up, Jenny retreats to the living room. *Maybe there's something on TV.* She flops into her recliner, grabs the lever on the side of the chair to ease it back and lift her feet.

Her thoughts are still with Rudy and retirement home living. The cliché she hears far too often pops into her head. *It is what it is.* She reminds herself that it's not all dismal.

She draws a deep breath, her mind turning to her volunteer time with Shasta House residents over the past three years. It's easy for her to engage residents, and usually it's fun dipping into their collective nostalgia. Hearing their stories. Some, over and over again, of course. Like Florence and the seal pups.

Jenny knows what it was like for most of them growing up in the 1930s, 40s, 50s. She can guide them to those memories. To the schoolyard games they played—Red Rover, Flying Dutchman, London Bridge, pick-up baseball.

They all relate to memories of fresh homemade bread with molasses. Some to sleigh rides. Hand-me-down clothes. Wiener roasts. Bed sheets fresh from the clothesline. Edgar Bergen and Charlie McCarthy on the radio. Frank Sinatra.

Mothers saying, 'Come home when the streetlights come on.' Childhoods with abundant freedom, so different from today with helicopter parenting.

It's not unusual to hear tales of family hardship, resilience and ingenuity during the Great Depression and World War II. Stories sometimes told with bobbing Adam's apples. Or tears.

"Rudy tells me you paint, Jenny," Cheryl had commented one day following a session of trivia the rec director had led with a group in the lounge. Questions gleaned from the internet, intended for Americans, anchored in an era too close to the present for many to relate to.

"I do some watercolours," Jenny said.

"You're here a lot, so I was wondering if you'd like to help with the art program for residents. It's a handful when I'm trying to deal with ten or more people at a time. Maybe, too, if you're involved, Rudy will come for art sessions."

"Let me think about it."

A few days later Jenny was at the art table, helping residents protect their clothes with men's old dress shirts worn backwards. Doling out blobs of air-drying modelling clay. Washing paint brushes. Removing caps from markers when arthritic hands couldn't do it.

She found it fascinating to watch creativity bloom through art. So much of what residents produced reminded her of her own children's, and grandchildren's, renderings that she'd so proudly displayed on her refrigerator door. Residents, she noticed, were equally non-critical, and as fully satisfied with their efforts as children were.

Rudy, who'd not wanted to be part of the art group prior to Jenny's involvement, did as Cheryl thought he might, and came to the sessions. And Jenny delighted in his new-found pleasure.

It was Rudy, though, who recruited Jenny to read stories to residents after supper by the fireplace. Perhaps he was remembering how the two of them had enjoyed reading to each other in front of their own fireplace in the fieldstone house, before they moved to the condo.

Once she brought flowers and slender milk glass vases and helped residents make simple arrangements for the dining room. In the middle of each table, two carnations and a sprig of baby's breath.

Martha pops into Jenny's head. Frail and quiet, Martha lived on the fourth floor with those needing additional care. She was the only one left at her table, her head nodding, waiting for a PSW to come wheel her back to her room. Jenny, waiting for Rudy to finish his tea, watched Martha absently.

Suddenly, Martha's thin arm stretched forward and she picked up the vase, brought the carnations to her nose, and sniffed. At that moment, Charlene arrived to take Martha back to her floor. Whisking the vase from the old woman's hand and recentering it on the table, Charlene tossed laugh-edged words toward Jenny, "Now don't that just beat all? A hundred-and-two years old and she still wants to smell the flowers!"

Charlene turned the wheelchair away from the table and pushed Martha toward the elevators. Jenny swallowed the lump that had risen unbidden in her throat.

Lately, though, Jenny volunteers less of her time to other Shasta House residents. Rudy prefers to spend more time in his room. Seems to want to keep himself apart from other residents. Prefers to be just with his wife where sexual overtures fly off his tongue like snow from a spinning tire. But she finds it easy to redirect his focus.

Jenny shifts in the recliner. Pulls up one knee and scratches the curve of her calf. *Dry skin. I'll need to put some lotion on tonight.*

Shasta House was never the life they had planned for their retirement years. They'd expected to travel. To make an ambitious trip to California. To Salinas, the setting for so many of the John Steinbeck novels Rudy studied in depth and Jenny read for sheer enjoyment.

She straightens her leg, pushes back deeper into her chair, senses her neck muscles relaxing. She remembers how she and Rudy sat at the kitchen table with maps spread out in front of them, plotting their journey. "Maybe after this trip we can do another. Follow the route Steinbeck took in *Travels with Charley: In Search of America*," Rudy had said.

But neither adventure happened because Rudy had a stroke.

After he recovered, his compromised driving skills made her nervous. When she pointed out that driving from southern Ontario to California would mean a great deal of time in the car—far more than she really wanted to spend—it surprised her how readily he agreed to cancelling their trip.

She returns to the present. To the way things are now. *Shasta House is it.* There is no other choice. Rudy must continue living there. His mind cloudy, his bodily functions deteriorating, his heart health precarious. And she will live alone in the condo they purchased when he found gardening and the home maintenance he once enjoyed had become too demanding.

Jenny tucks the afghan tighter around her legs. She shivers. "God, I miss him. The way he was." Her words echo against the walls. She shivers again, feeling oddly restless.

She pulls the lever to upright, tosses off the afghan, stands, crosses from her seat to the bay window. Arms wrapped around herself, she stares into the early evening scene. In the foreground small eddies of snow swirl in the dimly-lit parking lot of the apartment building directly across the street. A huge illuminated blue H glows in the distance atop Sonnenberg General Hospital.

Although Shasta House is nearby, the apartment building blocks the retirement home from view.

Sometimes she wonders if they chose the right place for him. There are lots of other homes in the city—recent-builds, more appealingly appointed. All slickly advertised as highly desirable places for seniors to pursue a vibrant, carefree, independent lifestyle. *As though retirement home living is a blissful, deeply desirable choice.* What she likes best about Shasta House is that it's conveniently close. *A hop, skip, and a jump.* In fine weather, a four-minute walk.

She saunters back to her chair. Settles comfortably and flicks on the TV. *Jeopardy.*

Just as Alex Trebek strides onto the set, the phone rings. She mutes the television and springs to the kitchen to take the call.

"Pam! Oh, how good it is to hear your voice."

Early in their long conversation Pam says, "We're thinking of getting a dog, Mum. Roger had dogs growing up. Beagles. That's the breed we're considering. Not before the holidays, though. We'll look for a breeder after we get back. We're going to Mexico this year for Christmas."

"But the next time you're off on one of your trips? What about your dog?"

"We've thought about that. I have a friend who runs a kennel in Dartmouth. She's a wonder with dogs. I'd feel fine to leave ours with her." She pauses. "Do you remember how Dave and I used to pester you and Dad to let us have a dog when we were kids? Then that Christmas when Santa brought us a tabby kitten? I was so upset that it wasn't a puppy, I sat on my hands on the sofa so I wouldn't have to touch it. And Dad thought I was afraid of the little kitten. He called me 'Pam, the Scaredy Cat.'"

"Yes, I remember." Jenny leans back in her kitchen chair and crosses her legs. It was a memorable Christmas. One of the few when Peter stayed sober. She swings one foot.

"Then I ended up loving Tiger as much as if he had been a dog." Pam laughs. "Especially when he climbed onto my pillow in the mornings and purred in my ear."

Jenny smiles as she listens.

Near the end of their easy chatting, Pam's tone grows serious, "Last night Roger and I watched a documentary. It was called *Alive Inside.* You've got to watch it, Mum. Right from the beginning we thought Mum *has* to get one of those for Rudy."

Intrigued by Pam's explanation, Jenny knows that tomorrow morning, after she calls Rudy's case worker, she'll go to Staples and purchase what Pam suggested. During the next few days, she'll leave enough time to do what's needed to make the unusual gift distinctly his.

Jockie Loomer-Kruger

Monday, December 14

Rudy's case worker is off sick. Ya Ping will call back as soon as she returns to work. If it's urgent, the voice on the other end can put Jenny through to someone else.

"It can wait," Jenny says.

Her trip to Staples is quick and successful.

As soon as she gets back she hauls the Christmas boxes from their basement storage locker. She's done it enough times to be able to unfold the artificial tree in a matter of minutes in its usual location in the bay window. Before lunch she also manages to string on the lights and hang the traditional rocking horse ornaments.

With a mere ten days left 'til Christmas Eve, she trundles off to Shasta House in the frigid early afternoon. Shasta House is laying out extra entertainment for the residents for the holiday season. She's not sure who it is this afternoon, but she'll join Rudy for the occasion.

The sidewalk is clear, the sky overcast. All the former button factory workers' stair-stepped brick row houses have Christmas wreaths on their doors. As she walks, Jenny thinks about holiday preparations. Is it harder or easier to prepare for Christmas these days?

When her children were in their mid-teens they took over the tree decorating. Pam could be persuaded to do some special baking. Beyond the tree trimming, it was a tussle to get Dave away from his comic book collection. Peter didn't help at all. He was either at the Chrysler dealership where he sold new and used models on commission, or sleeping off a bender.

Although she'd reached out to Al-Anon to help her cope during the worst crisis with Peter, in the end she'd let her attendance slide. She learned, however, she had choices. She chose to stop counting his drinks in a futile attempt to control his behaviour. She chose to stop pouring his liquor down the sink. When he accused her of badgering him all the time about his drinking, and 'Why can't you keep the kids quiet? That's your job, not mine,' she chose to wordlessly leave the room. And as she had, early in their marriage, Jenny maintained her choice to refrain from alcohol in her own life.

Two years after Pam started school, Jenny found a job downtown working in a flower shop. The family got by. But Christmases with Peter drunk and owly were a challenge.

Her Christmases with Rudy, though, were so different. He loved all of it. Finding the perfect tree, stringing it with mini-lights, hanging their collection of special ornaments. Setting the vintage rocking horse that dated back to her early years next to the tree. And Jenny's childhood teddy bear, a red bow around his neck, under the boughs among the gifts.

Oh, the joy Rudy felt in giving her gifts. Books of poetry, painting supplies, a soft green hand-painted silk scarf with delicate pink roses, an antique cast-iron trivet to add to her collection in the kitchen, an amaryllis bulb waiting to bloom. A winking tumbled tiger-eye stone on a silver chain because he knew she liked semiprecious gems. Tickets for plays and concerts for their mutual enjoyment.

Her gifts to him were equally personal and reflective of his tastes and interests. Antique postcards with street scenes of Saskatoon that she found on eBay, a Steinbeck novel in an edition she knew he didn't have that Duggar, the old bookseller, had located for her. Always the traditional new socks. She smiles thinking of the pleasure and appreciation he always showed when receiving Christmas presents. With every 'thank you,' a hug and a kiss.

Not far from Shasta House, Jenny spots a crumpled piece of Christmas wrap and a strand of red ribbon on the sidewalk. She nudges them to the curb, her ruminations running on like a tide going in and out. Past to present. Present to past.

For the second time she's on her own. After Peter died, even as she converted his life insurance into her own flower shop, grief played out with a confusing and agonizing stirring together of so many elements. Hope forever lost that Peter might reach sobriety, minimization of his faults, glorification of his virtues, emptiness, numbness, denial, guilt, anger, failure, relief. Emotions churning until, at last, what solidified was a conglomerate of acceptance and personal strength.

Missing Rudy, though, is different. Mourning is there every day like rain water through a downspout, sometimes torrential, sometimes drip, drip, dripping. What's the term she learned at the Caregivers' Support Group? *Yes, that's it; ambiguous grief.*

Oh, Rudy.

She misses their conversations. Their lovemaking. That thought startles her. Those times seem so long ago. She reconfigures her mental images.

She misses how helpful he was with every aspect of their shared living. If something needed repair, he was there with a screwdriver. He kept the car in perfect running order for her to use, even though he chose to bus back and forth to the university. And that phenomenal fruit cake he made every year for Christmas...

Meticulousness hammered into him by his fierce and fastidious mother created Mr. Neat-and-Tidy. He always cleaned up the kitchen when he was through. It bothered him when Jenny got sidetracked and didn't clear messes immediately the way he tended to. 'But, sweetheart, the mess isn't going anywhere. It will wait for me,' she'd say to him. He'd grin, and caution her, 'Messes are known to reproduce when they're left alone too long. They tend to get quite raunchy.' Then he'd proceed to fold the afghan she'd left in a heap on the sofa, scrub the pots and pans she'd left to soak overnight in the sink, empty the cloudy water jar she'd abandoned on the stand beside her easel. File the paid bills she'd allowed to stack up on her desk. Empty half-full waste cans. As she tramps under the retirement home's green canvas tunnel, she grimaces at the memory of Rudy's slightly obsessive-compulsive tendencies that, she admits to herself, had quite often annoyed her.

She signs herself in. Most residents are already seated when she arrives, including Rudy, alone on the grey sofa. She takes off her coat and boots and leaves them in the closet behind the reception area. She rubs her chilled hands together.

Threading a maze, she makes her way toward her husband through an assemblage of occupied wheelchairs or empty walkers, their owners on haphazardly placed chairs. She notices Helga standing not far from the sofa, surveying the scene. Helga catches Rudy's eye, and he beckons her to join him. With a dainty smile, his new friend lowers herself beside him.

Jenny reaches the couch just as Helga props her cane against the cushioned seat. "Hi, you two. Can you both slide over so I can sit next to Rudy, please?" They wriggle across the cushions to make room.

Rudy looks at his wife, "I'm a lucky man. Here I am between my best friend," he squeezes Jenny's hand, and reaches for Helga's, "and my brand new friend."

Helga yanks her hand free. "*Nein*. No hands yet."

Rudy shrugs, as though the rejection has no effect, and spreads his fingers over his knee.

Jenny clasps the hand he gave to her. Tight. "It's nice to see you again, Helga. I hope you like today's entertainment. My, that's a beautiful sweater you're wearing."

"I knit it myself," her fingers trace the buttons on her aqua, rosebud-embellished cardigan. "It's my own original design."

"Really! It's truly lovely. You're very talented." A twinkle glints in Jenny's eye. She grins. "I'm not a knitter. I tried it once, though, when I was in college."

"What happened?" Rudy asks.

"My roommate showed me how to knit plain socks. She showed me everything except how to finish off the toes. The socks were for my boyfriend at the time, who lived out of province and was coming to visit. I couldn't wait for my roommate to show me how to finish them properly, so I ended up with socks that looked like they belonged in those curled-up pointy shoes that Santa's elves wear."

Rudy laughs, "Did your boyfriend have pointed toes?" Helga smiles politely.

"No, but he likely had sore feet. He wore those long-toed socks wadded up in his loafers when we went to a movie. A few days later, he broke up with me. Do you suppose it was because his feet hurt?"

Rudy laughs again. But Helga merely rubs the fine ribbing of her elegant sweater. "Did you ever knit socks for me, Jenny?"

"Never. That was the end of my knitting career."

"I could knit socks for you, Rudy. Fancy ones with cables," Helga says. "It's very easy. You don't have to be smart to do plain knitting. Even *die Kinder* can do it."

Jenny raises her eyebrows. Did Helga just toss an insult at her? Jenny's not sure. *Perhaps it's a language thing.* She wonders how old Helga is. It's hard to tell about wrinkles under the careful makeup. And her hair... Helga's brown hair looks fairly natural. At least she doesn't dye it pitch black, like Evelyn over there.

Jenny glances at Evelyn. Short, wizened, ninety-five-years old. Wrinkled like a plowed field. Her pink scalp glowing through sparse fly-away coal black hair that she insists the home's hairdresser colour for her.

But Jenny can't help admiring Helga's sense of style, both in dress and makeup. Even her posture is straight, so unlike most residents, whose shoulders stoop. Jenny can see why Rudy, and perhaps other men at the home might find this newcomer appealing. Still, there's something about the way she's latched onto Rudy...how they've latched onto each other.

Jockie Loomer-Kruger

Something about this budding friendship....

At last the residents are in place. Today's entertainer, a heavy-set, middle-aged female singer in a red cowgirl outfit with white fringe around the hem of her skirt, readies her amplified guitar. Her outfit reminds Jenny of what Dale Evans wore in the old Roy Rogers films from her pre-teen years.

"Well, hello there, Shasta House!" The entertainer strums a chord. "My name's Pearlie." Another strum. "Good to see everyone. How're y'all doin' anyway? Everybody ready for Christmas?" Her voice is husky. "Y'all know this first song. How about singin' along with me?"

She plays a few more chords. then, in a surprisingly low range, belts out the familiar classic. "Rudolph the red-nosed reindeer, had a very shiny nose..."

Creaky voices join in. Jenny whispers directly in Rudy's ear, "She's singing your song, Rudolph. You better join her."

He adds his voice, "And if you ever saw him..."

Then Pearlie twangs her next selection, *Take Me Home, Country Roads*. Residents applaud.

While Pearlie retunes her guitar, Helga turns to Rudy. "I don't like this music. This is *der Abfall*—garbage. I don't like it here. I'm going to tell *mein Sohn* I want to leave this place. I like classical music." She picks up her cane and uses it to help steady herself as she stands.

"Please don't go, Helga," Rudy says. "I like classical music, too. I want you to be my friend." He reaches for Helga.

Jenny gently pulls his hand down. "If Helga doesn't like this kind of music, Rudy, she doesn't have to stay and listen. Not everyone likes every kind of music, dear."

He watches his new friend weave her way through the audience to the elevators. His mouth tightens, "You made my friend go away, Jenny. Why did you do that?"

"Shh. We're going to have another song." But she doesn't hear Pearlie announce the next piece. She's pondering Rudy's puzzling accusation.

He, though, is ready to sing along. "Frosty the snowman..."

Thursday, December 17

The lounge is transformed. Loveseats, wingbacks, and other furniture have been moved out. Dining tables covered in red plastic now crowd the space. Green and red crêpe paper streamers drape from the ceiling. Giant gold and red balls dangle from the tips of branches on the artificial tree in the corner near the fireplace. By the time Jenny arrives, most of the sixty-five residents and their guests are already seated for the Shasta House family Christmas dinner party.

At a table near the reception area, bookended by her two sons, their wives, and a handful of grandkids, Florence beams. Colette, fidgeting with her hands, sits with other residents who are without guests. Harry, now in full Santa suit, is at a table close to the fireplace. His moustache has been trimmed and he wears his ill-fitting dentures. Jenny sees him laugh at something his daughter says, then hears him burst into out-of-tune singing, "You better watch out, you better not cry."

"Not so loud, Dad."

"YOU BETTER NOT SHOUT!"

Jenny signals a thumbs-up to them as she turns toward the next table at the back of the room —a square one with room for two per side that is pushed hard against the wall. Rudy sits there, his chair beside Helga's, opposite a younger couple.

He points to the two remaining empty chairs facing the wall. "I saved a seat for you, Jenny. Next to Heidi and me."

"Why can't you remember? *Mein name ist Helga.*"

"Yes…sorry. That's right: Helga. I wanted to sit here with Helga. And you can sit beside us. Is that all right, Jenny?"

Jenny plants a kiss on the top of Rudy's head. "Sure. This'll be fine," *He's pretty determined about where we're to sit.*

An outstretched hand from the smiling young woman across from Rudy and Helga interrupts Jenny's thoughts. "Hi, I'm Marie. Helga's my mother-in-law." She motions to the man beside her."This is Nick, my husband."

He waves a greeting, offers a closed-lip smile, but doesn't speak.

Marie has curly red hair and freckles, and her gums show when she smiles. *Cute and perky.* Jenny guesses she's in her late thirties. Maybe early forties. *It's hard to fathom ages as you get older. Anyone under fifty looks so young.* Jenny assumes Nick, who is slightly overweight with fair hair and full ruddy cheeks, is about the same age.

Jenny leans forward to shake Marie's hand. "I'm Jenny. Rudy's wife." She sits, leaving the empty chair between her and Helga's daughter-in-law.

"We met Rudy when we first arrived. He and Helga were already here. Welcome, and Merry Christmas!"

The meal comes promptly: gravy-drenched bland turkey with cubed turnip, mashed potatoes, limp broccoli, dressing and a dollop of cranberry sauce from a can. As she eats, Jenny learns more about the new Shasta House resident who seems to have become her husband's instant friend.

Nick concentrates on his food. He appears to avoid looking at or speaking to his mother. Or to Rudy. Sometimes Nick runs his fingers inside his shirt collar the way Jenny remembers her father doing at the Sunday dinner table when he felt bored by his daughter's prattle or uncomfortable with his wife's neighbourhood gossip.

Between bites, Marie babbles Helga's history. Her mother-in-law was eighteen when she came to Canada in the early fifties. She married a few years later. There were no children until she was almost forty. Then, just the one son. When Nick was only four, her husband was killed in a freak accident at the rubber factory where he worked. Helga didn't remarry.

"Not that she didn't have offers," Marie chuckles. "Nick says she never lacked for admirers." She sips from her glass of apple juice. "She supported them by working as a seamstress. She's very gifted with sewing. Knitting, too. She got a knitting machine and designed and made beautiful sweaters for an exclusive shop in Toronto."

But Helga's not been well the last couple of years. Just too much for Nick and Marie, both with busy careers in IT. Nick felt his mother shouldn't live alone anymore. He felt she wasn't handling her diabetes safely, and sometimes, well, sometimes...

The arrival of a server offering coffee interrupts Marie's flow of information.

A cup of steaming beverage in front of her, Marie says, "Helga can be kind of feisty when things don't go her way. But look at her tonight! She always was a fashion plate. She still loves smart clothes. I mean, that dress she's wearing—she not only made it, but she designed it, too."

"It's beautiful. She can certainly wear gold lamé elegantly."

Jenny glances sideways toward Rudy and Helga. During Marie's long monologue they have been conversing in German. Their voices are low; only snatches of what they're saying cut through the general buzz and background of canned Christmas carols. She hears '*Nahmachine, Schlafzimmer*' several times, '*Nahmachine, Schalafzimmer.*' But Jenny has no idea what the words mean. She returns her attention to Marie.

"Everything you see her wearing, she made by her own hand."

"Remarkable creativity. And skill," Jenny says, resting her knife and fork across the top edge of her plate, near the wilted broccoli she didn't finish. "I'm glad Rudy has met someone he can speak German with."

She doesn't add that she finds his sudden interest in his first language a little odd. She remembers one of his stories.

> I spoke German at home until I started school. My mother had even taught me how to read in German before I was five. When I started school, the other kids teased me because I didn't talk like them. By the time I was ten, I refused to speak German any more. Mostly because the kids at school called me Little Hitler. They did the German salute and shouted, 'Heil Rudy.' I used to yell back at them, 'I'm not German. I'm Canadian.'
>
> Klaus got mad at me. He said I was being disrespectful to our parents. But I didn't care. I didn't want to speak German anymore. Ever. I was Canadian. I was only going to speak English the rest of my life.

After a choice of lemon or apple pie, staff in green Bellis-White aprons clear the tables. The evening's entertainer, a slightly hunched man in a tuxedo brightened with a sequined red bowtie, smooths his combed-back pewter hair, then checks the settings on his electric keyboard.

His fingers touch the keys like a lover, and the music flows. Sometimes he sings lyrics. Sometimes he plays instrumentals, teasing and tantalizing listeners with his comments. "Ah, here's one that will stir those delicious memories, *I'm in the Mood for Love.*"

He follows that song with *Embraceable You, I Only Have Eyes for You,* and *That's Amore.* A few residents and guests amble onto the floor to dance.

During a break in his patter and music, Jenny leans toward Marie. "They say he entertained on cruise ships for years."

Marie shifts her chair to better watch the musician. "He's very good.

Actually, very smooth. Kind of flirtatious too, eh?"

With staff as well as residents, Jenny notes, having turned her chair around in time to see Cheryl lift her long hair to fall over one shoulder when the musician tosses a risqué comment toward her. His fingers tickle the introduction of a new piece.

Rudy leans close to Helga. "That's *Moon River*. The name of that song. Would you like to dance?"

"Ach—*nein*. No. My knees hurt."

Rudy turns then to Jenny, his tone gruff. "You? Would you like to dance?"

As though I'm his disappointing default choice. "Love to, darling."

He takes her hand and leads her haltingly to a cleared area in the lounge near the snack bar. She folds into his arms with ease, but his awkward steps on the carpeted floor are hard to follow. *Where has our smooth, so-in-sync dancing gone?*

When the song ends, he's panting. Jenny wishes he understood the extent of his heart disease. *How little exertion it takes to wind him.*

"Let's sit a bit." She takes his elbow and helps him to a wooden armchair. He drops himself clumsily onto the seat, and she pulls a matching chair close beside him.

When his breathing grows easier, he says, "Heidi's very nice."

"Do you mean Helga?"

"Yes, yes, Helga. I like talking German with her. She told me she has a *Nahmachine*, a sewing machine. It's in her bedroom. In her *Schalafzimmer*."

Before Jenny can respond, Cheryl bounces over, smartphone in hand. "Mind if I take your picture? You two are such a great couple." She takes the picture. "Another one, just in case." Then, "How long have you been married anyway?"

Rudy turns to his wife. "Jenny knows. How long, Jenny?"

"Thirty years. It's a second marriage for us both."

"Someday, when I find the right guy, I hope he'll be just like you, Rudy." She winks at him. "Oh, I've watched you. You light up like a sunbeam when you see Jenny coming. The two of you, holding hands all the time." She pushes her hair back off her shoulder and looks at Jenny, "Rudy is always such a gentleman."

"And such a gentle man," Jenny adds with a wistful smile. *Where had that gentleness come from?*

Jenny remembers hearing about his mother's stern ways. Scolding him frequently. Praising him with a pat on the head only when he put his toys away. Making him sit for long periods on the uncomfortable wood box beside the kitchen stove. Sometimes a stinging swat from the end of the dish towel or a slap on the behind if he wasn't quick enough to get out of the way. And threats that his wicked ways would land him in the fires of Hell.

So different from her own country upbringing. Freedom to romp in the haymow anytime, Dish towels only for drying dishes. Parents who did not believe in 'spare the rod and spoil the child' and had made a pact that they would not spank their little girls. Household chores assigned to the children on Saturdays. An unwavering belief that Esther and Jenny would both, when the time came, be welcomed into Heaven.

Perhaps it was Mrs. Krantz, Rudy's godmother, with no children of her own, whom he had often visited, who nurtured his soft, endearing side. Jenny knew that story from his green binder.

> Mrs. Krantz had a fat calico cat. It would jump up in my lap and purr. Every time her cat was in my lap, she'd say the same thing, 'Lolly likes you because you're kind and gentle, Rudy. Always be kind and gentle with animals. And with people. That's how we make the world a better place.'

Cheryl has already strolled off to take pictures of other residents and their guests, and Rudy is no longer gasping for air.

"I don't know why I got so out of breath."

Jenny doesn't explain about his congestive heart failure. Instead she stands. At seventy-seven she's able to get up and down with relative ease, but Rudy, six years her senior, struggles to raise himself.

To help him up, Jenny slides her arm under his armpit and lifts. Then, hand in hand, they sloth-walk back to their deserted table.

Rudy surveys the emptying room. "Helga's gone. I don't see her. Where did she go?"

"Perhaps she got tired, love, and went to her room."

"Who were those other people at our table?"

"Her son and daughter-in-law."

"I didn't meet them, did I?"

"I think you did."

"Guess I forgot." He draws a deep breath. "I'm tired, Jenny."

"Then let's go to your room. I'll help you get ready for bed."

Unexpectedly, Rudy slips his arm around her waist and with his other hand turns her head toward him. He kisses her on the mouth.

She savours the sensation. There's something delicious about kissing a man with a beard and moustache, even at her age.

She remembers their first kiss. Not the night they went to the Italian restaurant to talk about Steinbeck and talked about everything but. It was on their second date. After the play at the City Playhouse—she doesn't recall the play, other than that it was by a local playwright and produced by the community theatre group.

Rudy had a love of amateur theatre, something she'd rarely attended but also grew to enjoy and appreciate. They both liked the way amateur theatre drew its cast from people who did other things for a living, but lost themselves in fantasy lives on stage.

It was after the play, when he'd driven her home and she was fumbling in her purse for her keys. He'd done the very same thing he'd just done in the lounge at Shasta House. Slid his arm around her waist and turned her head toward him. Then kissed her firmly on the mouth.

The first time she'd ever been kissed by a man with a beard and moustache. She'd relished the tingling that extended beyond her lips. Kind of like when she was a kid and used to hold a special fuzzy blanket against her mouth at night. Except the kiss was sexy and the blanket wasn't.

She smiles as they saunter to the elevators arm in arm. It doesn't surprise her that he forgot his walker. That happens now and then. They wait for an elevator to arrive.

"You're such a good wife, Jenny. I love you."

"I love you too, Rudy. I love you very much."

"Are you going to stay all night with me? Stay and have sex?"

Jenny sighs. *There it is again.*

"Afraid not. It's late. You need to get your rest. And I need to go home."

"You never stay all night. You should stay. I'm your husband. We could have sex."

"The elevator's here. I'll see you to your room." She knows she will not be the one to get him ready for bed after all.

As they enter his room, she presses the red button on the call pendant suspended from a green lanyard around his neck. "Someone will be here soon to help you get ready for bed. I'll see you in the morning."

She plants a fingertip kiss on the end of his nose.

Before settling in for the night she makes a journal entry: *This was a puzzling event. Rudy was so attentive to Helga all during the party, almost as though she was his 'date' for the evening. Then he pleaded with me to spend the night with him. He's not the only one feeling confused right now.*

And I don't have dementia as an excuse!

Jockie Loomer-Kruger

Friday, December 18

The morning after the party an episode of angina strikes Rudy. Anna, the charge nurse, calls to tell Jenny that Rudy is feeling unwell.

Something different every day. Jenny hurries down the hill to the home.

She had so many other things planned for this morning. Top of the list was finishing what she needed to do for Rudy's special gift. And the ironing—a task she detests. How had she described her best household hint years ago? 'If you leave the kids' clothes in the ironing basket long enough they'll outgrow everything, and you don't have to press a thing before donating to the Sally Ann.' She chuckles inwardly. Did she really do that, or was that a smartass thing she used to tell other women to make them laugh?

I wonder if my dislike for ironing started as a sibling thing? When it was Saturday morning chore time, Esther, claiming age seniority, always managed to get to use the ironer—the ever-so-modern tube-like machine set up on the dining room table. Comfortably seated, Esther would feed flat items through—sheets, pillowcases, dish towels—between the cloth-covered roller and the curved, heated metal plate. It fell to Jenny to stand at the ironing board in the kitchen, pressing her father's white shirt with starched collar and cuffs, to make it presentable for him to wear to church, along with the two girls' own fussy blouses and pleated skirts, and their mother's flowered house dresses.

Kids. It's a good thing Rudy and I didn't have children. She remembers just moments before the first time they made love, when he announced that he couldn't impregnate her. Because Addie didn't want to have a family, he'd had a vasectomy. Jenny had snickered, 'Not to worry, I've had my tubes tied.'

As parents, they'd have been at odds a lot of the time. He'd have wanted their children to be orderly. Organized. To keep their rooms clean. And she, well, she always felt it was more important to be spontaneous and playful with kids, tuned in to their feelings, tolerant of their messes. Growing up isn't easy, and it's never tidy. Neither, she concludes, is growing old.

Her Mr. Neat-and-Tidy isn't at home anymore or he'd have taken over today's ironing. She sighs. It really doesn't matter whether the Christmas tablecloth is creased. She's sure Dave and his family won't even notice. Or care.

Rudy's asleep in his bed when Jenny arrives. She brings his cork bulletin board up to date by adding three Christmas cards that came yesterday. One from his former dean at the English Department, one from his brother, and the third from Addie and her partner in Kamloops. She's amused by the irony of consistently tidying his room for him, but not being particular about keeping her own space in perfect order.

He wakens just before lunchtime, but doesn't want to join others in the dining room. Lucija, who told Jenny about teaching high school chemistry in her Croatian hometown before she came to Canada and became a PSW, brings his meal on a tray. He pushes the macaroni and cheese aside, eats only the bowl of green Jell-O with a swirl of artificial whipped cream on top.

In the afternoon, he naps some more, and Jenny lies down with him, curling herself around his back. She also dozes. The next time he awakens he feels better and, after gum-chewing Charlene changes him into dry underwear, he shuffles to the elevators with Jenny's hand over his on the black rubber grip of his walker.

In the lounge, he surveys the room as though he's lost something, "Why isn't Helga here?" His voice is plaintive.

"Perhaps she's having a nap." Jenny picks up the daily paper from the coffee table, "Here's today's paper, dear. Looks interesting." She leaves him hidden behind his newspaper.

As she treks up the sidewalk toward the condo in the early evening darkness, her thoughts drift. Is it possible he's feeling more than platonic toward Helga? *No. Surely not.* She feels shame for even letting herself imagine such a thing.

The night is exceptionally mild for December. One raindrop, then another, lands on her nose. The rain carries her back to the night they'd gone to a folk music concert. Was it their third date, or maybe the fourth? She's not sure.

They'd come out of the auditorium into an unexpected late spring thunderstorm. By the time they'd dashed to his car they were drenched. His goatee trailing rivulets onto his fawn jacket, her hair flattened into dripping strands. Her white blouse and red skirt soaked and clinging to her breasts and legs. He opened the passenger door for her, saw her flood herself onto the seat, then closed the door. He sprinted around to the driver's side. When he got in and shut the door, they looked at each other and laughed.

"Okay, Ms. Allen, what next?" She only grinned and pushed the wet wave off her forehead. "I was going to invite you to my apartment. Show you my Steinbeck collection, so we could have that conversation we keep setting aside for other topics. But I think you might prefer to go home."

"No," Jenny said, surprising herself, "you must have a robe and a dryer."

"Yes, both."

"Well, then let's go to your place."

And they did. He changed into dry clothes and ushered Jenny to the washroom to wrap herself in his frayed blue-and-green striped terry cloth robe. Together they settled themselves on the Danish teak settee across from the picture window while her clothes tumbled in the dryer.

Jagged lightning ripped the sky. Thunder rumbled. Jenny pulled her bare feet up onto the settee cushion, draped the robe over her knees, and hugged her legs tight. Like a skittery child seeking reassurance by making herself into a ball.

Rudy rested his arm across the back of the double seater, his legs outstretched. Looking as relaxed and comfortable as the well-worn fleece-lined slippers he was wearing.

A brilliant flash. Flickering lights. A deafening crash. Jenny shuddered.

"That was close," Rudy said.

She cringed, wishing she could tuck herself away like a turtle hiding in its shell. "I've never liked thunderstorms. They always scare me."

Rudy lowered his arm around her shoulders and she snuggled into the feeling of safety he offered. "I'm sorry you feel nervous about thunderstorms. I love them."

"You're kidding!"

"Thunderstorms on the prairies are spectacular. You can be under blue sky and watch a distant storm gather and erupt. It's a remarkable sight. Of course, when you're in a storm, you treat it with respect."

"I don't hide under the bed anymore, like I did when I was a kid, but sometimes I wish I could."

He laughed. "Thunderstorms, dust storms, snowstorms. I'm fascinated by weather. If I hadn't had that scholarship to study English, I might have become a meteorologist. Doesn't weather intrigue you?"

"Mostly it worries me. What I read about acid rain and air pollution."

Rudy shared the same concerns. Would the world wake to the threat of global warming in time? As he talked he snuggled Jenny closer.

She's not quite sure how long the conversation went on before they found themselves in his bedroom, but remembers that the storm had abated by then. And that her clothes remained rumpled in the dryer until morning.

Jockie Loomer-Kruger

Sunday, December 20

Jenny rinses the conditioner from her hair. They always showered together. Sometimes washing each other's curves and creases was sensual. But mostly it was merely a morning grooming ritual. Two people comfortable with each other's nakedness. She'd wash and dry his back. He'd do hers.

The morning he forgot to dry her back, that's when she knew something was wrong. His response to her question about why he hadn't dried her back delayed like a satellite connection. The odd twist to the side of his mouth and the way his words slurred when he said he just forgot. Stoic that he was, he hadn't yet mentioned the intense headache he'd had throughout the night.

She'd been so frightened he wouldn't survive the stroke. At the hospital they told her she'd brought him there just in time. His blood pressure was so high, he was on the verge of a massive brain hemorrhage. When he came home again, the only visible damage was an old man's shuffling walk and, for a while, a tendency to drool from one side of his mouth.

She steps out of the shower, tugs the thick blue towel off the chrome bar and dries her sagging skin. Drops the towel onto the built-in seat in the shower stall. Grabs another, rubs her wet hair, her grey hair—now so much coarser than when it was darker—then wraps the towel around her head.

It was after Rudy came home from the hospital, at a check-up appointment, that his cardiologist issued a prediction. Because of the nature of the stroke, when he got older, Rudy was most likely to develop vascular mixed dementia.

But even forewarned, she wasn't ready. Is anyone ever ready? How can you prepare to deal with a brain dying before a body is ready to let go?

Jenny dresses in a mauve pullover and black corduroy slacks. She sits at the kitchen table with the newspaper open to the comics. Rudy always read the comics first. 'It's healthy to start the day with laughter,' he would say. 'Makes the serious news more palatable.'

While she waits for her coffee to cool, she nibbles on toast thick with peanut butter. The portable phone on the kitchen table rings.

"Good morning, Jenny, I'm calling from Shasta House." Jenny recognizes the weekend receptionist's voice. "We've got a bit of a problem with Rudy."

Jenny's heart skips a beat. She clutches the edge of the table, pulling the poinsettia-patterned tablecloth askew. "Is he okay, Susan? Did he fall? His heart?"

"No, no, nothing like that. He wants to go to the drugstore," Susan says.

"What?"

"It's really Helga. She wants to go and she wants him to go with her. But I know he's not supposed to go out unaccompanied…"

"Is she allowed out on her own?"

"No restrictions, it seems. But she says she doesn't know this part of the city. Doesn't know where the drugstore is, and she asked him if he would show her."

"The blind leading the blind! They'll both get lost. He has no sense of direction anymore. See if you can talk her into waiting, Susan. I'll come take them both there in the car."

Jenny gulps a swallow of coffee. She leaves her mug on the table and hurries to the foyer. *At this rate I'll never be ready for Christmas.*

She opens the sliding doors of the closet. Lifts out her olive wool coat and puts it on. Grabs her purse from a hook on the antique oak hall tree. Checks in her bag for her car keys and scurries to the elevator. In the parking garage she starts the car and exits without waiting for the automatic door to close behind her as condo owners are supposed to do.

Through the glass outer entry at Shasta House she notes Rudy and Helga bundled up in their winter jackets, sitting together on a padded bench beside the sign-in table. She's pleased he has his walker with him this time.

As she steps through the door Jenny's eyes widen. The two sit close together, their gloved fingers entwined. *No, not this—he holds hands with me.*

Spotting Jenny, Helga instantly disengages her fingers from Rudy's and folds both hands sedately on her lap, over her large, flat black leather purse.

Jenny notices that Helga was the one who pulled her hand away. Rudy's new friend obviously knows it's inappropriate.

Jenny claps her own hands together. "So, you want to go to the drugstore?"

"I have to get some hand cream and toothpaste," Helga responds.

"And what do you need, Rudy?"

"I'll know when I get there."

Jenny signs them both out.

"Come with me. The car's waiting."

Under the canopy, Jenny walks ahead and Rudy pushes his walker beside Helga.

"Helga can sit in the front. I'll help you into the back, Rudy."

When he steps aside from his walker to open the car door for Helga, Jenny's mouth drops. Her eyebrows knit together. For years he played the thoughtful gentleman and opened the car door for her. But not often following his stroke.

Jenny peels back the rear door for Rudy. With difficulty he settles into the seat. "Here, I'll help you with your seatbelt."

She folds his walker and lifts it into the trunk.

In the drugstore parking lot, as she retrieves his walker, Rudy manages to unbuckle his belt, get himself out and once again hold the car door for Helga. Jenny shakes her head in disbelief.

Inside the store, Helga turns to Jenny, "I've never been in this store before. Where do they sell hand cream?"

Jenny points to the cosmetics aisle. Rudy has already pushed his walker toward the other side of the store. *Like a man on a mission.* She turns her full attention to Helga. "Do you want me to come with you, Helga?"

"*Nein.* I can shop on my own. Do you think I'm a *Dummkopt*? There's nothing wrong with me. *Nix.*"

"Okay." She ignores Helga's toss of barbed quills. "I need to check on Rudy."

Jenny searches the aisles for her husband, and spots him lifting boxes of chocolates into the wire mesh carrier attached to his walker. "Got a sweet tooth today, Rudy?"

"I want to get a Christmas present for Helga. Which kind do you think she'd like?" He points to the three boxes of chocolates in the basket.

"Actually, sweetheart, I think you shouldn't give her chocolates."

"Why not?"

"She's diabetic. They wouldn't be good for her."

"But I want to give her something for Christmas. I have to get a present for her."

So that was his mission. A must-buy gift for Helga. Jenny feels as though a bucket of cement has been poured into her boots. *But nothing for me.*

"What can I get for her, then?" He replaces the candies on the shelf.

"Look over there." Jenny points to the book and magazine section. "Perhaps she'd like a calendar."

Her feet lighten, but her chest tightens as she guides Rudy to the rack of publications. "You take a look while I see how Helga's doing."

Jenny locates her other charge staring at shelves of vitamins. In one hand, Helga holds a white plastic bottle of hand cream. In the other, the curved handle of her anorexic purse. Jenny wonders if Helga should have brought her cane. "Have you found everything yet, Helga?"

"I need one other thing, but I can't find it."

"Toothpaste, isn't it?"

"No, it isn't toothpaste. I don't need toothpaste. It's something else. Not toothpaste. Stop bossing me around."

What was the term Helga's daughter-in-law used? Feisty.

Helga examines her surroundings, her darting chestnut eyes widening. "This store is too big."

Jenny touches Helga's arm. "Let's take a look over here. Maybe what you need is in this aisle."

They survey rows of toothpaste on one side and hair products on the other. "I'll leave you here to look while I go back to Rudy. Is that okay?"

"*Ja.*" Helga, clutching her bottle of hand cream, is already heading down the aisle.

Close to the magazine display, Rudy is putting a final choice into his basket.

"Looks like you've found some things. What do you have?"

"This is for Helga," he holds up a plastic-sealed 2016 calendar featuring cat photos, "and so is this." In his other hand he holds up a puppy-themed calendar.

"And the book?"

"That's for me. It's about trains. I like trains."

He still hasn't thought of a gift for me. Rudy used to surprise her frequently with little no-occasion presents of jewelry, books, flowers, chocolates. She gulps down an unexpected bitter taste. It's as if she, his wife, doesn't matter today.

She hates his disease. Hates it. Hates it. Hates it.

She clears her throat. "Well, let's choose one of the calendars. Which do you think Helga likes better, cats or puppies?"

"I don't know. Which do you think she likes best?"

"Probably puppies."

With an edge of chagrin, Jenny thinks of how Helga has already barked at her. She puts the cat calendar back on the display rack. "How about I pay for your gift and book?"

"I want to do it. The present is from me."

He pulls out his worn brown leather wallet from his hip pocket. Extracts a five-dollar bill. "Is this enough?"

"Not quite, dear. Don't worry about it. I can pay. You keep your money for other things."

He likes to have a five and some change in his wallet at all times. What happens that makes his money disappear now and then, Jenny doesn't know. She doesn't ask. He wouldn't remember if she did question him. As needed, she replaces the cash.

The cards he carries in his wallet never disappear, though. His expired library ID, an out-of-date health care card with his picture on it—a photo taken long before he turned eighty-three in the summer. The only current card informs that he may be lost. His name is Rudy. Call the police. The card complements the stainless steel bracelet he wears with the same information on it.

"Rudy, dear, I need to check on Helga. I'll pick up a gift bag to put your present in. You can sit on your walker and wait here for me."

She watches as he locks the brakes and sits, then she hurries to where she last saw Helga. But Helga is not in the toothpaste aisle. She's once more studying the vitamins, with the bottle of hand cream in one hand, her purse handle and a green bottle of shampoo in the other.

"Are you finished shopping, Helga?"

"*Ja.*"

"And you don't need any toothpaste?"

"Of course I don't," she snaps, her eyes fiery.

Jenny reminds herself that it's best not to argue with people with memory problems. "The checkout is at the front of the store. Over there. Rudy is through shopping, so maybe we can all get ready to go back to Shasta House. You can follow me to the checkout."

Jenny hurries to Rudy, grabbing a blue-and-white snowflake-design gift bag on the way. She glances back to make sure Helga is following. She is.

I feel like a ping-pong ball.

Rudy is not where she left him. He is, however, close by, standing with his walker at the checkout. And she hears dismay in his voice.

"It's not enough money? But it's for Helga. It's a Christmas present for my new friend. She speaks German to me."

"Sir," the clerk is saying, exasperation in her every word, "that's only a five. Your purchases come to $37.50. I can't let you have those things."

"Excuse me," Jenny interrupts, stepping in beside her husband, "I'll look after it. You can put your money away, Rudy. It's all right." She rubs her hand on his back and feels his muscles relax.

As she inserts her credit card in the machine, Jenny notes from the corner of her eye that Helga is nearing the checkout.

With all purchases attended to, the trio returns to Jenny's gold Toyota. Again, Rudy holds the front passenger seat door for Helga before struggling to get into the back. He hugs his plastic bag of purchases close to his chest.

Back at Shasta House, Jenny hops out of the car quickly before Rudy can extricate himself from his seatbelt and push himself out. *She* opens the car door and escorts Helga through the canopy. Then returns to assist Rudy.

There is a darkening down one pants leg. He'll need a change. She wonders if she should have bought more protective underwear for him. *No.* She recently stocked a new box in his closet.

The two shoppers behind her, Jenny pushes the button to call an elevator. "These elevators are so bloody slow." She shakes her head in annoyance and something registers in her peripheral vision. She turns around to look.

Rudy has let go of his walker. Stepped back from it. Helga is in his arms, her face upturned, eyes closed, his mouth firmly planted on hers.

My god, what's happening here?

Jockie Loomer-Kruger

Part Three

I wonder how many people I've looked at all my life
and never seen.

— *John Steinbeck, <u>The Winter of Our Discontent</u>*

Jockie Loomer-Kruger

Monday, December 21

She comes to Shasta House earlier than usual, arriving in mid-morning to look for Ellen. The dingy grey walls and tired dark wood finish of the reception area deepen her feelings of gathering gloom.

Just as she's about to ask Nancy at the desk if the Director of Wellness is in, Ellen rounds the corner from the snack bar, a cup of coffee in her hand.

"May I speak with you, Ellen?"

"Is it important, Mrs. Hoffman? I have a meeting in a few minutes."

"Well, I think it's important. It's about Rudy…and Helga."

"Come into my office, then."

Ellen sinks into the padded chair behind her desk. She motions Jenny to sit opposite. "So, what is it?"

"I'm bothered by Rudy's increasing infatuation with Helga—"

Ellen cuts her off before she can say that she thinks his hormones may be unbalanced, he seems to have sex on his mind all the time, she's never seen him like this before, she's worried about Helga, too.

"Yes, I've heard." A thin curtain of spittle beads between Ellen's lips. "The PSWs say they're awfully cute together."

"What do you mean? Cute?"

Ellen takes a swallow of coffee. "The way they sit together in the lounge. There's really nothing to be concerned about. Lots of residents become good friends in retirement homes. Sometimes they even develop romances. Keeps them from feeling lonely. We don't discourage it. It's natural."

She pushes her chair back, breathes heavily as she stands and picks up the blue folder near the edge of her desk. "I'm sorry, Mrs. Hoffman, but I do have to get to my meeting. Now don't you worry about Rudy and Helga. It's all very natural. Very normal."

Teeth clenched, Jenny moves aside to let her pass. *Damn. Double damn. Don't a wife's concerns matter?*

Ellen lumbers to the staff room off the lounge.

Aware she's too upset from this brief encounter, Jenny decides to do what she rarely does. She will forgo seeing Rudy today. She hustles by the reception desk.

From sorting mail into the labeled slots behind the reception area, Nancy calls just as Jenny presses the code to open the inner door, "A magazine came for Rudy today. Do you want to take it to him?"

"Not now. I'll get it tomorrow. I'm not staying. I have to go home."

"Yeah, I know. So much to do at Christmas, isn't there? And never enough time."

Jenny nods and leaves the building.

At home she makes herself a cup of tea. Carries it to her favourite chair, and switches on the TV. Holiday commercials and talking heads. She turns the television off.

As she sips her tea, she relives her meeting with Ellen. Could Ellen be right? She is, after all, a registered nurse who likely knows a lot more about people with dementia than Jenny does. Jenny probes her own feelings. Is she upset because Rudy still recognizes her as his wife? Would it feel different if he didn't know who she is? Like Verna and George?

Every day they sit on those two high-backed chairs near the snack bar. Like a king and queen on their thrones. They never talk to each other, or hold hands or even seem to enjoy being together. Yet everyone treats them as a couple. When Rudy first moved in, Jenny assumed they were spouses.

Until the day they wandered near the reception area, just as Jenny was coming in the door. She saw Verna reach for George's hand. Saw him slap her hand away. Verna looked at him blankly before they turned around and sauntered back to their thrones.

"Well, that wife certainly got a rebuff," Jenny remarked to Nancy, who had also seen the interchange.

"Oh, they're not married. In fact, she's his third girlfriend. The first one died. The next one went to a nursing home." Nancy caught a stray strand of her auburn hair and tucked it into the bun on the back of her head, "Almost as soon as Verna moved in he grabbed onto her and she became his new girlfriend."

"Really?"

"Verna still has a husband." Nancy jotted something onto a sticky note, peeled it off the pad, and stuck it on the frame of her computer. "But she doesn't remember she's married. Her husband doesn't bother to visit because she doesn't know who he is anymore."

Is that what Ellen means when she says it's natural to develop special friendships, even romances, in retirement homes? Does she see Rudy and Helga as just another version of Verna and George? Can't she see the difference? That Rudy knows he's married? That Helga knows he's married? That he and Jenny consciously love each other? *Damn, I need to do something. Get my mind off this crap.*

She finishes her tea, then sets up the ironing board in the kitchen. The tablecloth will get smoothed after all. She busies herself with other pre-Christmas jobs, wrapping the last of the gifts, including the extra special one she got for Rudy and finished preparing by staying up late last night. She's sure he'll love it. How thoughtful of Pam to recommend it. Jenny remembers Pam's enthusiasm during their phone call.

"Mum, the documentary is about personal music for people with dementia. I know once you see it, you'll want to get a device for Rudy. The way he loves music and all."

Jenny had watched the show, then done as her daughter suggested. The next morning she'd purchased an iPod Shuffle and headphones. She left the earbuds that came with the device beside her computer. With hearing aids in both ears he couldn't possibly use the buds.

Now she has the items wrapped and ready for him. *Forget Christmas. I'll take it to him tomorrow, in the morning.*

Jockie Loomer-Kruger

Tuesday, December 22

She picks up Rudy's news magazine at reception and takes an elevator to the sixth floor. His door is unlocked, but that's not surprising. He often forgets to lock up when he goes to recreation programs. Even with his key dangling from his wrist on a green plastic coil as a reminder. This morning she assumes he'll be at exercise class in the activities room in the basement.

She tosses the gift and her purse onto his bed, but doesn't remove her outdoor garments. Merely unbuttons her coat after dropping into his recliner. Aimlessly, she looks around his narrow room. *A cell, almost.* Her thoughts go back to the first space he had at Shasta House.

A two-room suite on the third floor where he was content with shelves of books—mostly tomes from his vast Steinbeck collection—his TV and a CD player with a stack of his favourite classical discs. He also had a telephone and frequently called Jenny for casual chats. He could still shower safely by himself, was fastidious about his personal hygiene, the way he dressed, the orderliness of his room. Incontinence occurred only occasionally during the night.

He understood then about his impotence, that men have erectile dysfunction for myriad reasons. "I can live without intercourse, Jenny," he said well before he became a Shasta House resident. "Knowing you love me is enough. Knowing we can still touch each other freely, cuddle, snuggle. Hugging's the next best thing to making love anyway." During their years without sex they hugged often and tightly.

One of his dictated childhood stories pops into her head. It makes her smile.

> Joey, my playmate from the back alley, and I often sat out near the chicken coop in the backyard, and tried to figure out where we came from. Joey said it was from sexual relations with a woman. I couldn't believe my father would do THAT to my mother. So we argued.
>
> My mother had told me I'd come in Dr. French's black bag and

that's what I wanted to believe. I ultimately learned, of course, that Joey's version was right. And that it was a matter of love.

Sometimes Jenny stayed overnight with Rudy in his two-room unit. The two of them in the double bed they'd moved from the spare room in the condo. It felt warm, comfortable and normal to snuggle together, like a pair of spoons in a drawer—the way they'd always spent their nights.

He understood, in those early days as a Shasta House resident, that he needed help with certain tasks. Moving to a retirement home had been his own idea.

"I don't want to become a burden to you, Jenny," he said one day after an appointment at the memory clinic. A day when his thinking was clear and proactive, "I know I have dementia. And I know it will get worse. I think I should move into Shasta House. It's so close. I could come back and forth to home. It would make things so much easier for you."

She didn't jump on his suggestion; instead, tears welled. It was all true. She could see the changes happening. Some days he was clear-headed, and immersed himself in reading essays about the works of Steinbeck, making insightful notes he thought he might want to refer to later. He had a new paper in mind about the years Steinbeck lived and wrote in Paris. Some days, Rudy played a mean game of Scrabble and kept score with ease.

But other days, he wandered through the condo as though he didn't know where he was, or followed her like a puppy. Or asked the same question five times in a row, and she had to catch herself to avoid blurting that he sounded like a three-year-old. She knew he couldn't help what he was doing, but sometimes....

At the grocery store, relying on his cane for balance, he wandered the aisles, unable to locate the rolled oats she'd asked him to add to their shopping cart. "They don't make that stuff anymore," was his excuse.

Sometimes, while he still lived in the condo with her and she had to go out, she took him to Shasta House for an afternoon. The lifestyle consultant there, whose job it was to recruit new residents, welcomed him. Identified him as a potential room-filler. He liked the camaraderie of the staff and was not at all critical of the occasional mediocre musical entertainment offered to residents. When she flew to New Brunswick to visit her sister, Jenny arranged respite care for him in one of the rooms Shasta House kept available for such purposes.

Then came the time when Jenny's own health began to crumble. She needed a pacemaker. It was becoming too hard to do everything Rudy needed done for him. Leaving him home alone was no longer safe. She couldn't trust him around the stove. Because he didn't understand his licence had been revoked, she had to hide the car keys. He couldn't manage his own medications anymore. Or take a phone message.

Falls were the worst problem. He couldn't get up by himself and he was too heavy for her to do the lifting. She was glad they'd subscribed to a medical helpline for him. Four times paramedics came. Each time they sat him on the couch, checked his vitals and encouraged him to go to hospital. Four times he insisted he was fine, he'd just had a tumble. He didn't need to go anywhere. And the paramedics left without him.

So it was that, three years ago, at the end of August, days after his eightieth birthday Rudy moved from their condo to Shasta House.

The Friday before the official move, the head nurse who preceded Ellen gathered Rudy's intake information. "Welcome to Shasta House, Rudy. We're glad you'll be living here."

"So am I," he said. "Now it'll be easier for Jenny. And I like it here."

Six-foot Dave, with a dark lock of hair that tended to fall forward the same way Jenny's unruly cowlick did, came to help with Rudy's relocation.

On moving morning, Rudy joined others in the lounge while Jenny directed Dave on how to set up Rudy's rooms. She was glad her son was strong and muscular. With her heart issue it was safest for her to play boss lady. By evening Rudy was established as the newest resident of Shasta House.

Two weeks later, Jenny had her pacemaker and Esther, finally setting aside her years'-long refusal to fly, came to stay with her sister for a month. Occasionally going with Jenny to visit Rudy.

He liked living on the third floor, even though some of the others there exhibited behaviours that perplexed him. Like the man directly across the hall who frequently appeared outside his room after a high-pitched argument with his wife, with whom he shared a unit. Wearing a tee shirt, he wandered down the hall minus his trousers. Minus his underwear. And explained to anyone he met that his penis wouldn't get hard anymore. It used to, but it wouldn't anymore.

Rudy sometimes sat in the small common room opposite the elevators with Audrey, a former New York fashion designer and the widow of a brewery executive who liked to talk about the whirl of cocktail parties she'd attended, and what she wore. That's where he was the day Arthur, a tall heavy-set man from a different floor, minced back and forth in the hall on the third floor.

Through Rudy's open doorway, Jenny could see the man clutching his bottom with both hands. She was used to seeing peculiar behaviours from residents, so gave it no thought as she hung freshly laundered shirts in Rudy's closet.

Soon the man disappeared from sight. A short time later, Rudy poked his head in. "Jenny, come. Someone needs help. We tried to get him up but we can't move him. Come, Jenny, come."

Jenny tossed the last of the clean shirts back in the laundry basket and dashed ahead of Rudy to the common room.

Next to the cubby hole sink, unable to get off, a groaning bare-bottomed man squatted on a large metal waste can, with Audrey yanking on his arm. Rudy immediately moved in to pull on the other arm.

"You two can't lift him," Jenny said, fully aware she couldn't do the job either. Arthur, on his makeshift toilet, moaned his discomfort. "I'll call for staff to help," Jenny reached for Rudy's pendant.

Help came, but not for several minutes. The scene both amused and upset Jenny. Had Rudy and Audrey been successful in dislodging Arthur, all three residents could have fallen in a heap and been injured.

When she saw the predicament, the longtime employee who arrived —a full-timer, hired before Bellis-White changed its policy to part-time for PSWs—couldn't suppress a giggle. With practised leverage skills, she assisted Arthur to his feet. He moaned and grabbed at his scrotum, "Oh, my balls."

"You do that again, and I'll see that your balls hurt more than that," the PSW scolded as she hoisted his pants over his nakedness and escorted him to an elevator. Then she returned to remove the smelly waste can.

An outbreak of flu that winter among both staff and residents put Shasta House on quarantine status. The other homes where the same PSWs also worked part-time were similarly afflicted, and all closed their doors to visitors. Anxiously, Jenny awaited word that Rudy had recovered, and that she could resume her daily visits.

His bout of flu was followed not long after by inflammation around his heart following a dental cleaning. Jenny shudders as she remembers how the influenza combined with the endocarditis ushered in his dramatic decline, with significant changes in behaviour, cognition and memory.

Rudy began misplacing items. His toothbrush in his underwear drawer. His wallet under his pillow. He no longer remembered how to change the batteries in his hearing aids or that he should use his cane at all times. Dealing with the phone confused him. He needed absorbent briefs not just at night, but during the day. He couldn't remember how to turn on the CD player. If he went out on his own he became disoriented, paid no heed to traffic lights, forgot his way to the condo.

Yet still, he read. And he continued to play a sharp game of Scrabble, although Jenny now kept score. As he grew increasingly unsteady on his feet, Jenny bought him a walker.

His residency on the third floor was short-lived after the illnesses. The head nurse took Jenny aside one day, not long after Arthur and the waste can. "Rudy's having so many more difficulties. We'd like to move him to the sixth floor. A smaller room will be less confusing for him."

What will the next change be?

Still awaiting his return from exercise class, Jenny melts deeper into his recliner.

Tuesday, December 22, mid-morning

Continuing to lounge in Rudy's comfortable electric lift chair, Jenny recalls the most recent Wednesday afternoon gathering of the Caregivers' Support Group at the seniors' centre before the holiday break.

When it was her turn to talk about what was happening in her world, she'd said, "Change and adaptation, that's what I live with. He changes. I adapt. He changes again. I adapt again. But I change, too. I worry more. I cry more. And do you know what else? I swear more. Sometimes the whole thing makes me so angry. I feel so cheated out of what could have been. What should have been."

Others in the circle nodded. They understood. She considers the Caregivers' Support Group and her journal her coping mechanisms. Along with allowing tears to spill. And invectives to fly.

Jenny looks about Rudy's small room. Moving day from one floor to another pops into her mind. Again, she'd called Dave to help. She was grateful for her son's hug when he arrived. Grateful for his willing muscles. Rudy was happy to see him, too. He remembered Dave and his family and asked about Allison and the children. To Barbie and Alex, Rudy was Opa Hoffie. They'd been his grandchildren as much as Jenny's from the day they were born. Now, in their early teens, Barbie and Alex no longer send him homemade cards, but Jenny keeps their latest school pictures pinned to Opa Hoffie's bulletin board.

Together, Jenny and Dave pared down Rudy's belongings to a small bookcase, TV, and dresser. The double bed was too large for Rudy's new room. Some hefty men took it to a thrift store.

She didn't need that bed anymore since she'd turned the spare room into an art studio. But she was glad to fit Rudy's CD player into her art space. Painting and listening to music went together like peanut butter and jam.

Shasta House provided a single bed with an aluminum guard rail that Rudy could use to help himself up and protect himself from falling out onto the floor. Jenny bought him a new electric lift chair. Blue to match his eyes. Oversized. Cumbersome. Like a recliner on steroids. The attached control was simple. Two buttons. Blue for reclining, red for lifting. He struggled to learn the new technology. Just as he could no longer use the TV remote, but still wanted a television set in his room because it made the room feel like home.

Jenny surfaces from her reverie. She looks at her wristwatch. He should be back any minute. She gets up from his chair. Removes her coat and kicks off her winter boots. She opens the folding closet door to retrieve her slippers.

The sharp odour of dried urine assaults her. She winces. *Damn, he's done it again.* She checks his trousers, each pair neatly folded over a fat plastic coat hanger. She hates having to sniff his row of pants to see if he's hung up the ones he peed in.

There are three offending pairs this time, which she transfers into the white plastic laundry basket at the end of his shower stall. She doesn't like feeling upset about this. But it is a miserable task. She understands he's only trying to be neat and tidy the way he used to be.

She feels so lucky that he hadn't expected her to fulfil a stereotypical role in their marriage. He wanted her as she wanted him. To be a companion. A true friend. Someone to listen to his ruminating, as he listened to hers. Someone to be silly with when silliness surfaced. Someone to sit at ease with in silence. A lover when the feelings were mutual.

She washes her hands and catches herself in the mirror. Dark raccoon circles around her eyes betray the increasing fatigue she tries to hide. No time for the haircut she sorely needs. She'll snip away at it herself after tomorrow's shower. Her once slender figure carries a few extra pounds —the way most older women do. *Nature's health insurance, something to come and go on in case of illness.* She notes the pull of time and gravity on her neck and bust. The weary slump of her shoulders. But she knows in her husband's eyes she's still beautiful, inside and out.

As long as Helga's not around. The thought churns her stomach.

Jenny dries her hands, fills a glass with water, and carries it to the other end of his room, a drink for the vibrant crimson poinsettia sitting on his highboy bureau. Rudy loves flowers and she makes sure there are always blossoms in his room. She leans against his dresser.

Flowers. The summer he tore up the grass in the front yard and planted the area with perennials that came into bloom in sequence. From tulips and daffodils in May to dusky rose sedum in September. Jenny loved the seasonal colours in front of their fieldstone house.

Flowers. The fresh bouquets she'd find on the dining room table, garden-sourced or from a different shop—not hers—or from the supermarket.

Flowers. The Saturday morning in her flower shop, not long before she and Rudy married. A gruelling marathon of making corsages and boutonnieres for the university graduation dance. A time so busy that she'd recruited a temp to help her. Just as she stacked the final corsage box into the display fridge for student pick-up later in the afternoon, Rudy arrived.

He stepped into the workroom, a long, slim white box under his arm. "So how're things going?"

"I've had it. I don't care if I see another flower as long as I live!"

"Oh?" His eyes glinted and a wide grin spread under his trim moustache. "That's too bad, because I brought you something."

He passed her the box. She placed it on the leaf-and-stem-littered counter and pulled the attached card from its envelope.

'For Jenny, *mein dollink*,' his favourite term of endearment. Years later Rudy explained that *dollink* was not a proper German word, but a term he'd borrowed from Hans and Fritz, the *liddle dollinks* of the old Katzenjammer Kids comic strip.

Then she lifted the lid of the box. Nestled in green tissue paper, a magnificent long-stemmed coral rose.

When the temp saw what was inside, she covered her mouth and snickered. Jenny shook her head in disbelief, then burst into tears. She turned from the counter and bolted into Rudy's embrace. He stroked the back of her head, "Everyone needs a little beauty in their lives now and then."

Flowers, always flowers.

She rouses herself, crosses to the window, and sorts through the stack of magazines on the sill beside his chair. She pokes the dated ones into his closet to take home another day. She'll just have to remember to bring a shopping bag to slide them into for carrying. Some she'll want to read. Others she'll put in the magazine-share box in her condominium lobby. There's no use taking them to the lounge for other residents. The evening cleaning staff only clear them away and stuff them into the garbage.

She leaves the current issues: *Maclean's, Canadian Geographic, Humanist Perspectives*. As well as *Folklore*, a magazine from Saskatchewan with nostalgic provincial stories he likes because they remind him of growing up in Saskatoon.

She looks at her watch a second time. Rudy should be back by now. Exercises finished half an hour ago. She hopes he's okay this time. No angina. She issues herself a reminder. It's time to talk to Cheryl about some of those exercises. With his health problems he shouldn't be doing the ones that raise his arms above his heart. Too often he comes back exhausted and with angina. She'll go now and see where he is.

She locks the door behind her and strides to the elevators.

Tuesday, December 22, late morning

She finds him in the lounge. On one of the loveseats by the fireplace with his arm around Helga, whose head rests on his shoulder.

Jenny draws in a deep breath, releases it slowly, orders her fists to uncurl. *Natural. Ellen said it's natural in retirement homes.*

"Good morning, Rudy." She forces a smile. "Hello, Helga."

Rudy scowls. "What are you doing here?" His tone is accusatory.

She swallows before she answers. "Rudy, I'm your wife. I come to see you every day."

"Helga says you're mean. You got her a calendar with puppies on it."

Helga straightens up, "I hate *Hunde*."

"Oh, I'm sorry, Helga, I didn't know." Jenny looks directly at Helga, but Helga avoids eye contact, turning her head toward the fireplace.

"I don't want to talk to you." Helga pushes herself to a standing position. "I'm going to my room." Leaning on her multicoloured cane, she stomps off toward the elevators.

Rudy's thick white eyebrows pinch together. "Why are you being mean to Helga, Jenny? I like her. She speaks German to me." His brows relax. "And someday pretty soon we're going to have sex. And you can't stop us."

No. No. He didn't really say that. He can't mean what he said. It's his disease talking. Calm. Stay calm. Divert. Distract.

"Rudy, let's go up to your room. I brought you an early Christmas present."

He brightens. "You did? I like presents."

"I know you do. I think you'll like this one a lot."

Heavy-hearted, Jenny fetches his walker from its parking place behind the love seat. She walks beside him toward the elevators.

"Put your hand on mine, Jenny. I like it when we walk that way."

Without enthusiasm, she covers his left hand with her right as he grips the handles of his walker.

On the elevator neither speaks, but when they enter his room, he looks at her quizzically. "Are you mad at me—about Helga?"

Natural. It's natural. "No. I'm not mad at you. But I'm disappointed. You know you're married and you love your wife. Helga knows you're married..."

She catches herself. What is she trying to do? Instill filters in someone with dementia?

"Here, let me get your present." She riffles under her coat on the bed, finds the raffia handles of a small gift bag with a ruddy-nosed Santa Claus on it.

Rudy settles into his chair and she hands him the bag. "Happy Early Christmas!"

He peels off the gold tissue paper on the top, folds it into precise quarters and places it over a snow-capped mountain on the cover of his geographical magazine. Then he reaches into the bag and pulls out his present.

"Earmuffs?"

"No, Rudy love, they're headphones—earphones. It's a gift of music. Let me put them on you."

She fits the shiny purple ear pieces in place, clips the attached tiny square digital music player to the buttonhole edge of his brown cardigan. Fiddles with the slider button on the top of the device until it shows green.

"Hear anything?"

"No."

She presses the plus sign. "Now?"

"No."

More adjustment to the volume.

"Now! Now I hear it!" His eyes widen. "That's my favourite. *The Trout!*"

Jenny watches, smiling, as Schubert's *Trout Quintet* pours its melody into his ears. A dreamy look relaxes the furrows on his forehead. He lifts his head, closes his eyes, and begins to conduct an orchestra only he can see.

Jenny understands the sensation. She's tried the system at home. So different from listening to CDs that fill a room with sound. With headphones it's like dining on a gourmet meal of treasured music in the candlelit intimacy of one's own core.

As he listens to his miniature machine filled with the classical music he loves—music that took her hours to load—Jenny ponders the situation with Helga. She scratches the top of her head, then runs her hand through her hair and slowly down the back of her neck, sensing the tension in her body that is so at odds with the relaxation she sees happening in Rudy's. Natural or not, she's deeply troubled by Rudy and Helga's attraction to each other.

She glances at Rudy. She's glad she didn't wait to give him the magic music kit on Christmas Day. He's so happy with it. Apart from the obvious pleasure it gives him, perhaps she can use it as a distraction. It seems that when Helga's out of sight, she's mostly out of mind.

Jenny watches her husband, now miming playing a piano. She smiles. A feeling of deep tenderness floods over her. "What are you listening to?" She speaks loudly enough for him to hear through his cocoon of music.

"Chopin. I think it's Chopin."

Jenny hears Charlene's loud announcement to the very hard-of-hearing resident next door that it's time to go downstairs for lunch. Jenny repeats the same information for Rudy, then stretches over and lifts off the headphones, unclips and turns off the device. She places his magical gift on top of his tidied-up pile of magazines. Some other time she'll show him how to use the iPod by himself. She hopes he'll absorb the lesson.

"Let's go to the bathroom and get your hands washed before lunch. Here," she hands him the chair remote which, though attached to the chair by a short cord, has fallen over the side of the arm, "press the button. The chair will help you get up."

The chair slowly reclines and the foot rest comes up. "The other button." She points to the red one.

He pushes it and the chair returns to its standard upright position, then gradually tilts forward until he's standing comfortably. Jenny rolls his walker in front of him.

Once she sees him comfortably seated for lunch, she leaves for home. The rest of her day unfolds with more last-minute holiday preparations, greeting calls to and from friends, and climbing into bed early.

In her dream, Jenny is seated on a Toronto subway car with Rudy beside her. When she turns to tell him something, he isn't there. Frantic, she appeals to the strap-hanging commuters in front of her, 'My husband's disappeared. Please help me find him.' The subway riders become Nancy, Ellen, Dolly, Harry, Colette. They ignore her as though none of them see or hear her. Now, she yells, 'Please help. I've lost my husband. Please. Please.' The strangulated sound of her own cries yanks her fully awake.

She gets up. Goes to the bathroom. Returns to bed. She turns on her side, wrestles the pillow under her head, tosses off a blanket, pulls it back on. Rolls onto her other side. Pulls up her knees. Stretches her legs. Rubs out a cramp in one foot.

Finally she rolls onto her back, stretches one arm to the bedside lamp and snaps on the light. She picks up the top book on the stack lying there. Flips to an Alice Munro short story she hasn't read, "The Bear Came Over the Mountain".

Partway through, she sets the book aside. The story of a wife with dementia and a budding relationship with another resident cuts too close to continue. Instead, she opens a favourite Steinbeck volume and begins to re-read *The Winter of Our Discontent.*

At last, eyes and mind blurred from the printed word, she sinks into the welcome comfort of returning sleep.

Wednesday, December 23

After breakfast she makes a tuna sandwich to take with her to Shasta House, seals it in a plastic bag and pops it into the fridge until she's ready to leave. She'll have lunch with Rudy today. Show him how to use his new music system. Then leave in time to do her final holiday shopping. She hasn't yet picked up fresh cranberries. Or cabbage for coleslaw.

As usual when she stays for lunch, she sits beside him at his assigned table, close to the dining room entrance. Once he's served his plate of fruit salad and cottage cheese with a tea biscuit on the side, she unwraps her sandwich.

His tablemates slurp vegetable beef soup. Colette dribbles some onto her chin but doesn't seem to know it's there.

"You've had a little soup spill, Colette." Jenny picks up Colette's unfolded napkin. "Here. You can wipe off your chin." Colette brushes the red fabric over her chin and returns to eating her soup.

Rudy watches Colette and pushes his plate aside. "I want some soup, too."

"I'm sorry, dear, your doctor says no. It's too salty for you."

"But I like soup." Sudden excitement spices his voice. "Look! Here comes Heidi."

Jenny doesn't correct him. He pushes his chair back and tries to get up to greet Helga on her way to her own place near the back wall of the dining room.

"Sit down, Rudy." Jenny sounds bossy—authoritarian—even to herself. "Helga's going to have her lunch."

As Helga passes she blows Jenny's husband a kiss. Before he can respond in kind, Jenny grabs his hand, forces him to stab his fork into the mound of cottage cheese.

"Rudy, eat your lunch."

The meal over, PSWs bring residents their walkers. As Jenny wheels Rudy's to him she notes that Helga is still eating.

"Shall we go up to your room now, Rudy?"

"I want to wait for Helga."

"She hasn't finished her lunch yet. You'll see her later." She hopes not.
"If you come upstairs now, you can listen to some classical music."

"I'd like that. Let's go."

Good.

The lesson is difficult. He finds it simple to put on the headphones, but hard to manipulate the tiny sliding button that turns the device off and on. It confuses him trying to figure out volume control with minute plus and minus signs. In the end, he terminates the lesson.

"I'll listen later. I'm tired."

"Sounds like naptime." She scoops up her coat and purse and dumps them beside his closet door along with the shopping bag she brought her sandwich in. Then she walks him from his chair to the bed. He sits on the edge and she stoops to pull apart the fasteners on his black leather shoes.

He strokes the top of her head. "You know, you're a wonderful wife. I love you *mein dollink*."

"I love you, too, Rudy. Very much."

She stands again, bends slightly to lift his legs onto the bed. He flops back against his pillow. "You know what, Rudy, I'm tired, too. How about I cuddle in behind you?"

"How about you have sex with me?"

"Let's settle for a cuddle for now. I know you're very tired."

She kicks off her slippers, moves sideways into the narrow space between his bed and the wall. "Roll over on your side, darling, so there's room for me."

"I want us to have sex."

"A cuddle or I'll just go home now."

"Helga says you're mean because you won't have sex with me."

"Maybe there are things Helga doesn't know, Rudy. Now, roll over on your side, and we can nap together."

He grabs the guard rail with his left hand and pulls himself onto his side facing the closet. Jenny lies down at his back, drapes an arm over his chest. He catches her fingertips and raises them to his mouth, kisses them, and returns their clasped hands to his chest.

"I do love you Jenny Hoffman. Even if you won't have sex with me."

"And I do love you, Rudolph Hoffman."

As she feels him drift off to sleep she wonders, is there perhaps a medical solution? *A hormone treatment, maybe?* Or something else to lessen his raging libido? She'll explore that later. For now, fatigue demands sleep.

The sound of the door being unlocked, squeaking open, then closing awakens Jenny. She sits up on the edge of the bed.

"Sorry to disturb you," Dolly says softly. "You look so peaceful there together."

"I had no idea I was so tired."

Jenny rubs her eyes, and picks up her glasses from the stand next to the wall, "Is it three o'clock already?" That's the time a PSW is scheduled to change Rudy's wet Depend.

Dolly's answer is muffled, coming from the closet where she's retrieving a fresh pair of incontinence underwear from the large box in the corner. "Actually it's three-thirty. I'm late this afternoon."

Dolly, with the clown-like orange hair and kind heart, moves from the closet to the side of the bed. She holds a grey shirred brief in one hand, while with the other she jiggles Rudy's shoulder, "Wake up sleepy-head. We've got a job to do."

In the time it takes Dolly to fully rouse Rudy, Jenny rounds the end of the bed, puts on her coat, pulls on boots, tucks slippers into the closet, shoves magazines into her shopping bag and gathers her purse.

Groggily, Rudy sits up.

From the doorway, Jenny says, "I'm going home now, darling. I have a bit of last-minute shopping to do. I'll see you tomorrow."

She blows him a kiss and he returns the gesture.

As she closes the door behind her she hears Dolly. "Okay, big guy. Let's go to the bathroom and get you cleaned up."

Jenny purchases her groceries, and lugs them into the condo along with the magazines. The idea of medical intervention is still with her. But the extended nap means it's now too late to call Dr. Angus. The office closes at four. She'll have to call tomorrow.

She's glad she didn't have Rudy change doctors when he moved into Shasta House. It would have been easier for her. But she wanted better for the man she'd cared about all these years. She didn't want him to have to deal with the impatient older doctor who sees ailing residents every two weeks, depending on who the charge nurse has lined up for him to examine.

Dr. Angus, on the other hand, knows Rudy's full, complicated medical history. He'll see Rudy on very short notice. Plus, the Family Health Centre includes a memory clinic and a state-of-the-art clinic for people on Coumadin, the blood thinner Rudy takes for atrial fibrillation. They monitor him regularly to avoid internal hemorrhaging and extreme bruising should his Coumadin levels get too high.

At the clinic it's a prick of the finger, wait a minute for the reading, and the pharmacist on duty determines the appropriate dosage on the spot. Not like the system at the home when an outside lab technician arrives before six in the morning, wakes the resident, draws the blood, and the results come back more than twenty-four hours later. Then, more waiting for the pharmacy that serves the home to deliver dosage revisions.

No, it isn't convenient picking Rudy up and driving him halfway across the city to see his family physician, but that's the care Jenny wants for her husband.

At home she puts the foodstuffs away, then pads into the living room. Collects the periodicals she'd strewn on the brown leather sofa. Feels the softness of the Persian rug beneath her feet as she crosses to the mahogany rack beside her chair. She pokes the magazines in beside her recent issue of *Zoomer* magazine.

Maybe she'll have time to look at some of Rudy's magazines this evening.

Before bed she confides to her journal, *Rudy's in lust! I don't know what to do. Maybe it's irrational on my part, considering he has dementia, but, damn, I feel betrayed. And it hurts like hell. I'm scared. Please, please, Dr. Angus. Help!*

Thursday, December 24

What a crazy time to try to reach a doctor! First thing in the morning, the day before Christmas. Each time she redials, Jenny hears a busy signal. She'll try again in the afternoon.

It's almost eleven when she arrives at Shasta House. She finds Rudy in the lounge on one of the loveseats. Once again, he curves his arm around Helga as she angles her head onto his shoulder while her hand strokes the top of his upper leg.

Jenny grits her teeth and shoves her hands into her black corduroy slacks. "Hi Rudy...how are you today, Helga?"

"Why do you keep spying on us, Jenny?" Rudy says.

"Do you think I'm spying?"

"Helga says you are. Can't you see, Helga's my friend? My girlfriend?"

Jenny catches herself about to say, 'And I'm your wife,' and swallows the words. Instead, she sits on the edge of the ottoman. "That's very interesting. And Helga, is Rudy your boyfriend?"

"*Nein*. He thinks he is. But he's not. He's *dein Mann*, your husband."

She frees herself from under Rudy's arm. Smooths her snug grey wool skirt as she rises from the loveseat. Retrieves her cane. "I've got a headache. I'm going to find the nurse." She heads off toward the elevators.

"Now look what you've done. You've given Helga a headache. But you can't stop us, Jenny. Someday we *are* going to have sex."

"Rudy," Jenny leans forward, facing her husband, her hands pressed together between knees, "I'm sorry Helga has a headache. But she is right. You're not her boyfriend. You're my husband. I'm your wife. Rudy... please look at me."

He turns his head to face her. Crosses his arms. Jenny looks intently at him, "It makes me very sad to find the man I love more than anyone in the whole world with his arm around another woman. It tears me up inside to hear you talk about having sex with someone else."

"Well, you won't do it."

"There are so many reasons why, Rudy. Your health—"

"No there aren't. You're just making that up."

Libido in high gear? Testosterone out of whack? He's forgotten he's impotent. She must get through to Dr. Angus. Surely, their doctor can help.

"Do you mind if I sit beside you, Rudy?"

"Suit yourself."

She settles next to him on the loveseat. Reaches for his hand, but he pulls his crossed arms tighter across his chest and stares straight ahead.

"Rudy, I've loved you since our very first date. And I'll always love you." She exhales, breathes in deeply. "It's almost Christmas, Rudy, a time for good cheer and goodwill. Do you think we can at least be friends?"

"I suppose so."

She lets the topic go. "I noticed there are some peanut butter cookies on the snack bar. Would you like to have one, and a cup of tea?"

He brightens. "Peanut butter's my favourite."

Together they nibble their sweets and sip their tea. As Jenny is ready to return their ironstone mugs to the tray for dirty cups, he catches her hand. "I don't want you to be sad, Jenny. But I really do like Helga a lot."

She ignores his second comment. "I know, Rudy. I'm going to see if Dr. Angus can help us over this hump."

Cutting her visiting time short, she leaves Rudy immersed in a coffee-table book about trains and races home.

Back in the condo, boots off, coat and purse put away, Jenny carries the phone into the living room and folds herself into her recliner.

In tired sing-song, a recorded message answers her call. "You have reached the office of Dr. Phillip Angus. If this is a medical emergency, please call 911. The office is now closed for the holidays. It will reopen on Monday, December 28th at eight-thirty. Happy Holidays."

"Damn! Double damn! Fart! Shit!" Jenny spits at the dial tone. *Did I really say that? My dear departed mother would choke.*

Thursday, December 24, late morning

Despite her frustration at not being able to reach Dr. Angus, there are still things she must do before tomorrow.

First the cranberry sauce. The crimson berries pop like bursting bubbles as she boils them in sugar and water. She mixes pastry, rolls it, and fills it with fresh sliced apples. Before she adds the upper crust she picks a slice off the top. As she bites into her treat, she remembers her sister and herself, as little girls, begging their mother for just one more piece of apple sprinkled with cinnamon and sugar.

Today she bakes two pies, one for tomorrow when she'll bring Rudy home for Christmas. The other for Boxing Day when Dave and Allison and the grandchildren come. As the pies bake she opens a can of salmon and makes herself a sandwich.

Lunch finished and the condo spicy-fragrant from pies cooling on the counter, she dons her coat and boots. It's cold, but the mid-afternoon sun glows and sidewalks are clear. She'll walk. There will be adequate street lighting for coming home.

At the entrance to Shasta House she glances at the matching black urns on either side of the door. Each filled with fresh pine boughs and huge cones from a tree species she doesn't know. Both arrangements anchored with giant red bows. *Festive. Pretty.* Appealing to her florist's eye.

"Hi Nancy," she greets the receptionist, at the same time directing her focus toward the fireplace area where her husband usually sits to read the newspaper. He's not there. "Any idea where Rudy might be?"

"I saw him catch an elevator quite a while ago. Looked like he was following Helga. He's probably in his room." Nancy reaches for the ringing phone on her desk and trills, "Good afternoon, Shasta House, Nancy speaking. How may I help you?"

Rudy's door is unlocked and he's not in his chair. Nor lying down on his bed. "Rudy?" She opens the bathroom door. Not there either.

Jenny whips off her coat and tosses it on the bed, sheds her boots and slides into her slippers. A cold foreboding courses through her body. As she steps into the hall, an elevator door opens and Rudy, behind his walker, gets off.

With relief, she smiles, waves, and calls, "Oh, there you are! I was just going to search for you."

"Why were you looking for me?"

"I was worried about you."

"I was okay."

"So where have you been?"

"Visiting."

"Visiting where?"

"If you must know, I was visiting in Helga's room."

"What?" Jenny claps her hand over her mouth. Her eyes widen. She slides her hand down the front of her neck to rest between her collar bones. "Helga's room?" The words quiver.

He reaches into his pants pocket and extracts a scrap of blue paper. Looks at it. "It's room 715. See? Helga wrote it down for me."

"Why did you go to Helga's room, Rudy?"

"She invited me. She wanted me to see her sewing machine. She has a very nice sewing machine in her room. And I fixed her TV."

"You what?" Jenny opens the door of his room and he wheels in. He parks his walker in front of his bookcase and plops into his chair. Jenny sits on the end of his bed. "You fixed her TV?"

"She asked me to fix her TV, so I did. She said I was smart. She said it in German."

Jenny shakes her head. *He fixed her TV?* He can't figure out how to use his lift chair, let alone his new music device, and unless someone else turns his TV on and off for him he's unable to watch anything. He's utterly baffled by the remote.

"I came back because the nurse needed to see her. The nurse told me to go to my own room." He pauses. "Is it Christmas yet?"

"Tomorrow. And you're going to spend the day at our place—at the condo, where I live."

"Can Helga come too?"

Patience. It's natural. "I don't think so, dear. She'll likely be going to her son's place for Christmas."

Without preamble, his eyes downcast, Rudy announces, "Helga has a boyfriend. Some days he comes to see her." He pauses as though trying to sort out a dilemma. "But I like her, too."

"Yes, Rudy, I know you like Helga, but if she already has a boyfriend do you think you should be going to her room? He might be unhappy if he comes and finds a married man visiting her."

He brightens, "It's all right. I fixed her TV."

Jenny doesn't want to hear any more. Abruptly, she redirects the conversation. "There's time before supper. Would you like to play Scrabble?"

"Sure."

"The board's already set up in the common room."

"Where's that?"

"It's that cozy little sitting room on this floor, right across from the elevators." There's a similar space on every floor except the fifth, where there's a chapel instead, but she doesn't bother telling him this.

As he pushes his walker and she saunters beside him, she wonders if he remembers those early Scrabble games they used to play.

The funny prize she made to be placed on the winner's bedside table. A little cardboard bed. *Jenny*, *Rudy*, printed like game tiles on the checkered blue and white bedspread, their names intersecting at the Y. At the foot of the miniature bed, a silver cup fashioned from tin foil.

But the real Scrabble prize was something else. The winner got to take the loser to bed. So, win or lose, who cared? Scrabble led to bed. Bed led to nakedness. Nakedness to kisses, caresses, to Rudy inside of her. The clean spicy smell of him. The oak headboard drumming on the wall to the rhythm of their lovemaking. The groaning, moaning sighs of satisfaction…the falling asleep in each other's arms.

She catches herself. This is not the time to remind Rudy that Scrabble had been an aphrodisiac for both of them.

At the game board Rudy takes long periods to execute his moves, but surprisingly uses clever strategy and expert spelling. And emerges the winner. It is at that moment, when Jenny is congratulating him on a well-played game, that an elevator opens.

"Rudy, my man," chimes Dolly, without getting off, "it's supper time! Hi Jenny, Merry Christmas." The door closes and Dolly is gone.

"Are you staying for supper, Jenny?" Rudy takes hold of his walker.

"Not tonight, love. I'll see you in the morning."

As they wait for an elevator to arrive, she leans toward him, kisses him firmly on the mouth, "Please try to remember, Rudy, I love you very much. I've always loved you. And I'll love you forever."

"I know." He grins mischievously at her and pats her bottom. "I love you, too, *mein dollink*." He pauses. "But I do like Helga."

The elevator clanks to a stop. Jenny sees Rudy safely into the cubicle, now nearly filled with residents on their way to their evening meal. At the very back of the assembly she spots Helga. The door closes.

Head down, heart heavy, Jenny tramps back to Rudy's room to retrieve her coat and boots. Room 715. That's what he said. Room 715.

Back at the condo, she's almost ready for bed when the phone rings.

"Hi, Mom!"

"Oh, Pam, how good to hear from you."

"Thought I'd better wish you a Merry Christmas tonight, in case you were going to spend tomorrow at the home with Rudy. How's he doing anyway?"

Jenny clears her throat. "Excuse me. I've got a tickle." Then with a mere hint of sadness, "He's okay, I think. They tell me everything he does is 'natural', whatever that means." She doesn't want to go into detail. How can she tell her daughter that her stepfather is sex-obsessed and fawning over another woman?

"Remember that documentary you recommended—the one about personal music for dementia patients? I got an iPod Shuffle for Rudy. I gave it to him early. He goes into a whole different world when he hears his favourite music. The best gift I've ever given him."

There's static. Her daughter's voice cuts in and out, "You remember, don't you Mom, that Roger and I are in Cancun for the holidays?"

Jenny doesn't remember. It's hard to keep track of her daughter's trips. As often as possible, Pam and Roger flit off to exotic locations for what they call a 'breather' from their corporate law careers in Halifax.

"It did slip my mind. Mexico this time. Is that why your phone call is so jerky?"

"Probably. I'm on my cell. It does seem to be breaking up. So I'll just wish you Merry Christmas. Talk to you later. Love you, Mom." The connection sputters and is still.

Jenny finishes getting ready for bed. In her journal she records the day's events and her increasing worries. At the end she scribbles, *Helga —room 715.*

Friday, December 25, Christmas Day

It's snowing Christmas morning. Huge, fat flakes. The kind Jenny used to catch on her tongue when she was little. She loves this kind of snow. Reflection envelops her as she watches the fluttering flakes through the bay window.

When the students had gone home for the holidays, Rudy and she would walk around the campus in snow like this, holding out their arms, hoping giant flakes would linger on their sleeves long enough for them to marvel at nature's intricacy.

Rudy, always the playful romantic, would aim for the deserted gazebo behind the library. He'd bow low to Jenny and say, 'Oh, beautiful princess, we have reached the castle. Let us enter forthwith.' And they'd climb the steps. Go to the middle of the structure. Wrap their arms around each other, then kiss. Deeply. Or sometimes they'd laugh because they bumped cold noses.

Then they'd trek home. Make love on the sofa in front of the fireplace. Back when they lived at the edge of the campus in the quaint fieldstone house with leaded glass windows and exposed beams across the living room ceiling.

Full of delicious memories, she drives to Shasta House to bring Rudy to the condo for the day. As she parks the car close to the end of the caterpillar tunnel, she thinks of visits from the grandchildren every Boxing Day. When they were small, Rudy balanced Alex on one knee, Barbie on the other, reciting *'Twas The Night Before Christmas* in melodious tones that made their eyes dance.

She remembers fun at the kitchen table as the children cut out rocking-horse ornaments from the flour and salt modelling dough she'd mixed. How after poking a hole for ribbon to be strung through, she would bake their horses and they would wait impatiently for their creations to cool before decorating them with red and blue paint and silver glitter. How excited they were to attach their ornaments to low branches of the fragrant fir tree. This year those same ornaments hang on the artificial tree in her condo's bay window.

As Jenny and Rudy ride the elevator to her floor she sets the memories aside and lets the present crowd in. She dreads the prospect of dealing with Rudy's incontinence while he's with her. Rebukes herself harshly. *He can't help it. It's part of his illness.*

She bought plastic-lined soaker pads for him to lie on when he gets tired and needs a nap on their bed—her bed, now. Because he prefers to sit in her recliner when he visits, she smooths a soaker pad on the chair seat, too. At the Health Supplies Market she had found aluminum arms to fit around the toilet so he would have support to get himself up and down. Patted herself on the back when she installed them by herself.

"I like coming here," Rudy tells her as she helps him with his jacket. "I see things I remember." He points to a bas-relief carving on the wall, a typical French Canadian house romantically nestled in a grove of trees. "We got that in Quebec City, didn't we?"

"Yes, sweetheart. On our honeymoon."

The smell of turkey cooking in the oven drifts into the foyer. "Can you smell your Christmas dinner?" Jenny asks.

He sniffs as he pushes his walker along the hall to the living room. "I'm not sure. I think I can. A little bit."

So his sense of smell is disappearing. Something else that's changing.

She guides him to the recliner and he drops into it. "Want your feet up?"

"No, I don't think so. I'll just read for a while."

He reaches into the magazine rack, withdraws the dated *Canadian Geographic* magazine that Jenny had brought home from his room. "Oh, good, I haven't seen this issue."

"I have a few things to do in the kitchen." Jenny rests her arm on the back of the recliner. "Then we'll open presents."

"Did I get you a present, Jenny?"

She recalls his Christmas shopping at the drugstore with Helga. The gift he bought for his new friend. The nothing he chose for her. Before that happened, in late November she'd wrapped a couple of items she'd bought for herself. On the cards she'd written, *To Jenny, love from Rudy.* "Yes," she says, "you got me some gifts."

After her kitchen chores, she hands him his first gift from under the tree. She likes to watch his excitement. *He becomes such a kid at Christmas.*

"New socks." He jiggles them in front of his face. "I always like getting new socks."

"And you always need them." Jenny chuckles. "It seems the dryer at

Shasta House is on a diet of single socks. Plus your toenails get so sharp they cut holes through your socks in no time."

She tried for a long time to keep his toenails trimmed after he could no longer do it himself. But it was difficult. How grateful she feels that an RN comes to Shasta House on a regular basis to look after residents' feet, for an extra fee she gladly pays.

He also likes the new blue polyester cardigan she purchased for him. She learned the hard way that warm woolen sweaters and retirement homes are not compatible. When his expensive, Irish-knit, dry-clean-only, lamb's wool sweater accidentally got into his laundry basket, it came back to his room sized to fit one of Santa's elves.

He thanks her for the book of prairie photographs he unwrapped. She hands him the next gift.

He reads the tag, "This says it's to you from me." And he passes the package back to her. "Merry Christmas, *mein dollink.*"

She takes the package and sits across from him on the sofa. He watches as she pulls the wrapping off a new box of watercolour paints, and a pad of art paper. "Thank you so much, sweetheart."

Standing up from the couch she sidesteps the coffee table and crosses to his chair. She kisses him. "You always choose exactly what I like."

"But I didn't really get those for you, did I? I don't shop anymore, do I?"

"But that's what you would have picked out for me, if you could have, right?"

"Absolutely!"

"Then, thank you for the wonderful presents."

He plays their game and grins. "You're welcome. I'm glad you like my choices."

Jenny looks at her watch. "It's time for your noon meds. We won't be eating our turkey until later in the afternoon. So I'm just going to give you a little snack to go along with your pills."

She pops into the kitchen. Makes toast. Pours a glass of milk. Carries his food in on a tray. She opens the small dated packet which she'd picked up from Anna, the charge nurse. Shakes the contents into her palm and examines the assortment. A scored yellow pill; his diuretic. A pink-and-black capsule for digestion, two white round caplets for blood pressure, an oval coral one for his heart rate, and the tiny white one intended to slow the progression of dementia, which she's sure isn't helping any more.

After Rudy has taken his meds and eaten his snack, she suggests he nap before dinner. "Better get you into a dry brief, first."

She helps him up from the recliner and takes his arm. Slowly she walks with him to the bathroom.

As he stands holding on to the edge of the sink, Jenny kneels and removes first his left shoe, then his right. "Undo your belt and unzip your fly," she says. His trousers fall to the floor. He steps out of them and she pushes them aside with the toe of her slipper.

"Your brief is drenched. Here, lift up your leg so I can slip it off—good. Now the other leg."

She takes a fresh facecloth, runs it under warm water and rubs it with a cake of green soap. "I'll wash you off. Keep holding onto the edge of the sink so you don't lose your balance."

She reaches in front of him, swishes the cloth around his genitals, noting the only remaining evidence that once upon a time he'd been a redhead. A true 'carrot top' in his youth, he'd told her. Then she wipes the cloth over his buttocks, those sleek and slim—now wrinkled—cheeks she used to comment on in their intimate moments, 'You have such a cute little bum.'

She grabs a fluffy bath towel and dries him off. Again, she has him raise one foot, then the other into a new pair of absorbent underpants. "You can leave your trousers off while you nap."

Taking his arm, she steadies him as he shuffles to her bedroom. Just as she does at the home, she lifts his legs onto the bed and, when he's comfortable, spreads a satin-bound yellow wool blanket over him.

"Are you going to lie down with me? We could have sex."

"Sorry love, but I have things to do in the kitchen."

She leans over and kisses him on the tip of his nose. He reaches up and cradles her breasts. She lets his hands linger. A tiny bit of remembered pleasure for them both. "Have a good nap, Rudy. Merry Christmas."

Back in the bathroom, she picks up his trousers, folds and drapes them over the edge of the bathtub. Gathers the wet diaper, stuffs it into a plastic grocery bag, steps on the foot lever of the stainless steel waste can next to the sink, and drops the bag in. Then she washes her hands.

When Rudy awakens two hours later she repeats the underwear change. The final step is a combined effort as he tightens his belt and she mates the fasteners on his shoes. They wash their hands together in the bathroom sink. Both of them are now ready for Christmas dinner.

"I like eating here." At the dining room table he loads food onto his fork. "This is good." It pleases her to see him enjoying his classic holiday meal.

"More coleslaw, dear?"

"Please. You make the best coleslaw, Jenny." He's long ago forgotten it tastes special because she adds dried mint flakes.

Then it's time for dessert. Warm apple pie with vanilla ice cream. A crumb catches in his throat. He coughs. Coughs, and coughs again.

Even though Anna says, 'As long as he's coughing he's breathing,' each time Jenny sees him choke on his food, watches his face turn red, his eyes brim, it frightens her.

At last the coughing ends. His colour lightens.

"A sip of water now?"

He swallows the water without incident, puts his glass down, and ventures where she hoped he wouldn't go on this special day. "You know I like Helga. I like her a lot. You and she could be good friends."

Jenny's answer is curt. "I have lots of friends. I don't need Helga as a friend."

"Helga says you're mean to me." Jenny's brows pinch together. "You won't live with me. And you won't have sex with me. That's mean, Jenny, just plain mean."

Like a burst of acid reflux, Jenny's anger rises. She clamps her jaw shut while her mind rants. *We are sexual beings until the day we die.* She'd read that somewhere. It bugs her that nobody talks about sex when it comes to the elderly except in jest. Rudy's not the only one needing sexual release. It's not just a male thing. Women have sex drives, too. Her sexuality demands occasional pleasuring of herself. *Damn it. We are **all** sexual beings until the day we die.*

Still seething, after her protracted silence, she blurts, "Do you want to know why I don't have sex with you, why we don't make love anymore, Rudy? Do you really want to know?"

"Yes."

"Because you're impotent. You've had erectile dysfunction for years. For years! And also because of your fragile heart." Jenny senses she's being cruel. She won't go further. She won't add that the thought of it in his present condition makes her feel creepy.

"We can't do it anymore, Rudy." Looking into his pleading eyes, tears well in her own. "That's just the way it is. For us, sex—lovemaking—is over."

"But there are pills for that. For men who can't get an erection."

She's surprised to hear this. "You mean Viagra?"

"Yes, that's it. We can ask the doctor for some, can't we?"

Sadness replaces anger. "Sweetheart, the doctor won't give those pills to you. You have too many other health problems. They'd be far too risky."

"I don't believe you. Helga's right. You're just mean."

"Rudy, I'm going to take you to see Dr. Angus Monday morning. How about you ask him yourself?"

"I will."

Keen for him to drop this topic, she asks, "Do you want tea before I take you back to Shasta House?"

"Yes, please."

Before bed she communes with her journal: *An almost perfect Christmas with Rudy. Hiding in the background though, was Helga. I want to feel kindly toward her. But, damn it, I don't, and when Rudy quotes her to me, I don't feel kindly toward him either. Merry Christmas to all and to all in-the-bizarre-world-of-dementia, a Good Night!*

Saturday, December 26, Boxing Day

In the late morning Jenny once more brings Rudy to the condo. Dave, Allison and the young teens arrive shortly after. Greeting hugs for the Hoffman grandparents, hugs of welcome for the Allen family.

"You still put Teddy under the tree, Nana? Even when there aren't any little kids around?" Barbie asks, folding her legs under her on one end of the couch.

"Of course! It wouldn't be Christmas without him! Do you know that I was only two years old when Santa brought me that bear? He's seventy-five now."

"Wow! Nana!" Alex pipes. "He's ancient! Like, man! You're both ancient!"

Jenny laughs.

"What about the rocking horse, Nana? I loved riding on him when I was little," Barbie says.

"He actually belonged to your Great Aunt Esther. She gave the horse to your dad when he was born. So, I suppose if your father ever wants it I'll have to hand it over, since it's really not mine."

Rudy interjects, "Didn't I make new reins for the rocking horse when Barbie was little?"

"Yes, you did, dear. The old ones were weak, and you wanted her to have something strong to hold on to."

This Christmas Jenny has tied a bright red ribbon around the horse, and perched a dollar store Santa hat on Teddy's head. Dave reaches under the tree, lifts Teddy's hat off and plops it onto his own head.

Transformed, Dave becomes Santa for the day, "Ho! Ho! Ho! This present is for little Rudy Hoffman because he's been a very good boy all year long."

Rudy laughs, "Thank you, Santa."

The card on the next gift reads, *To Allison, with love from Rudy.* Allison hugs Rudy and thanks him for the mystery novel Jenny, not Rudy, bought for her.

The children, too, are lavish with hugs and thanks. Barbie, keen to read the set of *The Hunger Games* books Jenny found for her, pokes the gift card to The Gap into her pocket. Alex flips pages of *The Hobbit*, then shows his mother the Harry Potter board game Opa Hoffie gave him, and waves a crisp twenty dollar bill at his father.

"Now I can get that new video game, Dad."

It's lunchtime. No cold turkey for this crew. Jenny has ordered a kid staple, pizza. They'll have her own warmed-up apple pie with ice cream for dessert.

"Why don't you eat ice cream on your pie, Nana?" Barbie asks, "Why cheese? Yuck!"

"Well, your great-grandpa always ate a slice of cheese with his apple pie and I learned to like it that way, too. He used to say every time, 'Apple pie without cheese is like a hug without a squeeze.'"

Chatter, laughter and love abound around the dining room table. Rudy's smiles are broad and frequent. Jenny's heart is full.

Then to the bathroom for Rudy's change into fresh briefs. Help to Jenny's bed for a nap with the yellow blanket tucked under his chin.

The family is still there when Rudy awakens, is changed, and returns to the living room. Jenny likes the sight of the grandchildren kneeling on the floor while their parents lean forward from the couch, all of them concentrating on a game of Mexican Train set up on the coffee table. But cheers and boos, and the toot-toot of success at the end of the game etch a perplexed look on Rudy's face.

Dave notices Rudy's confusion. "Well done, Alex. You won this time. Congratulations, son. Everyone okay if we put the game away now?"

"Fine by me." Barbie clutches at her long auburn hair and shapes it briefly into a ponytail, then lets it fall back onto her shoulders. "I'd rather play something on my phone anyway." She gets up from the floor and pretzels into a corner of the couch.

Jenny lays her hand on her grandson's shoulder. "Alex, dear, would you like to help Opa Hoffie with the dog kit Santa gave him?"

She spreads a blue plastic covering over the dining table. "Dave?" she calls, "Can you bring Rudy here to the table?"

She removes the contents from the kit labeled 'for ages 6 and up' and spreads them out as she waits for Rudy to be escorted from the recliner to the dining room. Patiently, Rudy's step-grandson assists in putting together the pieces of brown foam that form a roly-poly dog figure with fat legs and googly eyes.

"Super job, you two." Jenny picks up the figure, examines it from all sides and replaces it in front of Rudy. "I'm sorry to break up the party everyone, but it is time for Rudy to go back to Shasta House."

"And time for us to go back to Toronto," Dave says. "There's a bit of traffic today, but not the big trucks. It shouldn't take us more than an hour to get home." He glances out the bay window. "And it isn't snowing anymore."

Thanks, and hugs, and the family is gone.

At Shasta House Rudy and Jenny go directly to his room. She doesn't plan to stay, so merely unbuttons her coat. When Rudy is nestled in his chair, she picks up his magic music square and headphones from the window sill, "Would you like to hear some music, Rudy?"

He nods and squirms in anticipation. She fits his headphones over his ears and secures the metal square to his sweater. "Just take it off when you're done and put it on the window sill. I'll check it tomorrow." She knows he likely won't remember to turn it off. She hopes he'll put it on the window sill.

Then she drives home. It's been a wonderful day. In her journal she notes: *Not once did Rudy mention Helga. Still, I'll call the doctor first thing Monday morning.*

Jockie Loomer-Kruger

Sunday, December 27

On the last Sunday of each month Jenny heads to Shasta House with a singular purpose. To keep Rudy from getting upset when staff hustle him, along with others, to the chapel on the fifth floor for the regularly scheduled church service. Although he can no longer articulate why he abandoned the evangelical faith he was raised in, finding himself in a church-like setting makes him anxious. He chews his nails, fidgets in his seat. After a while, his face reddens as his blood pressure rises.

For a few years he attended the Unitarian Centre services sporadically with Jenny. But the setting—coloured windows, rows of pews, a chancel with pulpit, and a flaming chalice in a building that originally housed a Lutheran congregation—made him uncomfortable. Until at last, one Sunday morning when both were ready to go to the Centre, he opened the passenger door for Jenny, held it ajar after she got in, 'You'd better slide over so you can drive yourself there. I can't go with you. It's not an answer for me anymore, Jenny. You keep on attending if you want to. But I don't belong there.'

One of the stories Jenny had transcribed into his green binder helped her understand.

> Klaus and I both attended ten o'clock Sunday School. Then we joined my parents at the morning church service, and the entire family went to the evening service too.
>
> Every night in the living room, right after supper, my mother conducted prayers, read from the Old Testament, and made us sing hymns in German.
>
> Whenever I did something naughty, and even when I didn't, she'd lecture me on my wicked behaviour. She assured me I would go straight to Hell for my sins. When you're a little kid with a big imagination, the idea of going to Hell can be pretty scary.
>
> The good part was when I was small, my father always held my hand on the way to church. During the service, he looked to

be half asleep.

By the time I was eight I began to doubt. It started during a thunderstorm. I was watching lightning through the living room window, and listening to the thunder. I asked my mother what made thunder and lightning and she said, 'God made it.' I thought God was far too busy sending bad people off to Hell to waste his time making storms. There had to be other causes.

Maybe that was the beginning of my interest in meteorology, along with my doubts about religion. By the time I was fourteen, I was no longer a believer.

Today, in the fifth-floor chapel, a brunette lady with a broad bottom sits on a bench at the electric organ. Jenny notes the incongruous placement of large orange chrysanthemums on the green dress she's wearing.

In front of a large plastic cross, made to look like wood, is an oak lectern. The visiting pastor, in clerical collar and black suit, clutches his leather Bible as he leans over the makeshift pulpit to speak to the organist.

Jenny spots her husband among the gathering of residents. He's in a back pew, sitting beside Helga. Jenny taps him on the shoulder. "Going to church this morning, darling?"

"Is this church?" He looks to Helga for the answer.

"*Ja*. We go to church."

"But I don't."

"Everybody goes to *Kirche*, Rudy. Why are you so stupid?"

"Helga, Rudy's not a churchgoer. Being here makes him uncomfortable. I'm going to take him with me."

Helga shrugs, "Do what you want. You're *die Frau*."

"Come, Rudy. We'll go do something else."

"But I want to be with Helga. Can Helga come with us?"

"You'll see her later. Come."

Jenny moves around the end of the pew and assists him up with a lift under his armpit. She finds his walker near the elevators. As they wait for their ride to the floor above, the minister bellies up to the lectern and in a loud voice addresses his congregation, "Welcome to the House of the Lord."

An elevator comes just as scratchy voices retrieve the words they learned so many years before. "On a hill far away, stands an old rugged cross..."

In his room, Jenny takes off her coat, hangs it in his closet, relieved that today the closet smells fine. She tugs off her boots and puts on her slippers, then gives Rudy the parcel she brought with her. "An after-Christmas present for you."

He tears off the paper, "Markers? And a drawing pad?"

"That's right. And we're going to take your new markers and go down to the art room."

In the basement, they wend their way past the specially-designed exercise equipment to the room set up with a long table, with coloured pencils and sheets of drawing paper scattered at one end. She gets him settled there, slides a piece of paper in front of him and opens his new box of markers.

"Anything special you'd like to draw?"

"Yes. But I can't tell you."

As he draws, Jenny leafs through a volume from the shelf behind him, her back to him. The book of watercolour paintings of birds intrigues her. She studies them intently, trying to figure out how the artist painted the feathers so realistically. Time slides away.

At the image of a mockingbird, she remembers Rudy and Mac, their mockingbird.

It had taken a few days before they realized the grosbeaks, sparrows, and even starlings were not coming to the large covered platform feeder close to the breakfast nook window of the fieldstone house. That a grey bird with yellow eyes had hunkered down for long visits. A bird they didn't recognize.

They eventually identified the newcomer as a northern mockingbird, the state bird of Florida. Had it blown off course in a storm? Why was it wintering in frigid Sonnenberg, in Southern Ontario? They read further that it liked a diet of fruit, not the seed mixture they spread in their feeder for their usual winter visitors.

The book didn't say mockingbirds also liked peanut butter, but this one seemed intent on pecking out the peanut butter-filled holes in a short hanging birch log on the fence behind the feeder. A favourite of the starlings, too.

They laughed to watch Mac dart at the starlings when they dared to land on the pegs sticking out of the stuffed log. Even though they were larger than Mac the Mockingbird, Mac sent them flapping and squawking.

All through the winter Rudy fed their solo feathered guest, even finding a recipe for mockingbird muffins made with cornmeal, blueberries and sand for the bird's crop.

Rudy interrupts Jenny's reminiscences. "I'm thirsty. Do they have water here?"

She leaves the art room to fill a paper cup from the water dispenser near the exercise equipment. When she gets back, she notices he has turned his drawing over so she can't see it.

"Enough art for today?"

"Yes."

"Okay then, let's get those markers into their box. We'll take them back upstairs. You might want to draw in your room sometime."

Together they gather the markers and poke them into place. "So what did you draw today?"

"I drew Helga."

"Oh, really? May I see your drawing?"

"No, it's a present for Helga."

Jenny pushes his walker to him, he places his markers in the bottom of the carry basket and drops the drawing in on top, right-side-up. Jenny looks. She recognizes his representation of a sewing machine. She assumes the dark-haired woman standing beside it is Helga. He has drawn her as a nude.

They go to his room to wash up for lunch, tossing his markers and drawing onto the bed. Jenny takes him early to the dining room to avoid the crowd leaving the church service.

Shortly after, the others stream to the main floor for lunch. Jenny waits for them to get off the elevators before she does the return run to Rudy's room. She sees Helga smile at Harry as they exit, her hand sliding flirtatiously onto his forearm. The former bank manager slaps at her hand and walks away from her.

Jenny remembers what Helga's daughter-in-law said. 'Helga had many admirers.' Now she has Rudy. And an outside boyfriend who visits her. But not Harry. *Good for you Harry.* Jenny steps into the empty elevator.

In Rudy's room she puts his markers away. Dons her coat and boots and picks up his drawing. She hesitates for only a moment before she tears the picture into a dozen pieces and pokes the fragments into her coat pocket. Trusting by the time he returns from lunch, his short-term memory loss will have erased the drawing from his mind.

As the residents eat, she hurries home.

Monday, December 28

Overnight, freezing rain glazes power lines and wraps tree branches in silver sleeves. From her second story bedroom window Jenny sees sidewalks glisten, but salting and enough back-to-work traffic have broken up the ice on the street. Still, she knows she can't take Rudy out in this.

At eight-thirty, as soon as the Health Centre opens, she makes her call, explaining that she'd like to bring Rudy to the office, but it's far too icy. Could she please speak with Dr. Angus about Rudy? Yes, it's urgent.

Dr. Angus listens as Jenny describes Rudy's elevated libido. "Is there something he can take that will calm this obsession with sex? A hormone treatment or something?"

"The trials on using hormones are somewhat inconclusive for situations like this," Dr. Angus says. "You realize, of course, that I don't usually prescribe without seeing the patient, but I'll make an exception in this case, Jenny. It sounds like this needs immediate attention. I'll fax a prescription to your pharmacy for Triadone. That should settle him down quite quickly. I'm sorry this is happening. It has to be very hard on you."

"It is." Jenny hears her own voice crack. She clears her throat. "It's damned bloody hard."

"Are you sleeping?"

"Not well. Not well at all."

"I'll fax an order for sleeping pills for you, as well. Something mild. Just to give you a little assistance. And only ten of them. A couple of renewals if you find you continue to need them. Triadone works very quickly. Things should be much more normal within a week."

"Thank you, Dr. Angus. Thank you very much."

She puts down her phone. She'll wait until salting makes sidewalks safer before going to the drugstore.

At the kitchen table she flips through the newspaper to pass the time. After she finishes with the latest news, she goes to the foyer, sits on the antique oak hall tree seat to pull on rubber forms embedded with cleats, securing them snugly at the heel and toe of her boots. *They don't look very stylish, but I don't want to slip and fall.*

She drives to the pharmacy, picks up the two prescriptions and continues on to Shasta House. Her ice cleats dig into the tight carpeting. She didn't fall on the ice but fears she might fall on the carpet.

Carefully, she steps onto the slate grey tile floor in the elevator. Wonders if the puddle in one corner is boot melt or from a resident unable to make it to the bathroom in time.

On the second floor she gets off and strides three doors down the hall to the nurses' station. She finds the long-term, full-time charge nurse seated in a rolling chair at the front end of a long desk. On the far end of the desk a multi-screen security monitor registers activities in various areas in the home, including what's happening in front of the elevators on each floor.

"Excuse me, Anna. Sorry to disturb you when you're busy..."

Anna swivels her chair. "Oh, hi, Jenny. What's up?" She leans back, runs her hand over the top of her muddy blonde brush cut that reminds Jenny of the way boys wore their hair when Jenny was a teenager.

"I brought you some new medication for Rudy." Jenny hands her the bottle of pills. "Something that should slow down the budding romance." It makes her stomach flipflop to speak so lightly of what's going on. Of what gnaws at her.

Anna reads the label. "Triadone? That's not what we usually use for lovestruck residents."

"You've been here a long time. I suppose you've seen it all before."

"Yes, ma'am. In one form or another. This does seem a little different, though."

Anna rolls the bottle of pills around in her fingers, then sets it on the desk beside the pile of charts. "Usually, it happens when residents are here without family visitors, or when they no longer recognize their spouses. Not like Rudy and you."

"I think that's why I mind it so much, Anna. Because he still knows I'm his wife. He still knows he loves me. And that I love him, and yet, Helga —"

Anna interrupts with the edge of a chuckle, "That Helga. She's quite a piece of work."

Shit. Even Anna thinks it's cute and funny. "What do you mean?"

"I probably shouldn't be telling you this, but I will. Helga blows hot and cold. One minute she wants Rudy around, then she comes whining to me and asks me to do something, stop him following her everywhere. She complains that he forgets things, that he can't remember even when she tells him in German. Then she's flirting with him again, and plunks herself down on the loveseat beside him, all mushy. Poor guy, he doesn't know what's going on."

"I didn't know that."

"And she has a temper, too. She hit my arm the other day when I wanted to check her insulin levels. I still have the bruise. I had to approach her three different times before she'd let me prick her finger."

"Do you think, if she gets angry with Rudy, that she might attack him?"

"I doubt it. I think she just doesn't like having her finger pricked."

Anna picks up the pill bottle again, "Hmm. Triadone. I'll get it started today. I hope it works."

Jenny goes next to Rudy's room. He's not there. She looks on his bulletin board near the door. On the activity sheet for December she sees there's a singsong session scheduled for the morning of the twenty-eighth. *Good, he likes to sing.* She'll come back later in the afternoon.

Without removing either coat or boots or sliding off her ice cleats, Jenny walks over to the window. Picks up his music device from the sill where he left it still turned on. She thought he would. She holds one headphone to her ear. No sound.

Disconnecting the tiny metal square, she pokes it into her pocket. At home she'll attach it to its short white cord, plug the cord into her computer in the den that used to be Rudy's office, and let it charge up again overnight. It'll then be ready for another fifteen hours of play.

Back at the condo, she clears up the clutter from the Boxing Day activities, the job she has been too weary to do for the past two days. By four in the afternoon the sky is deeply grey. She feels she should go back to Shasta House, but her legs ache with tiredness. She shakes her head. *No. I simply can't do it.* Tomorrow will be better. Besides, the new medication may be helping by then.

She makes a cup of tea, carries it to her rose recliner, places it on the end table beside the chair, opposite the magazine rack, and flops down. Shifting the lever on the side of the chair, she feels her weary legs and slippered feet rise off the floor.

"God, I'm exhausted." Her words echo in the stillness of the living room. "Rudy Hoffman, I love you with all my heart, but what you're doing is destroying me."

Tuesday, December 29

She awakens late and slightly groggy the next morning. A whole sleeping pill is too much.

After breakfast she considers when to go to Shasta House. She decides to wait until afternoon. Give Rudy's new medication time to start its magic.

From the hook on the back of the spare room studio door, Jenny lifts off her paint-stained blue smock and slips it on. At the bathroom sink, she fills a small container with water. She pulls up a chair to her easel, prepares the watercolour paper, then picks up her brush and begins to paint. A scene from memory—a frozen brook in a snowy evergreen forest. A place she and Rudy explored in New Brunswick the Christmas week they spent with her sister, the year he retired.

But the image isn't working. *All that somberness of the woods*. She needs something lighter today. She crumples her effort and tosses it in the wastebasket.

Then she opens her art supply cupboard, roots around until she locates a rarely-used box of oil pastels. *Colour*. She hungers for colour.

The next picture begins to draw itself. A little girl in red polka dot dress dancing through a green field of scattered daisies. The child's pigtails fly out behind her, as does the golden teddy bear she swings by one paw. In the sky, she draws drifting clouds and a vibrant yellow sun with rays protruding like bicycle spokes, the way children depict sunshine.

She smiles inwardly, noting that she has drawn the same way she did when she was in elementary school, as though she had never had an art lesson in her life. She's drawn herself in the field behind their house, with the old frayed teddy bear who still sits under the Christmas tree. It warms her to remember being so young on the family farm, climbing fences, feeding chickens, loving her teddy bear, playing with her sister.

Maybe she should call Esther. *No*. Her sister wouldn't want to hear what's going on. How often over the years had she grumped about women airing their wedded woes? Or tsk-tsked about divorce. 'If people choose to marry, it should be for life. For better or worse.' Esther's traditional beliefs were the reason Jenny had never told her the circumstances of Rudy's divorce.

When Jenny married Rudy, Esther found an excuse not to come to the small at-home wedding. Her flying phobia, she claimed. But Jenny knew it was because Rudy was divorced.

Even when her first marriage was entangled in Peter's alcoholism, Jenny avoided talking to her sister about it, dreading a pious lecture on a wife's duty to keep her family running smoothly.

Although they were often at odds, Jenny understood where most of Esther's strong views had come from. Directly from the betrayal her sister had experienced when her high-school-sweetheart fiancé, an air traffic controller at the Moncton airport, eloped with an airline stewardess, three months after his official engagement to Esther.

Jenny remembers her sister's sobs over the phone as she angrily related how she'd whipped off her engagement ring and tossed it onto the manure heap behind their father's barn. Her bitterness ran deep. Even translated into a refusal to set foot on an airplane. And softened only in later years as she plunged deeper into her faith for solace, and church activities to keep busy after retiring from years of secretarial and bookkeeping duties for a local greenhouse operation.

No. Absolutely no. She could not air the current situation with Rudy and Helga with her sister.

Jenny sprays her drawing with fixative to keep it from smearing. She'll take it with her this afternoon to show Rudy. He used to be so enthusiastic about her art. Insisted on framing and hanging many of her pieces, 'Your creative expression is such an important part of who you are, *mein dollink.* When I look at your art, I look into your heart.'

In the kitchen, she washes the pastel residue from her hands. There's still time to make a batch of peanut butter cookies.

After the cookies are done, she carries a lunch tray with a bowl of vegetable soup and a turkey sandwich to the table next to her recliner. She eats mindlessly. Turns on the TV news but watches only briefly. She doesn't want anything gloomy today. Quickly, she finds a music channel. Easy Listening.

Two hours later she jolts awake in her chair. "Good grief," she says aloud, "it's three o'clock. Time to go see Rudy." She'll leave the kitchen clean-up until she gets back. *Let the mess reproduce while I'm gone.*

Mild temperatures overnight along with morning fog have melted the lingering ice on the sidewalks. It feels safe to walk to Shasta House. How conscious she's become of the risk of falling. Maybe because Rudy has had so many falls and near-falls. He's so easily tilted off balance now. Almost like he could be pushed over with a mere tickle from a feather.

She braces herself before entering the home, fully expecting to find Rudy—and Helga—snuggled together by the fireplace.

"Natural. It's natural," she tells herself.

But he's not there. Nor is Helga. Lots of other residents are in the area, though. A musical entertainment has just finished. Fake Elvis, sparkly white satin shirt, splotched grey from sweat at the armpits, is packing up his guitar and amplifiers.

She hopes Rudy's upstairs with one of the PSWs, getting changed. Before it fills with residents returning to their rooms, Jenny catches an elevator.

Rudy's door is locked. She fumbles in her purse for her key to his room, the one with the pewter train fob, separate from her house and car keys.

The room is empty. She tosses her drawing and the plastic zip bag containing three cookies onto his bed.

On her way out the door, she almost collides with Lucija, "He's not there. I'm going to get him. I should be back in a few minutes. I'll buzz when we get back."

Aware that elevators will be full of residents returning from their Elvis session, Jenny hurries off in the other direction to the enclosed stairwell. She pushes the heavy metal fire door and climbs the single flight to the top floor of Shasta House.

715. She's pretty sure that's the number. Her rap on the door is gentle. No response. She tries the door handle. It's locked.

She knocks louder. No one comes, but she can hear muffled voices. She knocks once more.

A distant voice responds. "Who's there?"

"It's Jenny. Is Rudy there? I need to take him back to his room."

Hesitation. Then, "*Ja*, he's here."

Again, indistinct words being exchanged, and in a few moments, the lock clicks open. Helga yanks at the waistband of her sharply creased grey slacks to centre them comfortably.

"You found me." Rudy burrows deeper into the soft gold armchair near the window. A straight-backed wooden chair is pulled up closely in front of where he is ensconced. *Within touching distance.*

"Lucija came looking for you, Rudy." Jenny studies him from the doorway. "You need to go back to your room so she can help you."

"But I want to stay here."

Helga has stationed herself at one end of a long table beside a white sewing machine. Next to it, pinned with assorted tissue pattern pieces, is a length of emerald-green fabric flecked with tiny silver checkmarks.

Jenny steps into the room but not to where Rudy is sitting. She wants to see if he's able to get up from the low chair by himself. She edges close to Helga's table. "So, get up, Rudy. We need to go now."

Watching him from the corner of her eye, she speaks to Helga, "I see you're doing some sewing. What are you making?"

Rudy struggles to push himself up, fails, and sinks back down.

"I'm making a dress." Helga smooths her hand over the unpinned end of the fabric, "I like *naehen*. To sew."

"That will be a very pretty dress. Such lovely material."

Jenny turns her attention back to Rudy. After several more futile attempts, he manages to stand. He's out of breath. "I don't see your walker, Rudy. Do you know where it is?"

"I don't know."

"You really need to use it, dear."

"I think someone took it."

"It'll show up. Right now, though, you need to say goodbye to Helga and come with me to your room."

"I don't want to go to my room. I want to stay here with Helga."

Jenny is firm, "Rudy, you can see Helga in the lounge. Now, say goodbye. We have to leave."

She reaches for his hand, but he lurches out of her grasp to fold Helga into his arms. As he plants kisses on Helga's eager mouth, Jenny sees one hand enclose Helga's small breast.

Oh, my god. From hugs and kisses to fondling. Where the hell is the help from that drug?

Jenny tugs on the back of her husband's blue Christmas sweater. "Enough. We have to go."

"But I don't want to go. I'm helping Helga cut her cloth. You go by yourself."

This time Jenny speaks sharply, "Helga can cut out her dress by herself, Rudy. She's made clothes for many years. She doesn't need your help."

She sees Helga crinkle her nose and wipe her mouth with the back of her hand, as though Rudy's kisses have left an unpleasant taste.

Rudy turns toward Jenny and scowls. Reluctantly, he allows her to grasp his hand and lead him to the door.

But as she opens the door, he again pulls away. "I'm not going."

"Yes, you are." She grips his arm, "You need to go to your own room."

Then she remembers the cookies, and that it's often possible to redirect people with dementia. To bribe. Her voice softens, "There's a surprise for you in your room. A little present."

"A present? What is it?"

"You'll find out when we get to your room."

They step into the hall, and Jenny closes Helga's door.

But as quickly as he was distracted, Rudy's thoughts return to his new friend. "That took a lot of nerve."

He pulls his arm away from Jenny. She steadies him as he staggers. "You coming to Helga's room."

Jenny bites her lower lip. She makes no immediate reply, but holds tight to his hand as he scuffs along the hallway. Once inside an elevator, the silence between them simmers like a pot of soup about to boil over.

During the brief time it takes to reach his floor, Jenny finds her composure. "Want to know what your present is?"

He nods.

"I made cookies for you today and brought you a few."

"What kind?"

"Peanut butter."

"My favourite."

Before she opens his door, she reaches for his plastic pendant and presses the red button.

"What are you doing?"

"Calling Lucija. You're wet. You need a change."

"How can you tell?"

"I can smell it."

"Helga doesn't tell me I'm wet."

"She's not your wife. Maybe she doesn't notice. Maybe she doesn't have a sense of smell anymore."

"You don't like Helga, do you?"

Jenny opens the door, "Let's say she's not my favourite resident."

"Well, I like her. I like her very, very much."

Jenny accompanies him to his chair. "Lucija will be right along, Rudy."

From the bed, she picks up the bag of cookies, spreads open the zipper fastening and hands the treat to her husband. "I'm going home as soon as I find your walker. Oh, by the way, I did a drawing for you. It's on your bed. I hope you like it."

Behind a loveseat by the fireplace she locates the abandoned walker. She wheels it back to his room. He's in the bathroom with the PSW when

Jockie Loomer-Kruger

she parks it in front of his bookcase.
  Without saying goodbye, she leaves. *I'll wait 'til I get home to cry.*
  But she scarcely emerges from the end of the canopy before a gush of hot tears washes her cheeks. She sobs all the way up the sidewalk.

Wednesday, December 30

Half a sleeping pill gives her some restorative sleep. Jenny rises relatively rested and shoves her feet into her slippers.

Rudy immediately pops into her mind. Rudy *and* Helga. Maybe the Triadone hadn't kicked in yesterday. She'll go to the home early and see how he's doing.

The day is cloudy and hovering close to freezing; seasonal for late December in Southern Ontario. Although she dreads what she might find, she walks briskly down the hill to Shasta House.

She rushes by the reception area, not even stopping to sign herself in, directly to the elevators with only a cursory glance toward the fireplace where Harry, Florence and Colette are relaxing in their accustomed places. But Rudy isn't there. Nor is Helga.

He's not in his room either. *Exercise class?* She takes the elevator to the basement recreation area.

Participants are seated in a circle with Cheryl directing their movements. "That's it. Lift up one leg. Hoooold it. Put it down. Now, up with the other. Hoooold it. Leg down again. Good job."

Rudy is not among the leg-lifters.

As Jenny turns to summon an elevator, Cheryl spots her. "Is Rudy sick this morning?"

"I don't think so. I'm just on my way to find him. I'll bring him down for class."

Cheryl nods and waves, turns, and issues new instructions. "Okay, everybody. Let's try loosening up those ankles. You'll soon be ready to do the cancan!" She laughs at her own joke. Her class misses the humour.

Jenny boards an elevator and takes it to the seventh floor. To room 715. Her knock on Helga's door is loud, more insistent than she intends.

The door opens quickly. Rudy is perched on his walker, facing Helga's bed.

Jenny forces false cheeriness. "Good morning, Helga. I see Rudy is visiting again. I think he forgot about his exercise class. He needs to come with me."

"*Ja*," says Helga, "he forgets everything." There's disgust in her voice as she anchors her hands on her hips. "He forgets even when I tell him in German. It makes me sick."

She signals to Rudy with the back of her hand as though she's shooing a pesky fly out of her space. "*Geh*. Go. I don't want you in my room. *Geh mit deiner Frau*—go with your wife. Stop bothering me."

'Hot and cold.' Isn't that what Anna said?

Rising easily from his walker, Rudy stands and attempts to embrace Helga, but she pushes his arms down, turns her head to avoid his proffered lips.

He totters. Grabs the handle of his walker at the same time as Jenny lunges to steady him.

Helga's eyes are fierce, her mouth drawn down at the corners. "No hugs. No kisses. *Nein*. Just go. Get out of here. Go *mit* your wife. *Geh*."

Looking hurt and bewildered, Rudy settles his gaze on Jenny.

"Come on, dear. I'll take you down for exercise class."

They leave, with Jenny's hand over Rudy's on the handle of his walker. *Helga seems so volatile. Rudy's balance is so precarious. He could fall in her room. They could hurt each other.* Jenny shudders.

She and Rudy are the only ones on the elevator, and during the descent to the basement she leans over and kisses her husband. "Do you remember what we used to do on elevators? If we were the only people aboard, we always sneaked a little kiss? Our own funny ritual."

"I remember, like this." And he returns a quick puckered buss.

"I love you Rudy, you know that."

"I know. I love you too…but Helga—"

"There's a problem, Rudy, with your emotions. Maybe with your hormones. But we'll get it sorted out."

With Rudy now in the exercise circle, Jenny seeks out Ellen. She finds her in her office, peeling a fancy gold-foil-wrapped chocolate from the open box on her desk.

"Have one. My husband gave them to me for Christmas." She slides the box toward Jenny, who stands at the other side of the paper-strewn desk.

"No, thanks. I need to talk to you about Rudy and Helga."

"Oh, yes. I hear he's on Triadone. Is it working?"

"No—at least I don't think so. Not yet. The thing is, I found him in her room again this morning. Helga didn't want him there."

"He's pretty persistent, isn't he?" Ellen grins.

"It's not just Rudy I'm concerned about. It's both of them."

"I'm sorry I can't stay and chat about this right now, Mrs. Hoffman. I have a meeting in a few minutes." A drop of chocolate saliva forms in the corner of her mouth. "Are you going to be around for a while?"

"I can be." Jenny realizes she must look as though she's about to go home, standing there in her coat and boots.

"I'll talk to Anna. She has more direct contact with residents than I do. Let's plan to meet in the common room next to the nurses' station. Bring Rudy. Eleven-fifteen?"

Jenny returns to Rudy's room. Sheds her coat and boots and opens the closet to retrieve her slippers. "Oh, shit! Not again!"

She mutters a string of expletives as she sniffs out the offending soiled trousers, each smelly pair folded neatly over a hanger, looking as ready to wear as his freshly laundered pants.

Jockie Loomer-Kruger

Wednesday, December 30, late morning

He should be back from exercises by now. It's eleven o'clock. He must have gone straight to Helga's room.

Once more, Jenny goes to the top floor. She waits outside for a response to her knock.

Hair mussed and lipstick smeared, Helga opens the door with what Jenny interprets as an air of smugness. Rudy is in the corner easy chair, Helga's straight-back table chair close in front of him.

"I need my husband to come with me."

"He's visiting me."

"He has to go to a meeting."

"Oh, all right." Helga appears visibly irritated, "That's your business, I suppose. You are his *Frau*."

"Yes, I am." Jenny wishes to god Helga could remember and respect that Rudy is someone else's husband.

Sarcasm dripping, Helga says to Rudy, "Your loving *Frau* wants you for something. You'll have to go."

"But I want to stay. My wife won't live with me. She won't sleep with me. What kind of a wife is that when you won't have sex with your husband?"

Helga pulls the wooden chair away and tucks it under her sewing table. She crosses her arms. "*Nein.* Don't tell me about it. That's your business. *Geh.* Go with your wife. Get out of here."

He struggles to get up and Jenny steps in to assist. As soon as he's on his feet, he pushes Jenny's hand away and takes a faltering step toward Helga. "Don't be mad, Helga. Please don't be mad. I don't like it when you get mad at me."

Jenny notes a smear of bright lipstick on his moustache.

Helga unfolds her arms and Rudy hugs her, one hand automatically roaming to her breast. They kiss.

Jenny places her hand on her husband's rounded shoulder and presses her fingers into his soft flesh,. "Rudy, we have to go. You have a meeting. You don't want to be late."

To her surprise, he pulls Helga's arms away from his neck. Turns to Jenny, does up the buttons on his cardigan. "Can't be late for meetings."

Jenny remembers his penchant for punctuality. Not just for meetings, but early for concerts, plays, everything.

In the elevator he's silently sullen. Jenny takes a tissue from her slacks pocket and vigorously rubs the lipstick from under his nose.

"What are you doing? Do I have a drippy nose?"

"No. I'm just cleaning something off your moustache so you look presentable for the meeting." A hint of soft pink clings to the hairs.

They join Ellen and Anna, who are already seated at a small table in the second floor common room, the space where the home's doctor sees patients twice a month. Anna holds a clipboard and pen, ready to make notes. Ellen folds her pudgy hands on the table.

"What's this meeting about anyway?" Rudy asks when everyone is settled around the table.

"It's about you, Rudy." Anna poises her pencil to write. "So, how are you feeling this morning?"

"Cross. I'm very cross."

"Oh? And why's that?"

"Because Jenny's so mean."

"Can you explain why you think Jenny's mean?"

"She's my wife. She won't live with me. She won't have sex with me. That's no kind of a marriage."

In all their years together, Jenny had never heard Rudy disparage her to others. If the opportunity presented itself, he complimented her in public. As though he was so proud to have her at his side. Hearing this hurts. *Damn! Is that amusement on Ellen's face? Does she think what he said is funny? Fuck her.*

Anna asks Rudy, "And what about Helga?"

His face lights up. "She's very nice. I like her. She speaks German to me."

Ellen interjects, "German is your first language, isn't it, Rudy?"

"That's all I spoke until I started school."

Ellen directs her next comment to Jenny. "It's not at all unusual for residents to revert to their mother tongue here, Mrs. Hoffman. Take Nadia, for example. She stopped speaking English a few years ago. She only speaks Polish now, her first language."

Jenny knows exactly who Ellen is referring to. A resident on the sheltered fourth floor. A tiny woman bent-over like the top of a shepherd's crook, with her hair in a snowball bun at the nape of her neck. A

131

little woman who constantly flings her arms in the air in frustration because no one understands what she's saying.

Jenny's mind flashes to a scene in the basement at Shasta House. Rudy had lived there only a few months when it happened.

At that time, the amount of laundry he generated was minimal, so once a week, usually while Rudy napped, Jenny carried his laundry basket to the elevators, rode to the basement, traipsed down the hall from the recreation area to a cubicle with washer and dryer for resident use.

That day, almost finished, she was folding his pyjamas and adding them to the other clean garments in the basket when she heard something.

A cat? A baby? A meow? A whimper? She listened. Loud. Soft. Pleading. *What? Where?*

She stepped into the hall and looked toward the elevators. Nothing. More sound, now like an infant crying.

She looked in the other direction.

The stairwell exit was ajar, and caught by its weight was a small body with only one bandy leg showing and short fingers pushing on the heavy fire door.

Jenny raced to the end of the hall. She couldn't believe she was still capable of running.

She pulled the door open and caught Nadia in her arms. Between a flood of Polish words and tears, the petite woman sobbed in Jenny's embrace. The frail body felt like a bundle of loose kindling.

Immediately, Jenny pressed Nadia's pendant. Then slowly, supporting the woman's trembling steps on wishbone legs, Jenny guided her to a metal chair in the laundry room. Nadia perched like a bird with a broken wing. The toes of her shoes not quite touching the floor.

Jenny knelt in front of her. She held Nadia's hands. Watched the wee woman's terror-widened, milky-blue eyes shrink to normal size. Jenny knew Nadia might not understand her words, but she hoped their soft, calm, measured rhythm would sooth and reassure.

No one came. Jenny stood and pushed Nadia's call button again. They waited some more, Jenny now stroking Nadia's boney back and continuing to speak quietly.

After twenty minutes, a PSW appeared. "Oh," she said, "she really is here. The screen on my phone showed her in the basement, but I just couldn't believe it. I searched all over the fourth floor. She always stays on the floor unless someone takes her somewhere. She never uses the elevators on her own."

"She came down the stairs," Jenny said, suppressing her desire to lash out at the blatant neglect—or staff shortage—that allowed this to happen. "This fragile woman came down four flights. Four flights! By herself. But she didn't have the strength to open the door."

What if I hadn't heard her? When would someone have realized Nadia was missing? What might have happened before she was found?

The PSW made no comment. She slipped an arm around Nadia's waist and the two slowly made their way to the elevators, Nadia sobbing like a child between outbursts in her native tongue.

Yes, I know Nadia speaks Polish.

"But Rudy only spoke German until he started school," Jenny explains. "After that he wanted to be like his classmates, so he almost always responded at home in English. By the time he was ten he refused to speak German at all. That's what he told me. He said he wasn't German, he was Canadian. Isn't that right, Rudy?"

"I'm Canadian."

She doesn't continue with what else Rudy told her. About the trip he took to Germany with Addie. How he thought relying on his German heritage would make communication simple. But it hadn't. His vocabulary was too limited, his first language too long unused. Like other tourists he had to consult his little red *Travellers' Guide to German*.

Anna steers the conversation to other topics. "What special things do you like to do, Rudy?"

"I like to read." He thinks for a moment. "I like to play Scrabble." Another pause. "And I like doing art."

Before Anna can ask Rudy anything else, Ellen directs an inquiry to Jenny as though Rudy's no longer in the room, "What kind of work did he do, Mrs. Hoffman?"

She should know his background. "He was an English professor. He taught Modern American Literature."

"Really! You don't say!" Ellen turns to Rudy and says, "So, you like to read and you like to play a word game. And do art. Is there anything else you enjoy doing?"

"I like having sex."

But that's not even the term we used. We made love. 'Having sex' was for other people. For overanxious TV lovers. Or hormone-fueled teens. Their intimate moments were times of incredibly deep affection. An experience as close to being sacred as either skeptic could acknowledge.

Jenny remembers Rudy's stories of summer construction jobs when he was in high school, and the loose talk of the men he worked with. How it bothered him that they would speak of women—of girls—as nothing more than something to ease the pressure in their groins. Another story in his book.

> They called their wives nasty, vulgar names. Some of the men fooled around with other women and bragged about it. They said women and girls were good for only one thing. That all women were stupid. Some of them said women needed a good smack now and then to smarten them up.
> But I was a shy teenage romantic. I thought girls were special, and every bit as smart as boys. Someday I wanted to love a clever woman and be loved by her in return.
> I believed sex would be 'making love' and I was sure it would be exciting, tender and kind. And I knew, I, for one, would always be faithful to my wife.

From the beginning, Jenny had no doubts that, just as he had been faithful in his first marriage, he would also be faithful in his second. Dementia, though, has robbed him of those boundaries. *Damned, horrible disease.* Jenny sucks at the insides of her cheeks.

"So, Rudy." Ellen clears her throat. "is there anything else you like doing?"

He takes a moment to answer. "I like to listen to music."

Jenny jumps in, explains the device she gave him just before Christmas. Staff could use it as a distraction. She could show the PSWs how to turn it on and off. "He goes into another world altogether listening to his favourite music." But neither Anna nor Ellen react to her suggestion.

"Is that all, then, Rudy?"

Rudy nods.

Anna puts her pencil down. "Well, now that we've heard from you, let's hear what Jenny has to say."

Jenny chooses her words carefully. "I know Rudy likes Helga, but I wish he wouldn't go to her room."

"I like going to her room. She asks me to come there."

Jenny ignores his interruption. "My major concern is safety. He's wobbly on his feet. I'm afraid he could fall—or she could. He never pushes his buzzer himself, doesn't seem to understand what the pendant is for. And she doesn't wear hers."

Anna interrupts with a low chuckle, "More like she *won't* wear hers. She thinks it's a piece of jewellery. She told me she wasn't going to wear that ugly necklace."

"The thing is," Jenny goes on, "I'm concerned they could unintentionally harm each other. And another thing: he has a really hard time getting himself out of her easy chair."

Rudy is no longer listening. He has gotten up, pushed his walker across the room to where a fish tank bubbles against the wall. He taps his fingers against the glass.

"Is there any way we can have them meet where there are others around? I mean staff. Restrict them to just meeting in the lounge? Keep him out of her room?"

Ellen's response is sharp. "Staff are not policemen. They can't keep track of every resident every minute. I think you're worrying unnecessarily. Just relax. It's all very natural under the circumstances." She looks at her watch. "Oh, my! It's almost lunchtime, Rudy."

He turns around at the sound of his name.

"Thanks for coming and talking with us."

In silence, Jenny guides Rudy back to his room. She wonders what he got out of that meeting? *A goddamn waste of time for me*. She helps him wash his hands.

"I won't be staying for lunch," she puts on her coat and boots, "but I'll be back later on in the afternoon."

In the dining room she shows him to his table, says hello to his tablemates, pecks a fleeting goodbye kiss on the top of his head, and leaves.

Jockie Loomer-Kruger

Wednesday, December 30, late afternoon

Two loads of laundry later, Jenny is ready to return to Shasta House. December darkness has begun to descend.

As she fears, Rudy is not in the lounge. She steps into an elevator. Behind her, Sharon drives in on her red motorized scooter.

Jenny knows Sharon's story. A resident in her early sixties who still has her mental faculties but lives at Shasta House because of advanced diabetes and the need for exhausting every-other-day kidney dialysis at the hospital.

"Oh, am I glad to see you." Sharon maneuvers her scooter to face forward.

"Why? What's up?"

"It's Rudy—and Helga. They were just here on the elevator. He pushed his walker aside, and I don't know why she didn't have her cane with her. They were in a back corner."

Jenny closes her eyes tight, as if somehow by doing so she's also closing her ears.

"Their hands were all over each other. I thought they were going to get it on right then and there, be rolling around on the floor before they got off the elevator. It's disgusting. Can't you do anything about them?"

Oh, god. An acidic taste bubbles into Jenny's mouth. "I'm doing my best, Sharon. We've got him on some medication that's supposed to help."

But is it? He seems more agitated every day. More sex-focused all the time, and so angry with her. Jenny's never known him to be angry this way. Almost hateful toward her. Exposing an ugly side she didn't know he had.

She's watched others with dementia and Alzheimer's go from placid to angry like a light switching on, switching off. Is that where Rudy is in his disease? Why isn't the drug making the situation better?

Troubled and anxious, she enters his room to remove her coat and boots. She knows she won't find her husband there. But she does know where to look for him.

She knocks. This time Helga's door is unlocked. Jenny opens it and strides in. As she expects, Rudy is there. Sitting in the soft corner chair, two cut-out pieces of Helga's green and silver material draped over his shoulders.

Jenny ignores Helga, who stands by her sewing table, scissors in hand making cuts into the fabric. It surprises Jenny to see the pieces on Rudy are jaggedly cut. She lifts them off and drops them onto the floor beside the chair.

"Get up, Rudy. You need to go back to your room." She realizes being bossy isn't going to help and softens her tone, "Your beautiful music is waiting for you in your room."

He looks blankly at her.

"Remember? You have new headphones? Purple headphones? You can listen to your favourite, *The Trout*."

He allows her to help him up and she holds tightly to his arm.

"No time for goodbyes today."

"But I need to kiss Helga goodbye."

"Another time. You need to come with me. Here's your walker. Come. Now."

Helga, opening and closing her scissors as though they aren't working properly, appears indifferent to their departure.

On the way down the hall, Rudy lashes out, "You cut Helga's dress pieces all wrong. Why did you do that, Jenny?"

"I did what?"

"Ruined her cloth. You're so mean. Now, Helga can't make her dress."

"Rudy, I'm not the one who did that."

"Helga said you did it. She doesn't like you."

In his room, he glowers. Jenny picks up the wee metal square and headphones. "Music, dear?"

"I don't care. Do what you want. You always do." He balls his hands tightly at the end of the armrests.

She sets him up with his music and watches as his hands and limbs relax and the furrows in his forehead vanish.

"It's *The Unfinished Symphony*," he tells her, and slips into the soothing world of his favourite music, as though floating away on a magic carpet.

It's probably all right for her to go home now, she thinks. In her mind she plans a list of distractions she will type up for staff to use. There has to be a way staff can curtail this terrible infatuation.

She puts on her coat and boots, pops her slippers into the closet. It's then she spies a cane in the corner by the door. A lightweight aluminum cane with abstract metallic colours spiralling from black handle to rubber tip. Helga's cane. *Oh, damn. She's been in his room. They've been in each other's rooms.*

With Rudy lost in his music, she picks up the cane to deliver it; not to Helga, but to Anna at the nurses' station.

"I found this in Rudy's room," she passes the cane to Anna, "I believe it's Helga's."

"She must have left it last night. The night nurse told me they'd visited in pyjamas."

"Christ!" Jenny blurts, "There has to be something we…you…Shasta House can do. What about I bring you a list of distractions tomorrow? Suggestions for staff. Other things he likes to do." She pauses, "How long does it take for that damned drug to kick in anyway?"

"Maybe it already has. Like I told you before, it's not what we usually give in cases like this." Anna looks directly at Jenny. "You look terrible, Jenny. Go on home. We'll look after things. I'll take the cane back, talk to Helga—remind her Rudy's a married man."

But Jenny's not ready to leave. There's more on her mind. "Rudy told me Helga has a boyfriend. Is that true, Anna?"

"Yeah. A hulking big guy. He comes to see her now and then. Always unannounced. She tries to get pretty lovey-dovey with him the minute she sees him, but I think when she snuggles up to him in public it kind of embarrasses him."

"Does he know about Rudy?"

"I have no idea. Look, Jenny, you really need to go home. Get some rest. Let us handle things."

Jenny returns to Rudy's room. He's fallen asleep in his chair, his music calming him like a lullaby. He looks so content, so peaceful. Unexpected tears swim in Jenny's eyes. She pops into the bathroom to get a tissue.

Heaped in the laundry basket on the floor of his shower stall she notices his blue-and-white striped pyjamas. On the collar, a smudge of red lipstick. She kicks the basket. Stomps out of the bathroom and slams the bathroom door.

Rudy jars awake, takes the headphones off. "Is it supper time?"

"No, it's just time for me to go home." She turns, and without a goodbye, bangs his door closed behind her.

Thursday, December 31

There's a stillness over the city when Jenny awakens at five, despite the half sleeping pill she took at bedtime. It's the last day of 2015. The end of another year, one drawing to a close in the grip of debilitating stress.

She gets up in the blackness of the very early morning. With baroque music from the TV in the background, she does her household chores. The music eases the angst she can't articulate, but feels roiling inside.

She makes an egg salad sandwich, slides it into a plastic sandwich bag, and sets it and an apple aside for her lunch at Shasta House. Bad enough that Rudy has to eat their meals, but she doesn't have to.

She visualizes him, and others too, and how much weight most have gained from too many carbs. Bread, pasta, potatoes. Bread, pasta, potatoes. And starchy desserts. The slight paunch Rudy had when he moved in has bulged several belt holes into a proper Santa belly. With his beard and stomach and dressed in a Santa suit he could pass for the old saint himself.

That image takes her back to a warm summer day, some twenty years earlier. They had stopped to make a purchase at The Bay when Jenny noticed a young mother trying to calm a small boy who kept pointing in their direction. Finally, taking the youngster by the hand, the woman approached them.

"Excuse me," she said to Rudy, "would you mind speaking to my son? He thinks you're Santa Claus."

Rudy promptly knelt in front of the little boy, spoke a few quiet words to the child, and stood again. The youngster beamed.

"Thank you so much," the mother said, and the two headed off toward the toy section of the store. But she and Rudy both heard the excited high-pitched voice, "I saw Santa Claus. Santa Claus in the summer!" The memory brings a half smile.

Chores finished, Jenny takes off her apron and hangs it on the hook inside the broom closet. At her computer she types out what she'd been too tired to do the night before. She prints off a couple of copies to take with her.

Jockie Loomer-Kruger

Rudy's Distraction List
  1. set him up with his personal music system
  2. get a volunteer to play Scrabble with him
  3. invite him to have a cup of tea and a cookie in the lounge
  4. interest him in an art project
  5. offer him one of his magazines to read, or the daily paper, or his green binder of personal stories

The ground is white with fresh snow. She'll take the car today. *Silly, when I'm less than a full block away*. But there might be ice under the snow. Too risky for walking. Winter slipping and sliding, such fun in her childhood, such a hazard in old age.

She remembers how she and Rudy used to love walking after a light, pristine snowfall. Leaving their tracks behind them like they were the only people on the planet. All of it was theirs. Hushed. Serene. Holy.

She catches herself. 'Holy' is not a word Rudy would use, declared atheist that he became, but that doesn't mean he never experienced awe. Moments beyond explanation. Moments of all-encompassing love, wonder, beauty, reverence. 'There's still so much we don't know,' he'd often said when faced with wonders or surprising coincidences.

She intends to fetch her coat from the hall closet and get on her way, but as she passes the electric fireplace, she pauses and picks up a silver-framed picture from the mantle.

She doubts she could squeeze into the filmy emerald dress in that informal wedding photo now: a few too many additional pounds.

She studies the picture closer. *Hands, our hands always touching.* Rudy's over hers as they cut the two-tier wedding cake that Rudy had made and she had decorated with his favourite frosting. *Far more cake than we needed.* The excess assigned to the freezer for a month of cake and ice cream desserts.

It was such a simple, do-it-yourself, at-home affair. They'd read the vows they'd written to each other in front of their stone fireplace, with a Unitarian chaplain officiating. Pam and Dave fulfilled double roles—legal witnesses and sole guests.

Jenny had made her own corsage and Rudy's boutonniere. Esther had sent an apology floral arrangement to cover her absence. Klaus and his wife had sent another because they were on a long-planned Caribbean cruise.

Addie and her partner in BC, who maintained casual email correspondence with Rudy, surprised the bridal couple with a gift of daffodils and tulips. The accompanying note said how happy they were that Rudy had found someone special to love and to be loved by.

Jenny replaces the photo. She knows now, exactly what to do next. *Our little wedding album!* She will take it with her.

Maybe it will jog his memory. Help him sort this whole thing out. Help him remember he still loves his wife. She knows he does. But his filters are skewed—gone—he can't distinguish between exciting infatuation of the moment, and deep, lasting love that gives comfort and assurance. For a lifetime.

She finds the small, white, vinyl album in the mahogany bookcase in the hall. She's about to get her coat when she remembers her lunch in the kitchen, the distraction list, and something else. Just before she went to bed last night, she'd lain Rudy's new Christmas socks on the arm of the couch so she wouldn't forget to take them in the morning.

And here, she almost did. *Is memory loss catching?* She knows it's not. Still, she spends so much time at Shasta House…*That's ridiculous!* She's just emotionally overloaded.

At ten-thirty she leaves the condo.

Nancy opens the inner door automatically, "Good morning Jenny. Oh, hold on a minute before you go up to see Rudy. Ellen left something for you. She said it was urgent."

Jenny takes the Shasta House envelope and rips it open.

Dear Mrs. Hoffman,

I tried to catch you before you left yesterday but I was too late. After you were in Helga's room to get Rudy, she came to see me. She was very upset. She said you had yelled at her and threatened to hit her. She was very frightened. She feels extremely intimidated by you.

We cannot have such things happening here. In future, if Rudy is in her room, please ask a member of staff to fetch him. It is important for Helga's well-being that you have no further contact with her. Please do not speak to her if you see her elsewhere in the building.

> *Also, please try to remember that what's going on is very natural.*
>
> *Yours truly,*
> *Ellen DuPont*
> *Director of Wellness*
> *Shasta House Retirement Home*

Jenny is stunned. But not surprised. Ellen doesn't seem to hear, or want to hear, what Jenny has to say. How, though, can Ellen believe what Helga told her?

Jenny scrunches the message into a ball and rams it into her coat pocket. Then does the same with the envelope.

The door to the nurses' station is locked. She slides the two copies of Rudy's Distraction List under the door and across the sill, then bustles off to Rudy's room.

When she opens his unlocked door, she's surprised to find him, arms folded, in his chair.

"Ah! You're here!" She disguises her distress over the letter with an added, cheery, "Good morning, sweetheart." Takes off her coat and boots and puts on her slippers, then glides the few steps to his chair. Her kiss brushes his cheek, and her hug slips around his shoulders.

"You look unhappy. Is something the matter? Are you feeling sick?"

"I was in Helga's room. Bruno came. Helga kissed him."

Jenny is surprised that his poor short-term memory has retained this experience. She knows if she asked him what he had for breakfast, he wouldn't be able to tell her. Maybe not even be sure he had had breakfast.

"And where were you when this happened?"

"Sitting in her big chair."

"Did Helga introduce you to her boyfriend?"

"I think so. We shook hands. He squeezed my hand real hard. It hurt. He's big. He's a really big man."

"And then what? Do you remember what happened next?"

"Helga said, 'Bruno is my boyfriend.' And she told me to go back to my room. So I left."

End of story. She wishes.

"Maybe that's best, Rudy. If Helga has a boyfriend, she really shouldn't have a married man visiting in her room, should she?"

"I suppose not. When I'm with Helga I forget I'm married. That I love my wife."

Jenny gulps. It rips at her insides to hear his conflict of emotions.

"So, would you like to have staff remind you that you're married? Would that help?"

"Yes. I think so."

She'll speak to Anna and trust Anna to advise others. No point talking to Ellen. Anna's superior has yet to truly hear Jenny's concerns. Ellen, it seems to Jenny, would rather listen to Helga's fabrications and delusions.

Jenny touches Rudy's hand as she changes the subject. "I brought something for you to look at."

She sets up the black folding chair beside the arm of his recliner, slips the album from its plastic bag and leaves it on the seat.

"I'll put these away first." She holds up new socks so he can see them. "Your Christmas socks."

She adds them to the balled-up pairs and the lonely singles already in the dresser drawer. Then she sits, places the album in his lap, and flips the book open to the first picture, "Remember this?"

"Yes. Our wedding."

"Handsome devil, weren't you?"

He grins. "I don't know about that—but you were beautiful. Your hair was dark."

Jenny flips back the errant, once-dark wave from her forehead. "That was thirty years ago, Rudy."

"Is that a long time? I get mixed up with years. With then and now."

"I know you do."

"But I remember our wedding. We wrote our own vows, didn't we, Jenny?"

"Yes, and we chose a special word as a guide to making our marriage work."

"Yes. Yes, I remember that."

He hesitates, trying to pull the word from his memory. Jenny flips to another picture in the album, but he doesn't look at it.

"Now I remember, we chose the word 'accommodation'."

She's surprised by what has tumbled from his memory. Dementia is so unpredictable. "Do you remember why we chose that word, Rudy?"

"No, tell me."

"Most people think marriage is all about compromise—but that means one partner gives up something to please the other. We wanted 'accommodation' to be our word, because it meant we would make room for each other. We would make room for our differences in personality. We would make room for our differences in belief, our special interests:

Jockie Loomer-Kruger

your love of John Steinbeck's writing, my interest in art. We would make room for each other's friends, and even our differences in biological clocks, with me a morning person and you a night owl. You, Mr. Neat-and-Tidy; me, Mrs. The-Dishes-Can-Wait. We would make room for all the changes that happen in our lives."

Oh, dear, I'm going on too long. Rudy's asleep.

She stands, but leaves the album in his lap. Taking the folded, jade-green wool blanket from the end of his bed, she covers him tenderly with it.

Thursday, December 31, noon hour

At lunch, Jenny does what she can to engage the others at the table. Harry explains that he was a bank manager, that he grew up in a small northern Ontario town, that he and his wife, "she's dead now, God rest her soul," liked to travel. "We went all over the world. To Paris. To Marseilles. To France, even. We went everywhere."

Florence tells more of her story, that at the age of fifteen she took the train from her Cape Breton home to Ontario where an older sister lived. Lied about her age so she could get a job in a shirt factory. Met her future husband there, "gorgeous Polish guy," and married at seventeen. Two sons. "But everybody's kids was welcome at our house. Never knew how many would be there for meals. My husband, he didn't mind one little bit. He liked all them kids too."

Colette's responses are mainly, 'I don't know,' until she squints sideways at Rudy. Her eyes widen. "Papa? Is that you Papa? What happened to your hair? Where did it go?"

"Your father had a white beard, Colette?" Jenny asks.

"*Oui*. And a lot of white hair. Are you my Papa?" she leans toward Rudy, "Papa?"

Sensing something's going on that involves him, Rudy searches Jenny's face for an answer. "What's wrong with her?"

Jenny pats his hand. "It's okay, Rudy. Colette thinks you look like her father."

Gently, Jenny steers Colette onto another path, one she's walked along with this resident many times before. "Your sisters. Your twin sisters. Tell me about them."

"There were a lot of us in my family." Colette can't locate the exact number of siblings, but Jenny knows there were twelve children and Colette was the youngest. "My sisters. My twin sisters. They're artists. They got all the talent in the family. They were almost grown up when I was little. They tried to teach me to draw. But they gave up. They got all the talent in the family." Jenny knows the rest, what Colette doesn't tell today. The sisters never married, but lived in a house next door to their parents and sold their paintings for a comfortable living.

When the lasagna meal finishes, Jenny brings Rudy his walker. As he stands, both he and Jenny spy Helga, not at her usual table at the back, but seated at the small table beside the central dining room pillar, a place reserved for guests. Opposite Helga, with his hairy-backed hand eclipsing hers, sits a broad-shouldered, thick-chested man with a swarthy square face, and a shock of unruly steel-grey hair. Bruno. *Like Rudy said, 'a big man.'*

Rudy aims his walker in the direction of Helga and Bruno, but Jenny manages to hold him back.

"I want to see Helga," he says, loud enough for Helga to hear him.

She pivots in her chair, smiles and waves.

Jenny balls her fists. Ellen's orders pop into mind. "Not now, Rudy. This way."

She tugs at his walker until he turns back toward the elevators, "Let's go up to your room." They edge into the waiting lineup. "You're probably ready for a nap," she says softly.

"Will you stay?"

"For a while."

"Sleep with me, have sex?"

"Hush. We'll talk about it in your room."

An elevator arrives. There's room for them and some of the other returning diners.

Rudy, now angry, blares the same words she's heard before. "YOU'RE MY WIFE AND YOU WON'T LIVE WITH ME. WON'T SLEEP WITH ME. WON'T HAVE SEX WITH ME. WHAT KIND OF A MARRIAGE IS THAT?"

Alarmed by the ferocity and volume of his voice, residents inch as far away as they can from Rudy in the confined quarters of the elevator. The young PSW with them, however, stifles a snicker.

Jenny's sigh is audible, but she makes no response as Rudy subsides into smouldering silence and the elevator stops at each floor to disgorge its riders. On the sixth, they also exit.

As she unlocks and pushes open the door to his room, the smell of urine threads into her nostrils. She reaches for his pendant and presses its button.

After Dolly arrives and ushers Rudy into the bathroom, Jenny plops into his chair, activates it to recline and elevates her feet. She closes her eyes. Exhaustion makes her feel like what her mother used to say when she was tired out. 'I feel like a wet dishrag.' Maybe she'll stay and sleep a bit in his chair. Dolly can settle Rudy for a nap.

But Rudy, emerging from the bathroom seems strangely wide awake. Oddly energized. Unlike the familiar routine where he welcomes an after-lunch nap. When, often, Jenny cuddles in behind him and they both sleep wrapped together in a blanket of common tenderness.

"Well, I'll leave you two to your own devices," Dolly says at the door. "See you later, Rudy."

Jockie Loomer-Kruger

Part Four

How can we live without our lives?
How will we know it's us without our past?

— *John Steinbeck, <u>The Grapes of Wrath</u>*

Until the Day We Die

Jockie Loomer-Kruger

Thursday, December 31, after lunch

As Rudy sits on the edge of his bed, Jenny brings the recliner to its upright position. "So, do you want to nap, Rudy?"

"No, I want sex. I want you to sleep with me. Why won't you? We're married. Married people have sex."

Jenny takes a very deep breath. Then, another. *What the bloody hell? Maybe if he tries to have intercourse he'll remember he's impotent. Maybe it will end this insane sex obsession.* "Stand up, Rudy. Take your pants off. We're going to make love." She helps him remove his shoes.

Eagerly, smiling broadly, he undoes his belt and zipper and lets his trousers crumple to the floor. But he doesn't remove his faded pale blue sweatshirt with the kangaroo on it—a gift his brother sent him from a holiday in Australia a number of years before. And he keeps on his clean protective underwear. Jenny lifts his legs onto the bed where Dolly had spread a soaker pad.

Teeth clenched, Jenny moves around to the other side of the bed. She takes off her glasses and folds them onto the small bedside table next to the wall. Letting her clothes heap on the floor, she strips. Rudy struggles to get on his side with his back against the guard rail.

"You're beautiful," he says, as she reaches for the blanket at the end of the bed to cover them. Lying down, she rolls onto her side to face him.

Am I mad? Am I the wife who ramps up sex because she suspects her husband is having an affair? Classic wronged-wife behaviour. Jesus!

They kiss—his tongue searching her mouth—something she had to learn to enjoy after her first deep kiss so long ago...His hands find her breasts. *My god! That actually feels good.*

"Hold my penis, Jenny. Hold it."

No, Rudy, no. How could he forget that? Early on in their relationship she'd explained the stressful flashbacks such a request triggered. Once he understood, he never asked her to do it again.

She time-warps. At seventeen, Jenny's flattered that the twenty-six-year-old lawyer, articling in the town next to her New Brunswick village, has shown an interest in her. In her! A grade-twelve bobby-soxer attending high school in town. She'd met him at the soda fountain where high schoolers liked to hang out. He often appeared there when she and other kids were gathering after school for an ice cream float. She never questioned why he would want to be surrounded by the silly chatter of teenagers. Never wondered why he wasn't bored with them.

Now, he has invited her to meet him at the movie theatre to see *Three Coins in a Fountain.* She's disappointed that he hasn't offered to call for her at home. To meet her parents. She drives to the theatre with school friends. He's there waiting with a ticket for her.

No one else in her crowd has ever gone out with a sophisticated older man. A man nine years her senior. She feels a sense of smugness as they sit near the back of the movie house. When he searches for her hand, shivers run up and down her spine. Throughout the movie, he holds her hand

But she's puzzled afterwards when, instead of taking her home, he drives off in the opposite direction. She feels vaguely nervous when he pulls into a secluded lonely road, flanked on both sides by thickets of evergreens. Still vaguely nervous, but also a bit excited, when he stops the car and turns off its lights.

Pale moonlight filters through the windshield. Is he planning on some mild necking like she's enjoyed with the few high school boyfriends she's had?

Without a word he locks his arms around her. Kisses her hard, forcing her lips apart; his tongue thrusts deep into her mouth, hard and pointed like a crocodile's tail.

She's never been kissed that way before. It scares her. He won't stop. Gagging, she pushes at him. But he won't stop. She can't breathe.

Frantic, she clamps her teeth together.

He jolts back, clutches his tongue and mutters, "Whadyoudothatfor?"

"You wouldn't stop. And I don't like that. Take me home."

His bruised tongue back inside his mouth, he grips her arm. "Don't like French kisses, eh? Then I'll give you something you'll like better."

She tries to get away—he's hurting her arm—but he's so strong. She hears him unzip his trousers. He grabs her hand—the one trying to open the car door—forces it around his erection. She's never felt a man's penis before. His hand wrapped tightly over hers, feels like she's being forced to hold a weapon.

The rest remains a blur. The shove down onto the seat, the pushing aside of the crotch of her panties. The penetration. The pulling out before ejaculation. The large white hanky in his hand to catch his ejaculate, like a pale mini-ghost in moonlight.

But she remembers clearly what followed. The uncontrollable sobbing. The pain. The warmth of blood spilling between her legs. And his words.

"Don't tell your father. For god's sake don't tell you father. You're underage. He could have me arrested for statutory rape."

She doesn't know what statutory rape is, but it must have to do with age. Is it different from other rape? Because she was prepared to neck with him, was this her fault? How old does he think she is? Does he know she turned seventeen at the end of September?

"If you tell anyone, it could ruin my career. Someday I could be Prime Minister."

She knows he has political ambitions—likely a very promising future in government.

Enveloped in shame, fear, and self-loathing, she doesn't tell. It's the 1950s, after all. It's up to girls to keep fellows under control. To keep virginity intact until the wedding night. The sexual revolution has not yet arrived.

Dropping out of college at nineteen to marry Peter, she apologized to him for not being a bridal virgin. She didn't explain further. But he didn't care. His anxious hormones overrode his disappointment or moral judgment. He reached for her in their honeymoon bed.

"It doesn't matter, Jenny. I want you. I need you."

But it did matter. Throughout her first marriage she struggled to lift herself from the quagmire of emotions that teenage rape had left her with. Even as she agonized over Peter's downward slide into alcoholism, she wrestled with ways to build a healthy sense of herself. She volunteered at her children's school, at the hospital. Got a job in a flower shop where emotions were expressed in the beauty of blossoms.

Even as she saw her rapist's political ambitions reward him with a high-level cabinet position, she didn't tell.

She didn't tell until almost thirty years after it happened, when she confided in Rudy. He listened and his tears mixed with hers as he comforted her. He rocked her like a hurting child, and understood why holding his penis was something he would never, ever, ask her to do.

But today he begs, "Please, Jenny, hold my penis."

She can't. *No. Yes.* She has to.

Her breath shallow, she grits her teeth. Pushes his brief down a bit, reaches into his underwear, curls her fingers around his flaccid member and raises it above the edge of his underwear.

Instantly, she bolts upright.

"What's wrong?" He's startled.

"Christ, Rudy! You peed. I'm soaked. There's piss everywhere."

She hops off the bed, shaking her wet hand. Grabs her clothes and rushes to the bathroom.

At the sink, hysterics take over. One moment wild laughter, the next excruciating sobs.

From the bed comes his call. "Jenny...Jenny? Are you all right? What's wrong, Jenny?"

She hears him trying to pull himself up to the edge of the bed. *He could fall.* She forces her emotions to mute.

"It's okay, Rudy. Lie down again. I'll be there in a minute." She runs water in the sink to wash herself off and to cover the sound of her renewed, softer sobbing. Then dresses quickly, wipes her eyes, and returns to Rudy's bedside.

He lies against his pillow, his blue sweatshirt soaked below the kangaroo. A wet shape that looks like the southern continent the shirt came from. His protective underwear is still halfway down, his soft penis flopped to one side.

Suddenly, she feels angry. Ashamed of him. Ashamed of herself.

"So now," she glares down at him from her stance beside the guard rail, "now, do you get it? Why we don't make love anymore?"

"I don't understand." His eyes plead for an explanation.

"We don't because we can't, Rudy. You're impotent. You can't get an erection. You haven't been able to for a long time. You have no bladder control. We. Cannot. Make love. Anymore."

She feels tears rising again and swallows the sour lump in her throat. Her tone softens. "Rudy, we can't have intercourse. But we can still be loving. We can kiss. We can hug. We can snuggle. We can still show our love for each other by touching in other ways."

"But I want sex."

"Darling, I think there's something out of kilter with your hormones. We'll get it sorted out. We'll get it sorted out soon." Under her breath she mumbles, "We have to."

She escorts Rudy to the bathroom. Tells him to wait by the sink until she strips the bed, then she'll get him cleaned up. She won't call Dolly to look after this change.

And be damned if she's explaining this load of laundry to anyone either. Gathering the wet blanket, soaker pad and bedspread, she dumps them into his clothes hamper. Then she dresses Rudy in a clean tee shirt, sweater, and fresh Depend. Helps him into his trousers and footwear, and guides him to his chair.

"You don't love me anymore," he says, flopping down onto the soaker pad on the chair seat. "I see that you don't want a husband." He frowns. "What are you, anyway? Are you lesbian? You like to go out with your women friends all the time. Maybe that's it. You're a lesbian." Has Addie come into his mind?

Jenny doesn't reply. Instead she reaches across him to the window sill for his magic music and headphones, hoping to distract him with that, but discovers the device needs charging. She unplugs it from the headphones and pops the little square into her slacks pocket.

Then she picks up the wedding album and hands it to Rudy. He opens it to a picture of the two of them, arms around each other, their smiles joyful.

He snaps the album shut and throws it against the dresser. "That's a lie. You don't love me anymore."

Don't argue with people with dementia. What more can she say? What more can she do today?

She picks up the album and places it on top of the bureau. "It's time for me to go home, Rudy." She pulls on her coat and yanks on her boots. "I'll see you tomorrow."

Jenny avoids eye contact with the residents on the elevator, and ignores Nancy at the desk as she bolts from the building and races to the car.

Hot tears trickle down the side of her nose and she buries her head on the steering wheel. She sobs long and hard before turning the key.

At bedtime, when she tries to write in her journal, she can't. She slaps the book shut with nothing but a gigantic *X* filling the page.

Friday, January 1, 2016, New Year's Day

Still chagrined and oddly ashamed about the events that closed out the year, Jenny removes old calendars and puts up new. *Happy New Year! Happy Fucking New Year!*

She didn't bother to stay up to watch the ball drop in Times Square on TV. Nor was she awakened by the annual fireworks going off in the nearby park, a place she and Rudy often walked together before he moved into the home.

Memories of Lakeside Park surface.

It was right after their first summer of retirement, when they had to drive from their house to reach the park. Holding hands, they scuffed through crisp, crackly coloured leaves. The musky smells of autumn tantalized their noses.

As they strolled, Jenny placed her free hand on Rudy's forearm. "Let's sit on a bench, sweetheart. I want to talk to you about something I'd like to do."

And he did it again. That thing that always amazed her. He peeked into her mind and before she could tell him, he asked the relevant question. "You'd like to take a writing course?"

"How do you do that? Take what I'm about to tell you and present it to me as a question?" Like she couldn't have a private thought without Rudy knowing exactly what she was thinking.

"I don't know." He shrugged. "There are lots of things in the world we don't understand. Guess that's just one of the great unknowns." He squeezed her hand affectionately. "But is that what you want to do?"

"Yes. I looked at the fall courses being offered at the seniors' centre. There's one on creative writing. What do you think about me doing that?"

"I think it would be perfect for you. You already keep a journal. You're articulate. creative, artistic, imaginative…"

"But *writing* writing? I don't know, Rudy."

"Jenny, if you can talk you can write. It's just talking on paper—thinking on paper—dreaming on paper."

"Really? You really think I could do it?"

"I most certainly do. But I warn you, I will not critique your work. Others can do that for you."

"Why not you? You were an English professor."

"It would be like a husband teaching his wife to drive." He grinned suddenly, "I tried the driving lessons with Addie. We didn't speak to each other for days after each attempt. Finally, she squealed the brakes, opened the car door, yelled something vile at me, and slammed the door behind her. Within the hour she had signed up with a qualified instructor."

He tilted his head away from Jenny. "And she became a very competent driver. You, *mein dollink*," he said, looking directly at her again, "you will become a very competent writer. I know you will."

She felt she'd met Rudy's faith in her when her personal essay appeared in the *Globe and Mail*, and a short story in the *Antigonish Review*.

The corners of her mouth lift with that memory. Another walk-in-the-park memory vies for attention. A more recent one. On a warm cloudless day last summer.

Their outing lasted almost an hour. Sometimes walking, sometimes sitting on a bench where they could watch the geese and ducks swimming in the lily pond. Throughout, they played a *Who Am I?* game. She would take on the persona of a nursery rhyme or fairy tale character, and he would guess who she was.

"I'm a girl with long yellow hair, and I'm skipping along through the woods," one of her personas said. "I see this cute little house. I go in. And I smell something delicious. It's porridge. There are three bowls of it on the kitchen table—"

"Goldilocks and the Three Bears!" Rudy exclaimed.

"Perfect! You got the answer right again!"

Rudy didn't want her to stop the game. On the way home, when she'd almost exhausted her reservoir of remembered characters, she said, "You really like this game, Rudy. Why's that?"

He smiled at her, "It makes my head feel good."

She sighs with the memory. Then shakes herself back to the present. Her plan is to wait until early afternoon to visit Rudy. She'll dismantle the Christmas tree, cart everything to her storage locker off the parking garage. Maybe if she has time and energy she'll write a few notes to friends who sent Christmas cards—let them know she's still alive and kicking, even if she didn't get cards out this past season.

Christmas cards are important to her. She doesn't like losing touch with friends. Not at her age, when friends are disappearing through illness, dementia, death. Her caregiving role allows little time to cultivate new friendships. She hopes that later, some full-on friendships will come out of the Caregivers' Support Group. She's very fond of some of the people there.

Around two in the afternoon, having overdone things, she's too tired to walk the length of the block, so she drives to Shasta House.

Susan, working the holiday shift, opens the inner door remotely. "Happy New Year, Jenny!"

"Same to you!"

They exchange brief pleasantries. What did Susan do to welcome the New Year? A party at a friend's house. Jenny tells her she doesn't pay much attention to New Year's Eve anymore. Or to New Year's resolutions either.

Jenny feels no urgency to go to Rudy's room. Something tells her he won't be there. Something tells her he's again in Helga's room.

At the snack bar in the middle of the lounge, she pours herself a cup of coffee, her spirits as low and buried as the underlay of the carpet she stands on. She'll forego a chocolate chip cookie for herself, but she will take one for Rudy. She empties a creamer into her coffee and stirs with a skinny wooden stick. Tosses the stick into the waste can. Steaming mug in one hand and napkin-wrapped cookie in the other, she drags herself to the elevators, frees a finger from under the cookie packet to press the button.

Did Rudy go to the New Year's gathering last night, she wonders. Would he have remembered it was scheduled? Twice she'd attended with him for two hours of subdued revelry. Paper hats, noisemakers and a New Year ushered in at eight o'clock. She could have accompanied him last evening, but after their sexual fiasco, she chose to just stay home. Have a shower, curl up with a Steinbeck novel—*East of Eden,* worth reading again. And again. And to go to bed early with half a sleeping pill to help her through a tortured night.

As she expects, Rudy is not in his room. She wishes she was permitted to go get him herself. Now, she'll have to find someone to do it for her. But first she'll finish her coffee.

She sits in Rudy's chair. Connects his personal music device, which she's brought back fully charged, to its purple headphones. Her eyes wander aimlessly as she sips her coffee.

That's odd. There's a pair of glasses on his bookshelf.

She stretches from chair to shelf and picks them up. Black plastic rims with rhinestones embedded in the upper corners.

Oh, shit. Helga's glasses. She's been here again.

Jenny puts down her coffee cup—half full—on the floor beside the chair. Helga's glasses in hand, she jumps up from his chair and charges off to the nurses' station.

Anna isn't there on weekends or holidays. A substitute, whom Jenny doesn't know and who doesn't know her, is on duty.

"I'm Rudy's wife. I found these in his room. I think they belong to Helga."

"Oh, I'm glad you found them. She was complaining at noon that someone stole her glasses."

"They weren't stolen. I expect she left them in my husband's room herself."

"That could be. The night nurse told me, it was kind of funny actually, that she'd found Helga in Rudy's room when she took his eight o'clock meds to him. Seems neither one of them went to the New Year's party in the lounge. They were both in their pyjamas. She sent Helga to her room. And warned her that she could see her on video at the elevators if she tried to go to Rudy's room again."

The storyteller laughs.

Jenny wants to throw up.

"So about eleven-thirty the nurse went back into Rudy's room because she could see light coming from under his door. It was well past time for him to be in bed. There was Helga again. Both of them sitting on the edge of his bed. She had snuck down the stairs so the camera wouldn't catch her. She's a sly one, that one."

Ellen's words ring in Jenny's ears, 'It's natural.' *Like hell, it's natural.* Maybe when they forget who their loved ones are. But not when they know enough to sneak around to avoid detection.

"You can get the glasses to her." Jenny folds them up and plunks them onto the nurses' desk. She needs to go to the lounge to find someone to fetch Rudy from Helga's room. *I should be allowed to locate my own husband. This is so maddening.* All this wretchedness turns her stomach.

What possessed Ellen to write that letter forbidding her to fetch Rudy? Couldn't she tell Helga was delusional? Or deliberately lying? Was the letter a way of somehow protecting Ellen's own ass? *The same way she played ass-protection games with me when Rudy came to the condo in the fall?*

The week before Thanksgiving Jenny had developed a cold. As long as she was contagious, she knew she had to stay away from the home. For a full week she had phoned daily to ask Anna, or whoever was on duty, to please tell Rudy that his wife wouldn't be visiting that day. And why.

Her cold nearly gone, she would resume visits the next afternoon. She was in her studio with her paints when the door buzzer sounded. She wasn't expecting anyone.

"Yes? Who is it?"

"Me. Rudy. I came to see you."

My god! How did he get out? Find his way here? Cross the busy intersection?

"Stay where you are. I'll come down to the lobby and meet you."

She directed him onto the elevator and off, around the corner and down the hall to her suite. "How did you get here?"

"I walked."

"By yourself?"

"Of course."

He's on the Restricted Exit list. How did he get out? Who let him out?

"I was worried about you. I had to come, Jenny."

She got him settled in her recliner, then phoned Shasta House. The voice on the other end was unfamiliar. Maybe someone new had been hired to help with reception. "Put me through to Anna, please."

Assuming Rudy was likely in his room or in the lounge, Anna gasped to hear he was at Jenny's place.

"It's a miracle he found his way here. That he crossed the street safely. Let alone figured out how to use the buzzer to let me know he was here." Anna started to speak, but Jenny continued over her. "When I come back to Shasta House I want to see what happened. Will you let Ellen know I want to see the videotape that shows how he got out on his own?"

The next day, at the conclusion of her visit with Rudy, Jenny popped into the nurses' station. "I'm here to see the video, Anna."

Anna seemed oddly flustered. "Yeah, sure. Ah...Ellen said it was okay to show it to you. Just a minute now, until I get it set up."

Together they watched Rudy push his walker through the outer door and wheel it in under the canopy. "That's what Ellen wanted me to see? We both know he got out there. I want to see him at the inner door. That video."

Anna squirmed in her chair, "Ah..."

"I'm Rudy's wife. His primary caregiver. I have a right to see what happened."

"Yes, you do. I agree you do, but Ellen said to just show you this one."

"What's she trying to cover up, Anna? I want to see how Rudy got out. It mustn't happen again."

Anna adjusted the screen and controls until the footage appeared. They watched Rudy dressed for outdoors, his tweed cap jauntily to one side, as he stood at the keypad meant for those allowed to have the code to unlock the inner door. He pressed the numbers in vain. Then wheeled over to the reception desk.

The playback was visual only, so they couldn't hear Rudy speaking to the unfamiliar woman there. Without looking up at him, her attention fixed on the computer screen to her other side, the woman reached under the desk for the inner entrance button. The door opened. Rudy walked out.

So that's what happened. "How is someone new expected to know who can go out and who can't?"

Anna explained there was a binder with pictures of the restricted residents on the reception desk.

"You mean, she has to flip through a binder every time a resident asks her to open the door? That sounds like an inefficient system. It may be okay for Nancy and Susan, who've worked here for years and know the residents, but for someone new?"

At home Jenny wrestled with the problem. There was a ridge above the desk—the backside of the raised counter that people like to lean on when talking to the receptionist. What if they had small pictures of the wanderers posted there? An instant visual checking system. Much better than flipping through pages.

On her next visit she offered her solution to Ellen.

"Oh, no Mrs. Hoffman. We couldn't do anything like that. What if one of the residents noticed their picture there and asked why it was on display?"

"Tell them it's because they're special, and the receptionist just likes looking at their images."

"But that would be untruthful. Our binder system works just fine. And it protects everyone's privacy."

Like the unknown woman who had tried out for a reception job at Shasta House, Jenny's suggestion was promptly dismissed.

Friday, January 1, mid-afternoon

A newly-hired PSW, gossiping with Susan at the reception desk, agrees to get Rudy. Jenny waits in his room. She paces, dreading something, but not knowing what. *Why am I so nervous?* She senses her blood pressure is elevated. Her head throbs.

On the top of his dresser she spots a page from a small notepad she keeps there to scribble reminders of things he needs. There's a list in Rudy's now almost-illegible handwriting. She peers at it. Wonders what it means.

> *$500.00.*
> *Bank book.*
> *Penis hardness.*
> *KY Jelly.*

And something else impossible to decipher.

She pockets the note and sinks into Rudy's recliner to wait. When she hears the door unlatch she leans forward.

The door opens. Mouth set, eyebrows pinched, Rudy pushes his walker ahead of him.

"He didn't want to leave," the PSW behind him says, "but I told him you wanted to talk to him." She hurries off to other duties.

Scarcely into the room, Rudy spins his walker around. Locks the brakes, turns around and lowers himself onto the seat to face his wife. He folds his arms across his chest. "You wanted to talk. So talk."

Taken aback by his manner, by the hostility she hears in his voice, Jenny doesn't reply. *Who is this man in Rudy's body?*

"Well?" The hatefulness in his voice shocks her. "Go ahead. Say something."

"I was worried about you. I wanted to wish you Happy New Year."

He snorts. "Happy New Year to you, too." His eyes narrow, and he looks directly at her. "But it will be a Happy New Year for me."

"Oh?"

"Helga and I had sex last night. We're going to live together."

Jenny blanches. Her mouth drops open. Her stomach roils.

"We're going to look for an apartment right away. I need $500. Why don't I have a chequebook?"

"Because I have power of attorney, Rudy. I handle all our finances. Pay all our bills. Pay for you to live here."

"I never agreed to that."

"But you did—" she cuts herself off. *Don't argue with people who have dementia.*

"I'm not going to live here anymore. I'm going to live with Helga. But I won't divorce you," he explains in a slightly kinder voice. "I'll look after you financially."

Silence builds an invisible wall between them. He glares at her. She feels her heart shrivelling inside her like a woolen sock felting in boiling water.

Then Rudy speaks again. "I want to know, do you have a chequebook with you?"

"No, Rudy. I rarely carry a chequebook."

"Then, bring me one. And all the banking information."

She's conscious of how his illogical comments, expressed so forcefully, must sound balanced and sensible to him. Perhaps somehow reminding him of the man he'd been. Confident in his decisions. Flexible about changing plans when necessary. In a very peculiar way, because he's been so low-key, so cooperative for so long, this blast of assertiveness has a ring of remembered rationality to her, too.

She hesitates. Then she holds up the note she found, "I see you made a list. Do you want it?"

"No, it's for you. Things I need."

"I don't understand all of it. I see you want $500."

"Yes, for an apartment." *He couldn't rent a broom closet in Sonnenberg for that.*

"And you want a bankbook."

"Everything from the bank."

"Then it says, 'penis hardness.' What's that about Rudy?"

"Those pills for men. I want you to get those for me."

Jenny is caught in the bizarre nature of what he expects her—his wife—to do to accommodate his affair. "And I suppose you want me to pick up the vaginal lubricant, too."

"Yes, some KY Jelly. Helga needs it. Sex hurts her. That woman thing. Dryness or something."

Jenny cannot speak. She tries not to visualize them together in Helga's bed. Or perhaps in his. With a lead curtain of denial, she closes off that part of her mind.

"You have the car. So you have to get things," he reasons, "but you won't have to do the errands for long. I'll be getting a car soon for myself."

Although this entire encounter is rattling, Jenny remains amazed at how he has determined what he needs for his new life.

"And another thing: stop treating me like a child. Helga says you treat me like a child." He leans back, raises his crossed arms higher. "And that is all I have to say."

Jenny's hands tremble. Her mouth feels dry as a desert. *Is it possible to distract him?* "Rudy, would you like to listen to your music?"

"No. I want to go back up to Helga's room. But I want you to go home first."

"I'm not ready to go home just yet. I came to see you. I thought maybe you'd like to play Scrabble with me."

"I don't like Scrabble anymore."

Then silence. Silence, like the drawing in of a breath before a piercing scream. Jenny hopes he's finished with his wild words. But he isn't.

"So, how do you feel about all this?"

As if he cares, in the state he's in.

She answers slowly. Quietly. "Rudy, what you're telling me hurts. It's ripping me apart inside. Like I've been stabbed in the heart."

"Too bad, but that's your problem, not mine." *Icy. Cold as a slab of marble.* "You'll just have to get used to it."

Jenny tries her one remaining diversion. "Rudy, I brought you a cookie."

He hesitates. A spark of interest, "What kind?"

"Chocolate chip."

"Forget it. I like peanut butter. Eat it yourself."

The door opens. A holiday fill-in PSW pokes her head in. "Are you Rudy?"

"Yes, why?"

"I'm supposed to get you into dry pants."

"My pants are already dry."

The PSW steps in behind Rudy. "Are you sure?"

Jenny catches her eye. "Probably he's wet. He takes a heavy dose of diuretic."

"You keep out of this, damn you," Rudy shouts, his words thrown at her like a spear. "I'm fine. There's nothing wrong with me."

He sounds so vicious. In all their years together, Jenny has never seen this kind of nastiness. Never even imagined he would, or could, ever treat her like an enemy. *Who is he? Why has he become this way? This rapid change? Measurably worse each day?*

"Okay Rudy," the PSW purrs. "I'll come back later."

"Don't bother. I'll be out looking for an apartment."

But the PSW isn't listening. She's already closing the door behind her.

Upset as she feels, Jenny is also astounded that he's staying on topic for so long. That she can't distract him. Is this the way he'll be from now on? Tears well in her eyes and roll down her cheeks.

"Why are you crying?" His tone is hard, unfeeling, as though she's doing something to annoy him.

"Because I'm losing you."

"You'll get used to it."

But it's not just this loss. Jenny is sobbing about. It's years of loss—the steady decline in his judgement, in his cognition, his behaviour. It's watching the man with the golden mind, sharp wit, deep sensitivity, delicious playfulness turning inside out and leaving irretrievable bits of himself strewn where no one can find them to put him back together. She wants to stop the tears, but they keep coming.

"Come on, Jenny." He thumps his forearms on the armrests of his walker. "That's enough. It's not like you still love me—"

"But I do, Rudy. I do." She reaches into her pocket for a tissue and wipes the wetness from her cheeks.

"How can you say that when you won't have sex with me?"

"Rudy, we tried to make love, here, yesterday afternoon—"

"What are you talking about? We did not."

"Yes, we did. And you peed all over me."

"You're lying. That's a lie. You're a liar, Jenny."

He's forgotten, just like he can't remember what he had for breakfast—but he says he had sex with Helga. Jenny wants to believe that is merely delusion. A fantasy brought on by his disease. It's easier for her to call it something he imagined, like when some residents think they're conversing with long dead relatives, than to accept it really happened.

Suddenly, the rage drains from his face. "I'm very tired. I want to have a nap. Can you help me?"

Jenny doesn't answer. She waits until he gets off his walker and moves over to sit on the edge of his bed, positioned for her to remove his shoes and lift his legs onto the bed. She does as he expects, then covers him with a blanket. For the first time this afternoon, he smiles at her.

"Thanks, Jenny. You've been a good wife and a good friend."

She turns away, fishes in her pocket for the already used tissue, pulls it out and blows her nose. When she looks back at him, his eyes are closed. Fatigue, both emotional and physical, have claimed him.

Numb, broken, eviscerated, she stands beside his bed. *I can't handle any more. I need to go home.*

For a few moments she closes her eyes and breathes deeply trying to centre herself. Then, tiptoeing, she gets her coat from where she'd hung it in his closet. Tugs on her boots, and quietly departs.

Jockie Loomer-Kruger

Friday, January 1, late afternoon

At home she relives the shock and horror of what's just happened. She hates this. She hates all of it. She hates that ugly man who's taken over her husband's mind and body.

In a burst of sudden energy and without understanding why, she methodically removes every picture of Rudy she has on display. The one of the two of them, in the tiny Venetian glass mosaic frame on her bedside table. The professional portrait taken on a visit to Saskatoon that hangs beside her bed. Another of him looking so handsome in his academic gown, about to join other faculty at a spring commencement.

And the little one, in the standing oval frame on her dresser. Grinning broadly, he holds onto one handle of the Grey Cup with a husky young man who played for the winning team. The football hero, who dwarfs Rudy in stature, supports most of the weight of the huge trophy. She remembers how thrilled Rudy was to meet Adam and see the Grey Cup in person. Not that Rudy was a devoted football fan. But he always insisted on watching the final few games.

"It's a Saskatchewan thing," he explained, "Football's in our blood—although, I only got a few-games-a-year transfusion of it." It was her creative writing instructor, Adam's mother, who invited them to her house when it was her son's turn to bring the prize to Sonnenberg.

Jenny moves on into the living room. She whips their wedding picture off the mantle. Then the photo in the hall, taken at a New Year's Eve party that had a Victorian theme. They'd posed like people did in old sepia pictures: he, in his tuxedo, sitting on a straight back chair, she beside him, hand on his shoulder, wearing an authentic white Victorian dress that had belonged to her great-grandmother. Ramrod stiff, prim and proper. Neither of them smiling, except with their eyes.

She brings all the pictures to the dining room table. Opens the drawer in the buffet that harbours a few birthday cards they'd given each other, and their funny valentine.

She picks up the valentine. She remembers the card store where she bought it for their first Valentine's Day. The gift shop right beside the

Italian restaurant they'd gone to on their first date. She runs her finger over the plastic coil spine, around the edges of the die-cut shape of a beer stein and the embossed cartoonish images of a *Mann und Frau* in Oktoberfest costumes. Text below the illustration is printed to represent old German type and spelled to produce a distinct German accent.

When he first held the card and turned its pages, Rudy's rolling laughter delighted her. "I think this needs to be read aloud."

And so, in a full, guttural, German accent, he read the male parts. In a poor imitation, she read the female. Together they read the final verse.

> *Sveetie Pie,*
> *huggin's pleasin'-*
> *let's stop der teasin'*
> *Und get busy mit der*
> *squeezin'!!!*

Then they sealed their reading with a kiss, a hug, and bubbles of laughter. Through all their years together they'd exchanged that same card, and executed the same ritual. Even at Shasta House, in the privacy of his room, they'd gone through the same performance for each Valentine's Day.

That was one of the things she loved about Rudy. His playfulness. He may have been a professor, a Steinbeck scholar, a wannabe meteorologist, a deep-thinking philosopher, but his sense of fun—sometimes sheer silliness—was infectious.

She pokes the card back where it had been, and loads the Rudy pictures haphazardly in on top. Then closes the drawer with her hip.

The agony of today punches her again. She weeps.

When, at last, her tears are spent, she absently watches the sunset through the west end of the bay window. Like a living palette, colours shift from gold to pink, to mauve, into darkness.

Wait a minute! Could this be sundowning? She's seen other residents, mostly those with Alzheimer's Disease, 'sundown'—transform from placid, agreeable people throughout the day to angry, hostile, sometimes even dangerous manifestations of themselves in the late afternoon and evening. As though the sun going down panics their brains. Like Margaret, last summer.

Jenny had been sitting outside on the enclosed patio with Rudy when Margaret, pushing her walker, stepped onto the stained-wood deck. Margaret, straight and trim, always immaculately dressed in designer clothes. Makeup perfect. Never a white hair out of place. And with a voice deep and raspy from years of smoking.

Margaret's burnt-umber eyes darted. Confusion pinched her face. "Where do I sleep?" she asked the early evening air. "Where do I sleep?"

Rudy watched her. "What's wrong with that lady?"

"I think she's mixed up," Jenny said. "I'll be back in a minute. I'm going to see if I can find someone to help her."

Only a couple of residents still lingered in the lounge. Most had gone to their rooms. No staff remained on the first floor. Finding an available PSW in the evening was almost impossible. Most were absorbed in some aspect of residents' bedtime care. Jenny had learned early that under-staffing at Shasta House was most evident during morning and evening care.

Surely she could help out. She knew where Margaret's room was, at the end of the hall on the third floor. The floor Rudy had first lived on. It shouldn't take but a few minutes.

Margaret was still asking the summer air, "Where do I sleep? Where do I sleep?" Jenny quietly approached her.

"I'll show you where your room is. Come with me." To Rudy, Jenny called, "I'll be back soon."

But she wasn't.

On the elevator, Margaret focussed her blazing eyes on Jenny, raised a crooked arthritic finger and raged, "Why are you so rotten? You used to be so nice. Now you're so nasty. I hate you."

Then the plaintive concern, "Where do I sleep?"

Noting Margaret was without her pendant, Jenny wished she'd pressed Rudy's and waited for staff to come for Margaret. Jenny wasn't trained to deal with difficult residents. Now, she had no choice but to see this angry woman to her room.

Exiting the elevator, Margaret clamped onto Jenny's arm. "What did you do with my husband? My son? They'll help me."

Margaret's husband was long dead, and her son lived on the West Coast. Jenny patted Margaret's hand, felt the fingers loosen on her arm, and saw the hand return to grip the walker. "I'll help you, Margaret. Your room's this way." Touching the walker, Jenny tried to point Margaret toward her room at the end of the hall.

But Margaret pushed her hand away. "No, you won't help. You're just trying to hurt me."

Jenny wanted out of this. But how? If only Margaret was wearing her pendant. "I'll show you where your room is, Margaret, and then I'll get the nurse to come see you."

At the door they paused. Margaret rattled the handle. "It's locked. Why did you steal my key?"

"The key is right there, Margaret." Jenny pointed to the green plastic coil that wrapped itself around Margaret's wrist, with her key attached.

"That's not my key. Why are you so mean to me? I used to like you. I hate you."

"Maybe the key will work. How about trying it?" Jenny kept her words slow and deliberate, her tone soothing.

Margaret poked the key into the slot and opened the door.

"This is your room, Margaret. This is where you'll sleep."

Her eyes widening, Margaret grabbed Jenny's wrist. "Don't go. Don't leave me alone. I don't want to be alone. I'm scared."

"I can stay for a minute or two, Margaret, then I'll get the nurse to come."

Inside the two-bedroom suite, similar to the one Rudy had occupied when he first moved to Shasta House, Margaret made an immediate demand. "Make my bed. It's a mess. Make it."

But the bed wasn't mussed up. It was smooth and neat. Everything in place. Just the way Margaret kept herself.

"All right." Jenny pretended to smooth the bedspread.

"That's terrible," Margaret glared, her lips pursed, "don't you know how to make a bed? Are you stupid? Where's my extra blanket? Did you take my extra blanket?"

Jenny pointed to a carefully folded blue wool blanket on the shelf in the open closet. "Is that your blanket?"

"No. That's not my blanket. I've never seen that blanket before." Then, hand over her chest, Margaret stumbled her way to her pale turquoise armchair, and sank into it. She began to hyperventilate, "There. See what you've done? I'm having a heart attack."

More than anything, Jenny wished she could see the errant pendant lying somewhere, but she couldn't. She was so out of her depth. And she was afraid—for Margaret, for herself. She needed to notify the nurse.

Instinctively, though, she tried to calm Margaret, "Take a deep breath, Margaret. Deep. Slow. Breathe deeply."

Without drawing a single deep breath, Margaret's panting stopped as quickly as it had begun. "You'll be sorry tomorrow when I'm dead. Then you'll know what you've done."

"Margaret, I'm going to leave now and get the nurse to come see you."

With unexpected speed and strength, Margaret grabbed Jenny by the hand. "Don't go. Don't leave me alone. I'm scared. My head. My head is all mixed up. Don't leave me."

The frightened woman released Jenny's hand, and Jenny stroked Margaret's arm. "It'll be okay, Margaret. It'll be okay."

When she felt Margaret relax a bit, she said again, "I need to get a nurse to help you."

Like a Jack-in-the-Box, Margaret sprang up from the chair. "You aren't going anywhere without me."

"Okay, but you need to get your walker first."

Margaret headed into her bedroom, and Jenny held the door into the hall slightly ajar, fully expecting the troubled resident and her walker to join her. But instead, Margaret grabbed the handle on the other side, yanked the door shut with a bang, then blared through the wooden panels, "I'm going to bed. You go to hell!"

Margaret and her sundowning were done for the night.

Jenny had hurried back to Rudy on the patio, shaken by what she'd just experienced, hoping Rudy's dementia would never cause such a dramatic change in personality.

With the recollection of the incident with Margaret still haunting her, Jenny forces herself to eat an apple, a slice of cheddar cheese, and three soda crackers slicked with butter.

Could Rudy be sundowning or is it something else? Later in the evening she poses the same question in her journal, but she writes nothing else, just gouges a deep zigzag into the paper with the tip of her pen.

Saturday, January 2

Despite her sedative, Jenny sleeps fitfully. At three-thirty in the morning something awakens her and sends her to her computer.

She searches 'Triadone.' The first surprise is to discover that the drug is prescribed to relieve depression. Rudy hasn't been depressed. Why an antidepressant? She reads through the list of side effects. Not that, nor that, nor that either. But there, at the end of the list, 'may cause erectile dysfunction in men.' *Was that the side effect the doctor hoped would happen?*

But Rudy doesn't need an erectile dysfunction side effect. He needs something to reduce his desire. Cut down on his raging libido. It's as though his hormones are an uncontrolled wildfire. *He's not depressed. He's lusting.*

Jenny picks up the phone. Presses the numbers for Shasta House, knowing that during the night the nurse on duty will answer any calls that come in.

"Shasta House, Nurse Bradley speaking."

"This is Jenny Hoffman. Rudy's wife. Rudy in 610. I want you to stop a drug he's on. Triadone."

"It's the morning nurse that will be giving his pills to him, Mrs. Hoffman. I can't make that change."

"Then tell her to stop it. Absolutely no more. I don't want him to have any more of it."

"But I can't do that without a doctor's order."

"You'll get a doctor's order. But not for two days. I want it stopped. Now."

"I don't think you don't understand Mrs. Hoffman, our protocol is that we need to wait for the doctor's authorization before making any changes to medications."

"I don't think *you* understand. My husband's not reacting to that drug the way the doctor assumed he would. It's making him far worse, not better. I don't want him to have any more of it. None."

"But the doctor—"

"Never mind the doctor, damn it. I'm his wife. I'm his power of attorney. If you don't stop it, I'll sue."

She knows that's a bizarre thing to say, to threaten with litigation. "I'll get him to the doctor and on something else on Monday. But until then, I want that medication stopped. Do you hear me?"

"But Mrs. Hoffman, we aren't supposed—"

"Stop it, I tell you. Or else!"

Jenny bangs the phone back into its stand, not at all sure they will withhold the drug.

Saturday, January 2, very early morning

She stays awake after the call to Shasta House, wraps herself in her old frayed robe and roams into the living room. She should check out the information in the latest, still-unopened newsletter from the Alzheimer's Society that lies on the stand beside her recliner.

But she can't. Not right now. Instead she picks up yesterday's copy of the *Sonnenberg Herald* from the pile of unread daily papers she's allowed to accumulate on the coffee table.

In her chair, she lifts the foot rest, draws up her knees, and searches out the comics. None of the cartoons amuse her. She turns to the lifestyle page. Who cares whether bland neutral tones on the wall are the new must-have? She tosses the paper aside and bobs into the kitchen.

After an early breakfast—old folks' go-to of tea and toast—she crawls back into her unmade bed. Just a little nap, that's all she needs. A few catch-up winks.

At noon, she awakens. Still in pyjamas, she wanders into the kitchen for more toast and tea with the addition of a honey crisp apple, peeled and cut in wedges, and a chunk of cheddar cheese. Fresh fruit and some protein, that will do until she feels like eating something more substantial.

At one o'clock she picks up the phone to call the doctor's office. She doesn't expect the Health Centre to be open—and it isn't.

"—The office will reopen on Monday, January fourth. If this is an emergency—"

She plunks the phone down, and marches into the bedroom to get dressed.

It's mid-afternoon before she enters Shasta House, feeling as emotionally drained and haggard as she saw herself in the hall mirror before she left her condo. Other than absently opening the main door for her, Nancy, working on papers at her desk, fails to acknowledge Jenny's arrival.

But Jenny doesn't care. Today she doesn't care about anything. Her heart is hollow. Her marriage is shattered. Her life is in shambles.

Yet she is still her husband's caregiver. It is she who has power of attorney for his personal care. She needs to know if the drug that she believes has done him so much harm has been stopped. Or has it been given in spite of her middle-of-the-night phone call?

She chooses the stairs to reach the second floor. With a light rap on the door to announce her presence, she treads into the nurses' station where Anna is thumbing through a file drawer. When Jenny clears her throat, the charge nurse spins around.

"Jenny! My god, woman! You look like hell!"

"I look exactly like I feel. But never mind that. I need to know if Rudy was given Triadone this morning."

"I don't know. I didn't come on duty until noon. I'm not supposed to be here at all, but the day nurse had to go home unexpectedly. One of her little kids got sick. I'll check."

She unlocks the portable medication cart with its wide, shallow drawers. Pulls out the one marked *A – H* and finds Rudy's assortment of labelled prepackaged prescriptions. The morning packet is still there, with all pills given but one. Triadone.

"So the doctor ordered it stopped?" Anna says.

"No. I did. I think it's been making the situation worse. I'm convinced it isn't the right drug for him."

"Like I said, Jenny, it's not what we generally use here in cases like this."

She writes the name of a different drug on a piece of paper. "Ask your doctor about this. We've used it here numerous times. None of the guys ever had adverse side-effects. Well, other than eventually looking in need of a bra." She grins. "Listen, I've got a little time. Do you want to talk?"

Jenny sits carefully on a rolling office chair at the long desk. She faces the multi-screen video surveillance monitor. In a voice deep with sorrow, she recounts Rudy's New Year's Day pronouncements, but says nothing of the attempted intimacy of the day before. If Rudy has forgotten that, then so shall she. At least, set it aside as unimportant.

Movement on the monitor catches her eye. In an upper screen Rudy and Helga are waiting at the seventh floor elevators, perhaps going down to the lounge.

"You know, Jenny, Ellen doesn't believe in interfering in Shasta House romances because she considers them very natural in a setting like this. No interference unless there's the risk of someone being hurt. But I see *you* hurting."

Jenny dabs at her eyes and gulps, but listens intently to Anna's words.

"I also see how up-one-minute-and-down-the-next Helga is. I do intervene when I can. I tell Rudy he's a married man like you asked. But I don't know if anyone else says anything to him, even though I recommended it at a staff meeting. Unfortunately, Ellen pooh-poohed my suggestion. She said there was no need for staff to interfere."

"Figures," Jenny mutters. Then, louder, "But what does Rudy do when you tell him he's married?"

"Not much. Every now and then, though, he says, 'Yes, I am.' And I say, 'What you're doing makes Jenny very sad.' And he goes back to his room or to read his paper by the fireplace. Then I have Helga wild with me. But that's all right. I can handle Helga."

Jenny feels grateful for Anna's efforts, but irritated with Ellen. The feelings of both support and lack of support battle within as she takes an elevator to Rudy's room.

As she expects, he's not there.

Shoulders caved, she leaves his room. *I can't take any more. Wherever he is, I hope he's happier than he was yesterday.* And she hopes more than anything else that he's safe.

Holding back a bout of tears, she opens the door at the end of the hall and begins the trudge down five flights of stairs. When she emerges into the lounge she hustles to the front door, refusing to turn her head to see if Rudy and Helga are in the lounge. Bowed, blind with burning tears, she hurries through the canopy tunnel and back up the street to her condo. Her whole being feeling as grey and lifeless as the Shasta House walls she's left behind.

Numb, she turns on the TV to a home renovation show but, exhausted, quickly falls asleep. At midnight, she awakens in her recliner, the TV blasting an ad for a house security system.

She goes to bed, her journal unopened, and sleeps without the aid of a sleeping pill.

Jockie Loomer-Kruger

Sunday, January 3, mid-morning

With the need to spare Rudy from Shasta House church services happening only once a month, Jenny joins her own congregation for the first Sunday of the New Year. Cheery welcoming hugs greet her. Friendly comments, 'Happy New Year,' 'Good to see you, Jenny,' 'We've missed you,' 'You haven't been here for a while.'

Indeed she hasn't. Some Sundays she's taken the time to catch up on household chores. Others she's spent entirely with Rudy. A few times she's gone for brunch downtown with one of her women friends. But now and then she feels the need to tend to her battered, aching spirit and drives to the Unitarian Universalist Centre in the south end of the city.

The minister's talk is predictable. About new beginnings. What else for the first service of the new year? The words do little to salve her emotional torment. How can she start fresh when everything is so unfinished?

After the service, she follows congregants to the hall at the back of the building for coffee and conversation. Chatter bubbles, 'How was your Christmas?' Jokes about already-broken New Year's resolutions.

A hand touches her wrist accompanied by a soft, plaintive voice. Christine, a woman she knows by sight, but not well, speaks to her. Jenny does know, though, that Christine is also a caregiver, looking after her husband with Alzheimer's.

"It's rough, isn't it?" Christine squeezes Jenny's hand. "Are you holding up okay?"

"I think so. But some days, I'm not so sure. How are you doing?"

"Better. My husband's in a nursing home now. I don't have to do everything for him anymore like when he was living at home." Melancholy hangs from her words like icicles from the eaves. "He doesn't know who I am. He thinks I'm his old Aunt Rose, and he wasn't very fond of her."

Jenny sees tears well in Christine's eyes.

"It's just one day at time," the woman says. Then she blinks rapidly, throws Jenny a small smile, and moves on to speak to someone else.

Jenny finishes her coffee. *Enough of this for now.*

She leaves unobtrusively and drives to the supermarket in the busy mall not far from the UU Centre. She doesn't need much. Bread, milk, a box of Earl Grey tea bags. *Old ladies, gotta have tea with our toast.*

She's surprised by the sardonic smile that accompanies the thought. Surprised that the half smile actually makes her feel good, like finding something precious that you thought was lost. As though her ability to smile has been buried in a deep cave.

Coffee and cookies at the centre rob her of an appetite for lunch, so she does the fallback choice. Tea and toast. She knows she should eat better. The last thing Rudy needs is for her to get sick from malnutrition.

She finds the peanut butter jar and lathers sweetened protein onto her toast. She remembers how, when Rudy stopped attending the UU Centre with her, he made a point of preparing a special meal for her return. Marriage accommodation took many forms. Back then.

She's almost ready to trudge down to Shasta House when the phone rings. She hopes it's not the home calling about Rudy.

"Hi, Sis! How's it going? Thought I'd call to wish you Happy New Year."

"Esther!" Jenny's sigh of relief mixes with her response. "Happy New Year to you, too. Are you up to your hips in snow yet?"

She remembers enormous, well-packed drifts of snow when she was young, and the fun she and Esther had climbing on them. She especially loved the ones that formed by the front stoop. They jumped into those with whoops of laughter, the same way they leapt into heaps of crunchy, leathery-smelling fall leaves their father had raked from under the maple and chestnut trees.

"There's not that much snow here yet, but it's bitterly cold. Too cold to venture out to church this morning. What about you, do you have a lot of snow?"

"Not much. It's just a bit below freezing here. Not bad for the beginning of January. And I did go to the service this morning."

"Still attending a Unitarian church?"

"We call it a centre, not a church. Not that what a building is called really matters. And yes, I go there now and then. It's a good home base for doubters."

"You know," Esther says, "if mother was still alive—"

"But she isn't. And beliefs change. At least mine have."

"Mine haven't. I don't know where I'd be in life without my Baptist friends."

"Well, that's the key, isn't it? The friends, I mean. A place to belong. A sense of community. Isn't that what's at the root of why people go to church? We go there for human contact. I find it so interesting that almost all religions preach the golden rule in one configuration or another. One religion isn't all that different from another."

"Oh, Jenny, you're impossible. I'll never understand you. It's as though Rudy's lack of faith has somehow eroded yours."

"Don't blame Rudy. I'm a pretty independent thinker."

"High-spirited, is what Mum used to call you. And Dad said you were too bright for your own good."

Her sister's laugh tinkles in Jenny's ear. "No, I think what he said was, 'You're too bright for a girl.'"

"Maybe it was. Well, anyway, I just wanted to hear your voice, Jenny. To know you're okay."

"Yeah, Sis, I'm okay. Thanks for the call. Happy New Year, Esther."

Yeah, Sis, I'm okay.

When she arrives at Shasta House, half an hour after her sister's call, Rudy is once more missing from his room.

She locates a PSW in the lounge helping a resident locate her walker. She asks if, when the PSW is free, would she mind going to 715 and bringing Rudy back to his room where she'll be waiting for him.

Jenny settles herself in his power lift chair. To fill the time, she'll read.

She picks up the current issue of his *Canadian Geographic* from the window sill. An article on caribou migration catches her attention. It's a long article, but she has finished it before the door opens.

The shy, young PSW in a beige hijab stops in the doorway and rubs her hands together nervously. "I'm so sorry, I tried to get him to come with me. He wouldn't leave. I tried hard. He kept saying, 'I want to stay here with Helga.' I'm sorry. I'm very sorry."

"It's okay, thanks for trying."

The personal support worker closes the door.

Jenny wishes she knew what to do, but no inspiration surfaces. She gets up from Rudy's chair, dresses for the chill outside, and tramps home, her heart split in two.

That night, she does something she hasn't done since childhood. She picks up her old teddy bear from where he sits in the maple glider near the bedroom window and holds him close. Wrapping her bear in her arms, she crawls into bed. Like a snail pulling itself into the protection of its shell, she curls into a ball.

Part Five

*As happens sometimes, a moment settled and hovered
and remained for much more than a moment.*

— John Steinbeck, <u>Of Mice and Men</u>

Jockie Loomer-Kruger

Monday, January 4

As soon as the doctor's office opens, Jenny calls. The receptionist gives Rudy a mid-morning appointment.

Next she calls Shasta House to request that Rudy be in his room and dressed warmly, ready to leave when she arrives.

It's Charlene, popping gum, who does the job. "Here he is. All set to go. Handsome as a movie star."

He glowers at Jenny. "Where are you taking me?"

"To see Dr. Angus."

"There's nothing wrong with me. I'm not sick."

"It's just a check-up, Rudy."

In the elevator he looks at Jenny with what she interprets as either contempt or disgust. "You're having an affair with Bruno, aren't you?"

"I'm what?"

"Helga says you're having an affair with Bruno and it makes her mad."

Jenny shakes her head. Should she try to reason with him, or just shut her mouth? *Christ. I hate their diseases.* Their delusions. Their decline.

"Rudy," she speaks slowly, evaluating each word, hoping she's saying something he will understand, "I've never met Bruno. I've only seen him once, and that was when he was having dinner with Helga." In spite of herself she tosses in a barb. "When he was holding Helga's hand."

"Why do you lie to me, Jenny?"

At the table across from the reception desk, she signs her husband out, entering the time of departure, destination, and expected time of return. With his feet weighted in winter boots, his plodding shuffle behind his walker is even more pronounced. They inch their way to her car, and she helps him into the front passenger seat. Buckles his seat belt. Folds his walker and stores it in the trunk.

As soon as she slides in behind the wheel, his questions assail her. "Where are we going?"

"To see Dr. Angus."

"Am I sick?"

"No, not exactly. But the doctor wants to see you."

Rudy is silent in the examination room while the nurse checks his vital signs.

"I see from his chart he has atrial fib," she says to Jenny. "His pulse is a bit out of rhythm right now. But his blood pressure's good, and his respiration is all right."

She types her findings into the computer, then gets up. "Dr. Angus will be in to see you very soon." She closes the door behind her.

As they sit side by side in silence, Jenny automatically reaches for her husband's hand. Old habits interlace their fingers, and for a second, tears rise in Jenny's eyes. She swallows. Forces a dispassionate demeanor and prepares herself for the doctor's entrance.

A slender man in his early fifties, with an angular nose and thick black hair showing peek-a-boo streaks of grey at the temples, opens the door. "Well, hello, Rudy Hoffman. Happy New Year! Good morning, Jenny."

He speaks directly to Rudy. "So, what brings you here today, my good man?"

"I don't know. Jenny knows."

"Would you like me to ask Jenny?"

Rudy nods.

Jenny appreciates Dr. Angus' approach of always addressing Rudy first. Of appearing to give Rudy the opportunity to be in charge of his own health matters.

"So, Jenny can you help us out? What's going on with Rudy?"

"For one thing, he's off the Triadone. I had them stop it two days ago."

"And why was that?"

"I felt it was doing just the opposite of what it was supposed to do." She doesn't mention her husband by name. "Got very agitated, hostile, super-charged libido."

"You did the right thing." The doctor picks up a pen from his desk and tucks it behind his ear, "Obviously it wasn't the right choice of drug for Rudy. Not every drug does the expected with every patient."

She remembers something his cardiologist said after Rudy's stroke: 'I'm going to prescribe some poison for him, and we expect it will have desirable side effects. That's really what drugs are, and how they work.' It appalled her at the time, but over the years she began to think the specialist had spoken the truth.

She's reluctant to discuss Rudy's behaviour further in front of him, so she withdraws a folded type-written page from her purse. She had prepared it before bed last night, a detailed description of the events that occurred while he was on the drug. She left out their attempt at love-making. At the end of her account she asks if they could try him on something else.

When he has read her report, she shows Dr. Angus the slip of paper Anna gave her with the name of the medication generally used at the home for testosterone-gone-wild.

"We can try that, Jenny. Sometimes that particular medication can cause breast enlargement, but otherwise there should be no adverse side effects."

During the lull while Dr. Angus absorbed Jenny's letter, Rudy had picked up a brochure from a rack of medical pamphlets beside his chair. Tuning out from the conversation between his physician and his wife, Rudy carefully reads "Tips for Successful Breast Feeding."

Dr. Angus prints out the prescription. "Something new for you, Rudy."

Suddenly, as though a locked door has swung open in his brain, Rudy blurts, "Am I getting those pills for men?"

"Beg pardon?"

"Are you giving me those pills for men?"

"I think he means something for erectile dysfunction, Dr. Angus," Jenny clarifies.

"No, Rudy. I'm ordering something else for you."

"To give me an erection?"

"I can't give you that kind of drug, Rudy. It's too dangerous for you. You have too many serious heart problems. It would do you more harm than good."

A sneer curls Rudy's lips. "So, you, too. Jenny won't help me. And now you." He shifts in his chair, "I want to go home."

Does he mean the condo or Shasta House? "Home with me, dear?"

"No, home where Helga lives."

"Hmm. I see." Dr. Angus turns his full attention to Rudy. "Is Helga your new friend at Shasta House?"

"Yes, she speaks German to me. And I like her."

"And what about Jenny? Do you like Jenny, too?"

"Sure. She's my wife. She does things for me."

"So you like being married to Jenny?"

"Yes, she's a very good wife. I do like being her husband."

"Okay, Rudy. Try to keep that thought in your mind, because I know that Jenny loves you more than any other person in the whole world."

Jenny gulps.

The doctor stands, places his hand gently on her shoulder, "You're stronger than you realize, Jenny. Let me know in a couple of weeks if

Jockie Loomer-Kruger

there's no improvement."
   A new poison that she hopes will have the desired side effects.

Monday, January 4, mid-morning

Jenny pulls into the drugstore parking lot. "Rudy, I'll just be a few minutes. I brought your music along. You can listen while you wait for me."

She lifts off his blue-and-beige striped toque, fits the headphones over his ears, pulls the hat back on, and attaches the metal square to his jacket pocket. Then turns the sound on. In seconds his eyes glaze over, and he begins to hum along to a melody she can't identify from the sounds he's making.

"See you in a couple of minutes," she says, sliding out of the car. A few steps away, she remotely locks the car doors and strides briskly to the pharmacy entrance. The pharmacist fills her prescription promptly.

On the drive back to Shasta House, lost in his world of music and smiling dreamily, Rudy hums as he directs an imaginary orchestra. Even inside the home again, Jenny doesn't remove his headphones. So engrossed is he that, as they wait for an elevator, he fails to see Helga walking by on her way to the reception desk, probably, Jenny thinks, to pick up her mail.

Back in his room, his magic music dispenser now attached to his sweater, he sinks contentedly into his recliner.

Jenny takes the white paper bag containing his prescription from her coat pocket, tosses her coat on Rudy's bed, but doesn't remove her boots. She won't intrude on his communion with the classics. She'll just slip out and take the new pills to the nurses' station. He won't even know she's gone.

"Here's the new prescription, Anna. Let's hope it works."

"Oh, good. This should definitely help."

"The doctor said we should see significant improvement within a couple of weeks, or sooner—and not being on Triadone could ease matters somewhat sooner than that." Jenny says. "Already, off Triadone for two days, he seems less agitated." She pauses. "He's still fixated on Helga, but not quite so angry with me."

Anna wraps her fingers around the push bar on the portable medicine

185

cabinet. "Wish I could stay and talk, Jenny, but I have meds to give out on the fourth floor."

Expecting to find him still enjoying his symphony-concert-for-one, Jenny returns to her husband's room.

But he's gone.

Oh, shit. Here we go again. She feels helpless. Thwarted. Alone except for Anna, the only person at Shasta House who seems to understand. But even Anna is supposed to do Ellen's bidding. Now Jenny will have to find a PSW. Someone to drag Rudy back to his room.

She opens the door to start her search for help, all but bumping headlong into Ellen, emerging from the room next door.

"Why, hello Mrs. Hoffman. Happy New Year. I hope things are going better these days."

"No. No, they're not. I don't like this business with Rudy and Helga."

"But I told you, it's all very natural."

"Natural, be damned. Why doesn't anyone see that they're a danger to each other?"

"What do you mean?"

"They could hurt each other in one of their trysts. They could fall. Then what?"

Ellen's says curtly, "That's why residents wear pendants."

"But he doesn't understand how to use his. He's never used it. The only person who does is me, when I call someone to come change him. And Anna told us Helga refuses to wear hers at all. Why can't you people limit them to meeting in the lounge where someone will see them if something happens?"

"I told you before, staff are not policemen. At Shasta House residents have the right to make their own choices. We don't interfere."

"Bullshit!" Jenny is surprised at her outburst—at her dark-side vocabulary surfacing, "If you really let them make their own choices, half of them would be going out the front door and bumbling headlong into traffic."

"Well, they make their own choices within reason."

"Oh, fuck it! You haven't heard a word I've said."

"I certainly heard that! And that was very inappropriate. I'm going to have to ask you to stay away from Shasta House, Mrs. Hoffman, until you can calm down. It's obvious that you're overwrought and don't understand this very natural and normal behaviour by two residents suffering from dementia."

"Fuck you," Jenny hisses. She steps back into Rudy's room, slamming the door behind her.

She wants to scream. But she doesn't. Instead she pulls on her coat without bothering to button it, grabs her purse and marches to the elevators.

Anger holds tears at bay until after she has parked the car in its slot, ridden the condo elevator, and unlocked her door. Without removing her winter wear she stumbles to her bed, collapses onto it. Her body heaving, she howls into her pillow like a wounded animal caught in a leg-hold trap.

When her wracking tears subside, she wanders into the kitchen. Plugs in the tea kettle. She feels confused. Unsure. Maybe *she* is the problem. Maybe she does need to stay away.

The rest of the day she putters about the condo, sweeping, dusting, barely conscious of the blank places on walls, mantle, and furniture surfaces where pictures of her husband once eased the emptiness of living alone.

Her journal entry is brief: *I've been ordered to stay away from Shasta House. Should I comply? Can I comply? I'm so bloody confused.*

Jockie Loomer-Kruger

Tuesday-Thursday, January 5-7

The next morning she strongarms her urge to go to Shasta House. Several times she picks up the phone to find out if Rudy is all right, but each time she puts it down without making the call. Maybe it will be easier when she goes back. The effects of the Triadone should be gone. She wonders if the new hormone treatment will be making a difference by then.

She calls two friends to join her for lunch at a nearby Thai restaurant, but senses she's poor company. She does what she can to be part of the upbeat chatter. Did her friends realize she was putting on an act? Neither of them probed beyond what she presented.

The second day of keeping-her-distance, she reconnects with her Caregivers' Support Group for their first get-together in the New Year. Kate, a former nurse who herself had travelled the caregiver's route—first with her mother, then with her husband—invites attendees to share their holiday catch-up stories.

One member spent most of the Christmas season at the hospital, where her husband with Parkinson's disease remains a patient after a fall at home that fractured his hip. He's doing poorly. Another's mother was able to spend Christmas Day at her daughter's home, but the mother was convinced her daughter was a neighbour from years ago. The sole man in the group explains his wife is expected to start another round of chemo as soon as her platelet count can be built up. And on around the circle.

"Jenny," Kate says, "do you want to tell us about your time over Christmas?"

"Christmas and Boxing Day were wonderful, but since then it's been pure hell." She recounts the drama of the past several days, leaving out the part about trying to make love with Rudy. Sometimes, she pauses to wipe her eyes.

She expects no wise counsel from any of them. It's enough that she feels heard. That she senses empathy and compassion. That she knows she is not being judged for feeling rage, grief, confusion, jealousy, rejection, failure.

That night she climbs into bed, weary, but with slightly less weight on her shoulders.

And then it's Thursday. In the morning she turns on the TV three times but finds little other than scripted reality shows and news that depresses. Reading the paper offers no comfort. At last she goes to her studio, not to paint but to sit quietly, playing CDs. The same kind of music she downloaded into Rudy's iPod Shuffle. Her memories drift to symphony concerts they attended together and trips into Toronto for opera performances. She recalls their mutual enjoyment of live theatre.

"Oh, Rudy, how I miss who you used to be. How we used to be together," she laments to the silent walls.

I've got to get out of here.

She calls Ivy, her one remaining Lavender Lady friend. Would Ivy be okay to drop everything so they can hit the thrift stores together? Do some of their kind of special retail therapy?

'Thrifting' is what they used to call it. Something the Lavender Ladies plus Rudy occasionally did after lunch together at the Red Lobster. Jenny relished those light-hearted outings. Everyone coming back to the Hoffmans' for tea and to show off their prize finds.

Jenny tells herself she shouldn't still be collecting. But it *is* fun. And it feels like eons since she last did anything she could call fun, just for her own pleasure.

Ivy's game for a thrifting session, and they spend the afternoon browsing. Jenny doesn't mention Rudy. Ivy doesn't press.

Jenny brings home a hand-painted Noritake candy dish, with a picture of a house on a treed hillside beside a lake and symbolic white cranes lifting from the water. She knows she doesn't need the dish and she will never serve anything in it. Instead it will go on the plate rail in the dining room with other 1900s hand-painted dishes.

She didn't find any antique beaded purses today to add to that collection on another wall in the dining room. But she did find an artist-signed Brundage postcard, post-marked 1906. On the back, a happy birthday message to a long-ago child from an Auntie Bea. The image on the front shows a rosy-cheeked little girl in a fur-trimmed, deep-pink cape and matching leggings, with a blue-mitted hand outstretched to catch snowflakes. She'll poke that into a page of plastic sleeves in the black album she keeps in the bookshelf in the hall.

She's sorry she didn't find a little something for Rudy.

Jockie Loomer-Kruger

Alone at home in the evening, she can't shake him from her thoughts. Staying away is far too wrenching. She needs to see for herself if he's okay. If he's safe. She *is* his primary caregiver with a right—a duty—to be there as his advocate. After all, Rudy Hoffman *is* her husband. She'll go back tomorrow.

Then she searches out a book of poetry. Poets have a way of expressing the things she can't. In her recliner, with feet up and knees bent, she reads aloud wise and accessible words by Mary Oliver. She reads three poems and closes the book before her thoughts begin to drift.

Sometimes on winter nights like tonight, she and Rudy would sit on the rug in front of the flames dancing in the fireplace, each with a mug of hot chocolate. Take turns reading verse to each other until the fire fizzled and embers grew cold. Filling the evening with the exquisite language, captivating cadence, and penetrating insights of poetry.

Jenny goes to bed late, describes a fun-filled day in her journal, and compensates for the lost hours by sleeping in the next morning.

Friday, January 8

She's still in pyjamas and housecoat, coffee cup in hand, at the kitchen table when Rudy's caseworker phones. The person she's been aching to hear from.

"I apologize for taking such a long time to get back to you after I saw Rudy at the end of November," Ya Ping says. "I was off sick for a couple of weeks, and then the holidays. I just wanted to let you know that Rudy has been moved up on the waiting list for Parker Place. He's now number one."

"Really? Number one?"

"Parker Place is still your first choice for long term care?"

"Yes, yes it is." Jenny makes no attempt to hide her excitement at this news.

"Good, I just wanted you to know."

Finally, after all these months, a nursing home bed for her husband looks possible. *Number one!* She can scarcely believe it. She feels like dancing with the phone at her ear. "Do you have any idea when?"

"We never know. But likely before long. You understand that if a bed is offered, you have twenty-four hours to accept or reject? And then three working days to move in."

"I'll start his packing right away. And I'll try to be patient."

"Is he doing all right these days?" Ya Ping asks.

Knowing enough about the system, Jenny hedges on Rudy's current situation. If Ya Ping were to hear what's *really* going on, she might rank him as an emergency and he could be assigned the first nursing home bed that became available. Anywhere. In the city, or outside of it. "Oh, there's some decline, but he's doing okay, I guess. It's time, though. I'm so glad he's number one."

By the time the conversation ends, Jenny's coffee has grown cold. But it doesn't matter. She has a new stimulant now. Hope. And she hopes against hope that Parker Place will be his final home.

As she gets dressed for the day, her thoughts circle back to the encounter with Ellen. Jenny knows she was unnecessarily crude. Shame

Jockie Loomer-Kruger

flushes her cheeks. She'll apologize to Ellen first thing when she gets to Shasta House.

Friday, January 8, mid-morning

Not long after Ya Ping's call, Jenny hurries to the retirement home, ignoring the thin layer of new snow on the ground.

Nancy greets her with enthusiasm. "Hi Jenny. We haven't seen you for a few days. Have you been sick?"

Jenny stomps a bit of snow off her boots on the mat at the door. "No, just couldn't be here for a while." *No need to explain.* "Is Ellen in?"

"I think she's in her office."

Jenny knocks.

"Come in."

Ellen sits behind her desk licking the tips of her fingers. An empty pleated brown chocolate cup rests on the document in front of her—an open box of chocolates beside her phone. "Mrs. Hoffman! I'm surprised to see you so soon. I expected you'd take more time off than that. Get yourself fully calmed down. Pulled together."

"I'm okay, but I need to talk with you." Without being invited to, she sits. "First though, I want to apologize for my uncouth language the other day. It really wasn't called for. And I am sorry."

"You're right. It wasn't called for. It was totally inappropriate. I expected much better than that from you, Mrs. Hoffman. A woman your age."

Why the further upbraiding? "Yes, well, I truly am sorry."

Jenny pauses, crosses her ankles and knits her hands together in her lap. "I've been doing a lot of thinking of how we can change this situation. I just got word that Rudy's now number one on the list for Parker Place —but who knows how long it will take before there's an opening—so I wondered, could he get respite care for as long as it takes, at one of Bellis-White's other retirement homes? There are three of them in the city, aren't there?"

"Oh, I don't believe that's necessary, Mrs. Hoffman. Our staff here are on top of things."

"Not in my opinion, Ellen. I don't feel Rudy is truly safe here. I don't think staff recognize the risks to both him and Helga. And there's something else, I want to talk to you about. Does Helga's son know what's going on? Have you asked him whether Bruno—he's a big brute of a man—could be a danger to Rudy? I mean, if Helga's son hasn't been informed, isn't it time he knew what's going on?"

Jenny wonders why she hasn't seen Nick or Helga's daughter-in-law, whose name has slipped her mind, at Shasta House since the Christmas party. But then, most families don't visit as frequently as she does. And Nick and Marie—*Ah! That's her name.* Both work. *Busy lives, I guess.*

"We haven't felt any need to involve him."

"Why not? Why is it only Rudy—and me?"

"Well, ah, ah..." She reaches into the box of chocolates, pops one into her mouth, chews, swallows, then says, "Perhaps I'll give him a call. Oh, would you care for a candy?"

"No thanks." Jenny uncrosses her ankles and re-crosses them in the other direction, "So what about respite care elsewhere for Rudy?"

"I'll have to find out from administration."

"Thank you. And thanks for your time. I'm going to find Rudy now."

"You know, you're to stay away from Helga, Mrs. Hoffman. Remember that."

Jenny makes no response, simply rises from the chair and walks out of the office.

It surprises her to find her husband by the fireplace reading his newspaper. She kisses his cheek, "Hi, darling."

He lifts his head but doesn't smile, "Why are you here? You never come to see me. Helga says you're mean."

He closes the newspaper and folds it over, lays it in his lap. He looks stern. "You don't come because you're having an affair with Bruno, aren't you? Helga says you're having an affair with her boyfriend. She doesn't like you."

Jenny draws a deep breath, pulls the other wing chair over to face him. *The Bruno story again.* How can she counter the things Helga tells him?

"Rudy," she looks him in the eye, "do you like me?"

"I don't know." He shakes his head. "I feel confused. I don't know."

A suggestion jumps onto the end of her tongue like one of those fizzy popping candies her grandchildren once insisted she sample. "Maybe tomorrow you'd like to do something different. How about I come and get you and we go to my place? We can make a cake together."

His response is enthusiastic. "Can't we do it today?"

"I wish we could, but I have to get some boxes and start packing."

"Are you going somewhere, Jenny?" His eyebrows lift like the peak of a tent.

"No, love, but you are."

"Where?"

"To another home where you'll make new friends and have very kind people to look after you. I need to start packing things in your room. So you just stay here and read, and I'll see you in a little while."

He unfolds his paper and resumes reading. The same words, Jenny suspects, that he has already read but can't remember.

Bill, the ever-congenial longtime maintenance man at Shasta House, finds boxes for Jenny, telling her that her timing is excellent. He was just about to break the boxes down for recycling.

Jenny has Nancy add the visitor's noon meal charge to Rudy's monthly expenses and, as his visitor, joins the four residents at the table. A sandwich with deli ham, and a bowl of chicken noodle soup for her and others; but only the sandwich is offered to Rudy.

"Please," Jenny addresses the server, "could you get an egg sandwich or even peanut butter for Rudy? He's not supposed to eat deli meats."

He's lived here for three years. The kitchen staff should know he's not allowed deli meats. That was a dietary restriction she learned about the hard way, after he survived the 2008 Canada-wide deli-meat listeriosis outbreak. After he spent thirty-five days in hospital, hovering between life and death.

An infectious diseases specialist told her that people with artificial body parts should not eat deli meats, smoked salmon, unpasteurized cheese or sushi because of the risk of contamination by listeria bacteria. Rudy has artificial body parts—replaced heart valves. How often, she wonders, when she's not at Shasta House do they serve his no-no foods?

He's tired after lunch, and she helps him onto the bed for a nap. His snoring is quiet, and it makes her smile. Before she met Rudy, she used to joke with friends that she would only marry again if she could find a man who purred like a cat. *When Rudy snores that's exactly how it sounds.* When she told Rudy he'd laughed, 'I hope I'm a calico.'

For most of the afternoon she fills boxes with books, summer clothes, pictures off the wall. Even a few magazines. By three o'clock, when Lucija comes, Jenny has stacked half-a-dozen packed boxes in front of his empty bookshelf, close to his chair.

After Lucija leaves, Rudy asks a question that astounds her. "Jenny, do you still love me?"

"Of course I do, Rudy."

"I love you, too. But I think I make you feel bad."

"Sometimes you do. That's true."

"Because of Helga?"

"Yes, because of Helga."

"I know I love you, Jenny. But I have a crush on Helga. My crush won't go away. But I don't want to hurt *you*."

Is that the new drug talking? "So, what do you think you can do about it?"

"I want to write a letter to Helga. I can't read my handwriting anymore. Will you write what I say?"

Jenny searches for paper, and remembers the drawing pad she gave him. She finds it under his magazines on the window sill, fishes a pen from her purse.

He dictates:

> *Dear Helga,*
> *I am a married man. Jenny is my wife. I don't like it when Jenny feels upset, because I love my wife.*
> *But I have a crush on you.*
> *It makes Jenny sad when I go to your room and when you come to my room.*
> *I think we shouldn't do that anymore. I think we should just sit together in the lounge. I think we should just be friends.*
> *From Jenny's husband,*

He scratches his squiggly signature on the bottom and Jenny folds up his letter.

"We can give this to Nancy at the desk. She can put it in Helga's mail slot."

Pushing his walker, and with Jenny's hand over his, they deliver the letter to Nancy.

At home that evening. Jenny pulls out the drawer of the buffet. She removes their wedding picture, but leaves the others where they are. Hesitantly, hopefully, she places the silver-framed photo back on the mantelpiece.

In her journal she writes: *Rudy floored me. On his own he assessed his infatuation with Helga and came up with his own solution to simmer things down. I was stunned. I long ago stopped believing in miracles. But surely, this was one.*

Part Six

*Try to believe that things are neither so good nor so bad
as they seem to you now.*

— John Steinbeck, <u>East of Eden</u>

Jockie Loomer-Kruger

Saturday, January 9

Jenny arrives at Shasta House just as the residents are finishing their lunch. Before Rudy has a chance to go to Helga's room—or to nap. She pulls a chair up beside him and keeps him company as he drinks his tea.

After lunch, in his room, he sits on his walker and waits while she packs a couple of absorbent underpants from his closet into the fabric bag she's brought with her. And, just in case, a clean pair of trousers. She remembers to check his music square; it needs charging. She tucks it into her slacks pocket. Then she helps Rudy into his winter garments.

At the front desk, she signs him out, noting he's going to her place and expects to return before supper. At home, before they set about the afternoon's culinary adventure she bobs into her den and plugs in Rudy's device for recharging.

Then they walk arm in arm to the kitchen sink so they can both wash their hands. From a drawer she removes a folded pink checkered bib apron, shakes it out, lifts it over his head, and ties it in the back.

"You look pretty spiffy, Mr. Hoffman. Think you remember how to make a cake?"

"Sure, I've made cakes since my kidhood. My mother showed me how."

She hands him the portable electric mixer, measures out butter and sugar. He beats them until they're fluffy. "Want me to crack the eggs for you?"

"I can do it." With expertise long unused, he adds eggs to the mixture, and whirs the mixer again. He slowly adds the other ingredients Jenny has carefully measured. A cup and a half of flour into which salt and baking powder have been stirred, then milk, finishing with a bit more flour. Finally, he beats in a spoonful of vanilla.

"I'll put it in the pan, Rudy, and after it's in the oven, I'll help you clean all those spatters off your hand. You got sprayed when you were holding the bowl."

Rudy examines his speckled hand. "That looks delicious!" He licks the back of one finger. "Can I have the beaters?"

While he again washes his hands, Jenny readies a chair for him at the kitchen table. She knows, these days, people are advised not to consume uncooked dough or batter. But she'll take the risk, just to give him the pleasure of doing what he wants to do.

Childlike anticipation flashes across his face. With abandonment he darts his tongue around the bars of the beaters. He lifts his head and looks wistfully up at Jenny. "This is the best part."

It makes her heart swell to see him happy again, and it makes her grin to see the state of his whiskers.

"We'll need to wash your beard, sweetheart. It's full of cake batter."

"Enough for a snack later?"

She leads him by the hand to the bathroom. Gives him a soapy washcloth to clean his beard, then gets him into dry underwear.

"As soon as the cake comes out of the oven, I'll take you back to Shasta House."

"Can't I stay here? Live with you?"

"Oh, Rudy I wish you could. You have no idea how I wish you could. But I can't care adequately for you anymore. Come, have a seat in the recliner. A little rest while the cake's baking."

She pulls the lever on the side of the chair, fits a small cushion behind his head and takes the knitted afghan from the end of the couch to cover him. As the sweet aroma of his made-from-scratch cake fills the kitchen, Rudy sleeps. Jenny cleans up the cooking mess, including the spatters on the backsplash.

Not one mention of Helga. What a good afternoon this has been! Rudy's so much calmer than he was on Triadone.

With the cake cooling on a metal mesh rack on the kitchen counter, Jenny prepares to take him back to Shasta House. She drapes his jacket over the arm of the hall tree bench, checks to see that his boots are fully dry, then brings them to the living room. Gently she touches his shoulder.

"Rudy?"

He opens his eyes. "Helga?" But it's his wife looking down at him. "Where's Helga? I thought Helga was here. Where is she?"

"I think you were dreaming. You're at our place. At the condo. Helga doesn't come here. You just made a cake."

"Oh, yes. Now I remember. I made a cake. Will you decorate it Jenny, with your good frosting?"

"Yes, my love. And I'll bring the cake to your table tomorrow for lunch."

"And give some to Helga?"

"We'll see. She has diabetes, you know. She likely isn't supposed to eat cake."

"I forgot."

"I'm going to help you with your boots now." She flips the chair lever to right him, and kneels to pull his boots on.

She raises herself by holding onto the arms of the recliner. The effort momentarily winds her. Getting down is easy, but it's becoming increasingly difficult to get up. She teases herself, *Is it possible that I'm growing old?*

"Okay, my fella, let's get you out of this chair." She tucks her arm into his right armpit and assists him to a standing position. Then she links arms with him as he shuffles to the foyer where she fits him with his scarf, jacket, toque and gloves, and pulls his waiting walker into reach.

"There. You're ready. I'm going to dash and get your magic music machine, then I'll get ready for outdoors, and off we'll go."

At Shasta House, she repeats the underarm lift maneuver to help him from the car. As they come in under the canopy, they step aside to let Bruno pass on his way from visiting with Helga. Mouth firm, the huge man glares at Rudy, but doesn't speak.

Rudy appears not to recognize Helga's boyfriend. *A good time for Rudy to have been away.*

That night she draws smiley faces around her journal paragraphs.

Jockie Loomer-Kruger

Sunday, January 10

Jenny brings the decorated cake to Shasta House and places it in the centre of Rudy's table at lunch time.

"So pretty," Florence says. "I want a taste of that frosting right now." She reaches toward the pink rosettes and green leaves on one corner as though she's about to stick her finger into the icing, then slaps her own wrist, and laughs. Jenny grins.

Jenny has brought her iPad and, before the cake is cut, takes a picture of the four tablemates gathered around Rudy's special dessert. The tablet-size photo is easy for all of them to see. Smiles curve as they look at themselves on her device.

She cuts the cake and portions some to each. To her surprise, Rudy, who scarcely touched his ravioli first course, declines the treat he made himself.

"What's wrong, Rudy?"

"I don't know. I'm not hungry." He swings his left hand across his chest to touch his right shoulder. "My arm hurts. And my shoulder. They really hurt."

Back in his room, Jenny slides his cardigan off.

"Ouch! That hurts."

She unbuttons his dark striped dress shirt and gingerly pulls the sleeve down. "Oh, my god! No wonder your shoulder hurts. You have a terrible bruise there."

She raises his arm slightly. He winces. "And you're black and blue in the armpit and down the inside of your arm."

She's dealt with his unexpected bruising from too much warfarin before. Once on his thigh. Another time around his navel. For certain, his Coumadin levels are too high again. She's glad the blood thinner clinic is tomorrow. She'll get him there first thing in the morning.

"My shoulder and my arm hurt, Jenny. Why do they hurt so much?"

"They're badly bruised, dear." Did the repetitive motion of the mixer strain his shoulder? She's sure lifting him under the armpit did the rest.

"What's wrong with them?"

The tablet. She can take pictures and show him why he hurts. She snaps several images, lets him see his discoloured flesh, then drapes his shirt and sweater over his shoulder. Cautiously, she helps him into his chair. But this time she offers no under-the-armpit assistance.

"I'll go to the nurses' station and get you something for the pain."

It's the weekend nurse on duty. "I need some Tylenol for Rudy, please."

"Does he have a headache?"

"No, he's having arm and shoulder pain."

"Which arm?"

"His right."

"If it was his left I'd have to come check his vitals. And I'm really busy right now."

Whichever PSW gets him ready for bed is bound to report the excessive bruising, so the nurse will understand why his arm hurts. They know he's on Coumadin. They'll understand what's happening.

Back in Rudy's room, Jenny gives him the painkiller. "Would you like to nap here in your chair rather than on the bed?"

"Yes, please. Oh, Jenny, my arm hurts. It really hurts."

She presses the button on his chair and it unfolds like the opening of a book, his feet mechanically lifted well off the floor. She covers him with the blanket from the end of his bed. In a matter of minutes he's asleep, and Jenny busies herself filling the remaining boxes Bill found for her and left out of the way at the far side of the bed.

At suppertime, she walks slowly with Rudy to his table. He picks clumsily at his food with his left hand, his sore arm hanging over the edge of his chair. She sits beside him until he's finished, and accompanies him back to his room.

"I want to go to bed, Jenny."

Without calling for staff assistance she changes him. Helps him into clean pyjamas, tucks him into bed and kisses him goodnight.

Because a PSW didn't get him ready for bed, Jenny wonders if she should ask the night nurse to have a look at his bruising. *No, the night nurse would have heard during shift change that there was a problem.* Jenny's sure they'll check on him.

She dons her coat and boots and slips out the door. *Poor Rudy.* It upsets her to know he's in pain. The only good thing is that there will be no trip to Helga's room tonight.

Jockie Loomer-Kruger

Monday, January 11

The blood thinner clinic opens at eight-thirty Monday morning. Jenny and Rudy are among the first patients there. She opens her tablet to show the pharmacist the extent of Rudy's bruising and explains what she thinks caused it. The clinic nurse pricks Rudy's finger, checks the monitor, and reports the results to the pharmacist.

"His reading is pretty high. That much bruising is not surprising considering the numbers," the pharmacist tells Jenny. "We'll cut him back—no Coumadin tonight, and only half a pill tomorrow. Another half on Wednesday, and we'll check it again on Thursday. In the meantime, I'll let Dr. Angus know what's going on."

He writes out the dosage changes and hands the altered prescription to Jenny to take back to the nurses' station at Shasta House.

Rudy spends a quiet day favouring his sore arm while Jenny packs more of his belongings.

"Am I moving?"

She repeats the information that any day a call could come from the new place. She has to have him ready to vacate this room on very short notice.

"Is Helga going there too?"

"No, she's staying here."

"But why can't she come too? She's my friend. She speaks German to me."

"Someday, maybe she'll move. But not right now."

He seems satisfied with Jenny's response.

She needs more boxes and goes to find Bill in his basement workshop. She pushes the button to call an elevator, but almost immediately a door opens and Ellen steps into the sixth floor lobby.

"I was just coming to see you, Mrs. Hoffman. Do you have a minute?"

Jenny watches as the elevator she was about to take closes and creakily descends without her. "All right."

Ellen lifts her clipboard, rolls a page over the top and catches it underneath. "I spoke with management about respite care for Rudy. They tell me it's far too complicated. So much paperwork. It would take almost two weeks to set up the accounting for such a move. Of course, you'd have to pay for both places to retain his space here."

Jenny's amazed at what sounds like fabricated difficulties. "Thanks for looking into it anyway."

"I'm sure he'll be just fine here until he moves," Ellen adds before swaying off down the hall.

Ellen really doesn't get it, Jenny thinks as she summons an elevator a second time. *If they can't keep him safe at Shasta House, I may have to take him home.* Have him spend his days with her until she hears from the nursing home.

She knows she's asking almost the impossible of herself. But she'll find a way to do it if she has to. Determination doubles up her fists and sets her jaw.

It's suppertime when, totally exhausted, Jenny returns to her condo.

Jockie Loomer-Kruger

Tuesday, January 12

After lunch at home, Jenny arrives at Shasta House. As she walks around the corner past the reception area, she spies Anna pushing her medications cart into an elevator. The charge nurse holds the elevator for Jenny to join her. Arthur, of the waste can incident, is the only other person aboard.

"As soon as you can, meet me in the nurses' station, Jenny. I need to talk to you. It's important."

"Give me time to check on Rudy."

Her husband's arm is still tender. And he's tired. She doesn't add to his discomfort by having him remove his shirt to let her see his bruising. And she's particularly careful helping him get settled on his bed. Despite the hurting, he succumbs quickly to sleep.

Jenny wishes she could lie down beside him, not only to feel their physical closeness but to assuage her own fatigue. Instead, she slips out of the room to the second floor.

"What's up, Anna?"

"Come, sit down."

Question marks crinkle Jenny's forehead.

"Look, I know I shouldn't be telling you this, but Ellen suspects you're abusing Rudy."

Jenny gasps, "What are you talking about?"

"One of the PSWs told her she could see finger marks on Rudy's right arm when she got him dressed this morning. And there are bruises on his chest that look like he was struck with something."

Jenny hasn't examined his bruising yet today. Perhaps it's spread. Maybe withholding of the warfarin—Coumadin—*the pharmaceuticals don't want it called 'rat poison'*—hasn't worked yet.

"Ellen said she'll be reporting suspected abuse to the Ministry. It's messy, Jenny. Very messy."

Jenny feels the blood draining from her face. Her hands shake.

"Jenny, you look like you've seen a ghost. Listen to me. I know you haven't hurt him."

"Jesus, Anna, this is terrible. I don't know what to do."

"Leave it with me. I should be able to convince her that this is a blood thinner problem. I have his change of dosage orders. Even if I have to call your doctor for confirmation." She pauses. "Look, I know there have been conflicts between you and Ellen—"

"Yes, but surely she's not vindictive."

"I don't know. I'll talk to her."

Jenny hurries back to Rudy's room, her thoughts tangled like a roll of barbed wire. Anna said bruises on his chest? There were no bruises on his chest yesterday.

She makes enough noise entering his room to disturb his sleep.

"Rudy," she stands beside his guard rail, "I need to see your arm and your shoulder."

He pulls himself up with his good arm and sits on the edge of the bed.

Gently she exposes the bruising. His arm and shoulder look much the same, perhaps less purple and a tinge greenish, but there are three distinct, deep-blue bruises on his chest, each the size of a mason jar lid. *Where the devil did those come from?*

"Rudy," she asks, "did somebody hurt you? Did somebody hit you?"

"I don't know. I don't remember."

"I want Dr. Angus to see you."

She calls his office. "No, this is not a 911 emergency, but it is very urgent. Rudy needs to see Dr. Angus as quickly as possible."

"Well," the receptionist says after a long pause, "if you and Rudy can be here in an hour, I think we can fit you in."

One of the things Jenny likes about being connected to the Family Health Centre is that they always hold a few time slots for the unexpected. She races home to get her tablet and the car. They reach the doctor's office exactly on the appointed hour.

Her iPad under one arm, she steers Rudy to the examination room. Before he looks at Rudy, she shows Dr. Angus the pictures she took.

He studies the images, then peers at the bruised shoulder and arm. "Your photos are very consistent with the report from the Coumadin clinic. But these on his chest look different. Quite fresh. What do you know about them, Jenny?"

"Nothing. I didn't even know they were there until the charge nurse told me I'm suspected of causing all of it."

"In what way?"

"They think I hit him. Squeezed his arm, maybe. Pounded him on the chest. I know I didn't help the situation with his shoulder by lifting under his armpit, but these marks on his chest—I don't know what caused them."

The doctor touches the new bruises. Rudy shudders. "They're obviously tender, but I don't feel anything broken. And there's no swelling. I don't think he was struck with much force. If, indeed, that's what happened. When Coumadin levels are too high, bruising happens very easily. Sometimes quite spontaneously. And I know you didn't do this."

"I can curse like a sailor sometimes," she says, "but I don't hit."

"Take him back to Shasta House, and make sure he does limited activity. He's going to be amazingly colourful for the next little while."

Back at the home, after Dolly changes him, Rudy wants to lie down. Jenny lifts his legs onto the bed. Helps him lower his upper body onto the mattress. She drops a finger kiss onto the end of his nose.

"Thank you," he whispers. Then closes his eyes.

Tuesday, January 12, mid-afternoon

Exhausted beyond weariness and wishing more than anything that she could take the time to cuddle in beside her husband, Jenny rests for a few moments on the side of his bed at the end of his guard rail. She lets her gaze wander to the stack of packed boxes in front of his empty bookcase.

Something looks odd. *What in the world is that?* On the floor, between the boxes and his recliner, lies a smooth, fist-sized, oval beach stone.

Where had she recently seen stones like that? *Somewhere? Of course! Helga has a rock collection on her windowsill.*

Jenny notes something under the stone. She steps over to the boxes and picks up the rock. Below it, torn in two and crumpled, is the letter Rudy dictated to the woman on whom he has a crush. She shoves stone and paper into her slacks pocket.

With Rudy already softly snoring, she hustles out the door. She strides purposefully off the elevator on the first floor, and heads for the Director of Wellness's office.

Ellen is there, munching on a candy bar. Jenny doesn't wait for niceties or for Ellen to tuck the wrapper over what remains of her treat.

"We've got a problem, Ellen." Jenny's voice is flat but firm.

"It seems so."

"Rudy has been injured."

"Yes. I'm aware of that, Mrs. Hoffman. Do you want to tell me how it happened?"

Cripes. She thinks I'm here to confess. "I didn't hurt my husband. Well, yes, in a way I did. I'm sure his initial injury came from using the portable mixer at my place when he made a cake. Then I helped him up from a chair, and again out of the car. But I'm not responsible for the bruises on his chest."

Ellen leans forward, presses her finger tips together on her desk like the prow of a boat. "You can tell me about it. About all of it. I know you've been upset and angry. It happens sometimes that family members lose control and lash out physically."

"Yes, I have been upset. I have been angry. But I didn't hurt him. Those bruises on his chest, they weren't there when I took him to the blood thinner clinic yesterday. The first time I saw them was this morning. About an hour ago."

"Bruises don't always develop immediately."

"You don't believe me, do you? Hold on. I'll be right back."

Jenny darts out the door, with Ellen's shouted words flying out behind her like a cape clipped around her neck. "You know, I'll have to report this to the Ministry."

Jenny ignores the icy wind as she opens the car's back door and scoops her tablet off the seat. She strides purposefully back inside. Directly to Ellen's office.

"Here's part of what you need to see." Jenny turns on her device. She touches the photos icon and immediately finds the pictures she took of Rudy's shoulder and arm. "This is what was there Sunday afternoon, and this is from yesterday morning when I took him to the blood thinner clinic."

From her slacks pocket she withdraws the smooth grey beach stone and the torn letter. "And this is what I found in Rudy's room just a few minutes ago. This stone is from Helga's room. The letter is what Rudy had me write to her."

Ellen doesn't speak. She smooths the paper and fits the two halves of the letter together. Reads the message. Picks up the stone and puts it down again on her desk. "Mrs. Hoffman, I'll have to investigate what you're saying. Check the video monitor footage. Staff can tell me whether Helga has a collection of stones. Is there any proof that Helga ever received this letter?"

"Ask Nancy. Rudy gave it to her to put in Helga's mailbox. She'll know whether Helga got it."

"I'll get back to you with my findings. You understand, I'm sure, that we're dealing with a very serious matter."

"Oh, yes, I understand." Jenny's jaw is set. "It's a very serious matter."

White knuckles gripping her tablet, she turns toward the door. Lifts her head high and exits Ellen's office.

Back in his room, she finds Rudy still asleep. She drops a kiss from her index finger onto the top of his head, as softly as the landing of an apple blossom petal.

Then she drives herself home.

She's in the condo less than twenty minutes when Ellen phones. "Mrs. Hoffman, I'm still checking out the things you've alleged, but in the meantime, I've set up a meeting with Helga's son for ten o'clock tomorrow morning. Can you make it?"

"I'll be there."

Wednesday, January 13

Nick, Helga's son, is already in Ellen's office when Jenny arrives. His full cheeks look ruddier than they did at the Christmas party and his fair hair has been recently cut. His black leather jacket is unzipped, and he runs his fingers back and forth inside his open shirt collar. It's apparent he's already been talking with Ellen.

"Is there anything else we should know about your mother?" Ellen says.

Nick clears his throat before he speaks and rubs his hands together as if they're chilled. "Yes. My mother has a very short temper. She can easily get physical." He looks down at the floor. "She punished me a lot as a kid. Sometimes she beat me with an old leather belt of my father's, so hard I had red welts for days." He draws in a breath, "And not just physical with me…"

The ruddiness of his cheeks spreads around his eyes, up into his forehead. Jenny senses he's embarrassed by what he's about to reveal. "She would get mad at her boyfriends. She had lots of them. I heard her yell at them. Saw her hit them. Sometimes they hit her back. She doesn't hit Bruno, though. I think he's too gigantic. Maybe she's a bit afraid of him. Of his size."

Feisty? Crap. The woman is dangerous. Jenny listens without comment. Although anger burns like red hot coals inside her chest, she senses this meeting is also exceptionally hard for Nick. Every bit as hard as it is for her, as Rudy's wife.

"When she began showing signs of dementia, she started hitting me again whenever I said or did something that didn't please her. When we took her home for Christmas she attacked me with a belt my wife had given me. I was able to get it away from her easily. She's not as strong as she used to be."

He runs his fingers along the inside of his collar, then swallows. He zips up his jacket. "I should have told you. I'm sorry. I'm really sorry I wasn't fully upfront with you."

In so many ways, to so many people, dementia is viciously cruel. Jenny feels a deep sadness for this hurting man.

She stands, extends her hand. "Thank you for telling us this, Nick. It couldn't have been easy for you to do that, but it helps me understand."

He lets go of Jenny's hand, shakes Ellen's, and leaves. Jenny turns toward the door.

"Wait. Don't go yet, Mrs. Hoffman, please." Ellen points at the chair Jenny just vacated. "Have a seat."

Jenny sits.

"I saw the monitor footage. Monday night Helga came off an elevator onto the sixth floor with a piece of paper in her hand. She headed toward Rudy's room. She appeared to have something else in her other hand. Dolly checked her room. There *is* a rock collection on the window sill. And Nancy told me she gave Helga the letter Rudy wrote."

Her face blank, Jenny sits in silence, waiting for what Ellen will say next.

"I'm not going to contact the Ministry."

There's a pause, a deep silence. Then, very softly, "I'm sorry, Mrs. Hoffman—Jenny."

Wordlessly, Jenny gets up and walks out of Ellen's office.

Jockie Loomer-Kruger

Wednesday, January 13, late morning

Jenny spends the remainder of the morning with Rudy, reading poems to him from a book she found in the home's sparsely stocked library. *A Child's Garden of Verses.* He seems content sitting in his chair, listening to poems for children by Robert Louis Stevenson.

At noon she returns to her condo, relieved, but exhausted. She'll nap before she goes to see him at suppertime.

In the back of the freezer drawer, she finds a chicken pot pie. Her poor eating habits sometimes mean foodstuffs hang around too long, so she checks the due date. This choice is safe. She heats it in the toaster oven.

When the timer dings she takes it out, flips it upside down on a plate, pours a glass of milk and sits at the kitchen table. She picks mindlessly at her meal. Eats half of it. Puts the remainder in a bowl and sits a saucer over the top—something she and Rudy began doing years before to cut down on their use of plastic wrap. She pokes her leftovers into the fridge. For tomorrow.

Suddenly she remembers that her sister's birthday is coming up at the beginning of the next week. She rummages through a disorganized drawer in her desk where she keeps a supply of cards. Mostly sympathy cards these days

She finds a birthday card with daffodils on it and a stock message. She scribbles, 'Have a wonderful birthday, Sis, Love Jenny'. Addresses the envelope and attaches a stamp from the hundred-pack roll she'd bought before Christmas, when it had been her intention to send out her usual assortment of holiday greeting cards.

Then she plumps a couple of cushions for her head and stretches out on the couch, pulling the afghan her sister made over herself. Like a ship bumping against rubber tires on the side of a concrete pier, she edges toward sleep.

Ya Ping's phone call jars her awake.

"I have news for you. There's a bed available at Parker Place and they'd like to offer it to Rudy...Jenny? Jenny? Are you all right?"

Only gut-wrenching sobs respond.

"Oh, Jenny, I had no idea it was that bad."

"Far worse than I dared to tell you. Far worse," Jenny sniffs. "Please, tell them 'Yes'. We'll take the bed."

"Because this is Wednesday and you have three working days beyond the twenty-four hours for acceptance, you won't have to be there until next Monday," Ya Ping says. She gives contact details for Parker Place and hangs up.

Jenny honks her nose. She sits at the kitchen table to call the nursing home and learn what preparations she needs to make.

The admitting nurse is pleasant but businesslike. It's clear she's had this conversation many times before. She moves straight to the essential information.

The single bedroom is small. Bring the minimal. Jenny can decorate any way she wishes to make it feel like home for her husband. No, there won't be room for his electric lift chair. The facility provides an armchair with a washable vinyl covering that residents find quite comfortable. No room for his bookcase, but there is a ledge along the outer wall that he can keep a few books and other things on, and the drawers for his clothes are built in, so no need for a dresser.

Bring only a few changes of clothes. Tee shirts and lounge pants are the easiest things for residents to wear. And several pairs of pyjamas. Protective underwear is provided, so she won't have to buy them anymore. No, they're not the brief style like she's been purchasing. The ones they use are more like adult diapers with sticky closing tabs. Yes, he could wear cotton briefs over them. In fact, a good idea, as it would likely make him feel more comfortable.

Jenny eats an egg sandwich for supper, then walks briskly under the streetlights to see Rudy before he goes to bed. He's reading in his recliner when she arrives.

Surprised to see her, he says, "Are you here to stay all night?"

"Only to kiss you goodnight. I came to give you some good news. You'll be moving in just a few days."

She knows he won't remember. She'll need to tell him the same news every day until his relocation happens. But she needed to share her own excitement with the man whose life will be deeply affected by this change.

She stays until after the PSW who gets him ready for bed moves on to help other residents. Then she leans over the rail on his bed and kisses him full on the mouth. His hands rise to cover her breasts. She makes no move to disengage from his touch.

"Goodnight, Rudy. Sleep well. *Ich liebe dich.*"

"You said it perfectly this time," he smiles. "Good night, *mein dollink.*"

At home again, before she settles into her own bed, she rehangs and replaces all the photos of Rudy. For the first time in what feels like forever, she's warmed by the memories the images evoke. When she finishes her journal commentary about her happy day, she fills the margins with Xs and Os.

After a day stoked with emotion she crawls wearily, but relieved, into bed. She pulls her goose down duvet over her, and searches out deeper physical and emotional comfort with her own hands. As her body reaches climax, she remembers lovemaking with Rudy—spontaneous, tender, mutually gratifying. *As close to something sacred as either of us skeptics could acknowledge.*

Sleep envelops her like floating away on a cloud, with her last thought being what she's understood for many, many years. *We are sexual beings until the day we die.*

Part Seven

*...they had gone through pain and had
come out on the other side.*

— John Steinbeck, <u>The Pearl</u>

Jockie Loomer-Kruger

Until the Day We Die

Thursday, January 14 through Friday, May 20

On Thursday, Jenny takes Rudy to the blood thinner clinic. His readings are better. It's the last time the clinic will see him. A new doctor and new method of assessment will be part of his care as a resident in a nursing home.

For the remaining four Shasta House days, Jenny brings her husband to the condo. Difficult, disheartening, and draining as it is to keep him with her all day, she's comforted knowing he's safe there. And that he's happy to be home with her, napping, listening to his music, and occasionally reading.

Helga, out of sight, is mostly also out of mind. After supper Jenny drives him back to Shasta House, trusting that a now fully-alerted staff will prevent the two German-speakers from visiting each other.

Dave comes on Monday to help with the move. By evening Rudy is tucked into his new bed, in his new room at Parker Place Long Term Care Facility.

Throughout the first week Rudy complains that he doesn't like anything there. He likes his old place better. He misses Helga. Could Jenny bring her for a visit? Jenny fabricates car trouble.

At night, Jenny begins to wean herself off the sleeping pills.

The second week, he tells Jenny he had a friend at the old place. A woman who spoke German to him. He can't remember her name. Does Jenny know her name?

"No." *Let the memories fade.* "I have no idea who you're talking about."

At night she sleeps fitfully, but without assistance.

In the third week, sitting in his chair by the window, Rudy studies the painting of a grain elevator hanging above the head of his bed, "That's out West, isn't it?"

Jenny nods. "Yes, on the prairies. Do you like that picture?"

"Yes. And I like this room. It's a very nice room to be staying in until I can go home. When can I go home, Jenny?"

She sucks in a deep breath. "Not for a while. You still need people to help you."

"But when?"

She thinks quickly. "You need to stay here until you can manage without your walker. The doctor will tell you when he thinks your legs are strong enough."

Rudy doesn't respond. Activity in the tree top that's level with his second story window, draws his attention. "Look, Jenny, there's a squirrel just outside my window. He's fat."

At night, Jenny sleeps deeper and feels refreshed in the mornings.

Just as she did at Shasta House, she comes daily to Parker Place. Some afternoons she naps with him on the narrow bed, snuggled against his back, her arm around his middle. Rudy never mentions sex. His new doctor takes Rudy off the hormone treatment.

Sometimes Rudy confuses Jenny with Addie. He's happy to see his first wife. Jenny plays the role.

At the end of April Jenny brings Rudy a potted pink azalea, some coloured markers and an unpainted wooden plaque with an attached chain for hanging—gifts for their thirty-first anniversary.

"The flowers are my anniversary gift to you. I know you would want to give me an anniversary gift too," she says. "So I thought while I'm over at the mall doing a few errands you can make something for me with the markers and this blank sign."

When she gets back, the oval is turned upside down on Rudy's lap. "Here's your anniversary present, *mein dollink*, but I need a little help."

He flips the gift over.

She sees a sprinkling of red hearts and across the top barely legible green letters, 'Happy Anniversary, Jenny'. In the centre is the word 'to'. Below that he has scribbled his name in purple.

"I want to put the year we were married on it but I can't remember it."

"1985."

He removes the cover from the blue marker and writes the numbers on the left side of the 'to'. Recaps that marker and uncaps the orange one. On the left side, he doesn't add a date as she expects him to do, but instead configures three question marks.

Then he passes the finished gift to his wife. Jenny blinks away the wetness in her eyes.

The days pass. Jenny observes that, along with his memory, Rudy's legs are also weakening. He can no longer safely maneuver his walker. She rents a wheelchair for staff and herself to push him in.

One day, when she hears his common refrain of 'I can't remember,' she asks him, "Rudy, does it bother you that you have trouble remembering things?"

He laughs as though she's asked a ridiculous question. "Not a bit. I don't know what I can't remember. I just like things when they happen."

A burden she's carried since his initial diagnosis lifts. Vaporizes. Vanishes. If it doesn't bother him, it needn't bother her. They will both enjoy what happens in the moment for as long as they have left.

They will play together.

A few days later, when she's looking for a colouring book for Rudy at the Dollar or More store, Jenny spies something else. A calico cat. A mischievous looking, upright, battery-operated cat with shiny black plastic shoes. When she squeezes its front paw, the cat twists, turns, and jiggles to a loud, twangy, garbled song. The only words she can pick out are 'love you all my life.'

Without a second thought she buys it for him. How could she not? It's the calico cat he's always longed for.

He lifts the gift from the fancy bag she'd put it in. Jenny suggests he place it on the low shelf beside his closet as she readies her cell phone for video.

"Press his paw," she says.

The cat gyrates and the song throbs into the room. Rudy leans back, his gaze fixed on the furry entertainer. Then, to Jenny's surprise he doubles his hands into fists, bends his elbows, rotates his shoulders and joins the dance from his wheelchair.

Jenny films. A keepsake of joy for sad times to come.

Days pass. She watches the gentle man she married regress deeper into a gentle boy. A youngster with a full white beard who likes to draw, sing old familiar songs, dance with his calico cat, and hear her read from the green binder of his childhood stories. Or from the *The Wizard of Oz*. She makes no attempt to alter his identification of the illustrated Oz characters. 'Alice. A knight. A clown. The Cowardly Lion.'

But it is his personalized music flowing through his headphones that is his constant source of contentment. Jenny is grateful for a staff that recognizes how important the music is to his well-being, and who often set him up with it, and make sure the device stays charged.

Her family continues supportive. Her daughter Pam phones weekly from Nova Scotia. On a particular Saturday Dave, Allison and the grandchildren make another of many visits. They wheel Opa Hoffie outside to watch brown bunnies hop in and out of the hedge by the front entrance.

While they pursue the delightful wildlife with Rudy, Jenny hikes next door to the mall. A chance to buy fresh flowers for Rudy's room.

Jockie Loomer-Kruger

In the flower shop she spies something unusual for herself. Beside the cash register hangs an angel pendant on a silver chain. It has a large, featureless bead head with embedded bling, pewter wings, a grey, fabric-covered bosom, and skinny, dangly metal arms. Its skirt shimmies with what looks like tiny silver shingles, and its dangly legs are encased in sparkly knee-high boots.

She buys the angel—a gift of creative whimsy for herself. On each daily visit to Rudy, she wears the funky angel necklace.

Saturday, May 21 through Saturday, July 2

Throughout the latter part of May, friends who'd stopped visiting Rudy at Shasta House come by Parker Place to say a hesitant hello; an early goodbye. Rudy thanks them for coming, but not by name.

At the beginning of June, he begins to suffer daily episodes of unstable angina. Narcotics fail to eliminate the pain. He describes a pressure, a weight on his chest that also makes his left arm ache. When his doctor asks Rudy to calibrate the pain level—one being very little, and ten the worst pain he's had in his life—Rudy can't comply. Numbers cause confusion.

Jenny suggests something else. "Rudy, let's pretend there's an animal on your chest. What's lying there right now? A cat? A dog? A goat? A big fat pig?"

He grins through his discomfort. "It's a cat. A calico."

Some days a kitten rests upon his chest, or a cocker spaniel, or even a heavy German shepherd. The doctor notes the increasing pain levels while Jenny knows the day is coming when a butterfly will alight, pause, and fly away.

Close to the end of the month, Rudy no longer wants to be dressed. He asks to stay in bed. He declines food. "I'm on my way out, Jenny."

A far-away look glazes his eyes. "I wonder what it's like to die."

His energies fade, but the enjoyment of his music remains. Often he falls asleep to the sounds he loves weaving through his headphones.

On the thirtieth he's more lucid than Jenny has heard him in a very long time. He asks about funeral and burial plans. Will she bury his ashes in Saskatoon, in the same grave where his brother Gerhard has lain for almost eighty years? Where her ashes can be placed later?

Over and over he tells Jenny he loves her. Thanks her for loving him. Scarcely audible, he sings along with her. 'Oh, give me a home, where the buffalo roam...' And tells her those words are about Saskatchewan.

"I like that song," he whispers.

As she sits on the side of his bed, holding his parchment hands, he pulls one hand free and reaches for the long-legged angel pendant she's wearing yet again. He holds the articulated figure away from her chest. "I haven't seen this before. Is it new?"

An idea sparks. She smiles. "Yes, it's brand new. It's a gift From my husband."

He lets go of the pendant as if raising his arms required more effort and energy than he could maintain. His thin, bleached hands fall onto the sky blue blanket. A shadow of sadness dims his milky blue eyes, accents his sallow sunken cheeks. "I don't think I've bought you anything for a long time."

"But if you could have, you'd have chosen this for me, wouldn't you?"

"Oh, yes."

"Then it's from you, to me."

She lifts the necklace over her head, and gently rotates his hand. The jewellery trickles onto his palm.

Instinctively, he cups the other hand above the tangle of pendant and chain and arches the hidden gift toward her. He pauses to catch his breath.

"I have a present for you."

Slowly, with straining effort, he reveals the necklace.

"Rudy, it's beautiful! You always choose the best gifts. Thank you."

His grin is feeble but, for an instant, his eyes twinkle. "I'm glad you like it."

"I love it—and I love you." She kisses him on the forehead, then slips the playful angel back on.

He exerts one more extreme effort and plants both hands over her pink flowered blouse. "I've always loved your breasts, you know," he whispers.

His hands slide off onto the blanket.

"I know." *Sexual beings...*

He draws a laborious breath, and closes his eyes.

Two days later, Jenny sits in his vinyl-covered chair pulled close to his bed. She cradles his motionless hand in both of hers. Listens to his shallow, staccato breathing.

Then, just as she knew it would, a butterfly lands on his chest and, unseen, silently flies away.

Epilogue

Jockie Loomer-Kruger

Tuesday, January 1, 2019

With fireworks popping in the city night, Jenny turns off the television. Unable to sleep, she'd watched the ball drop in Times Square.

She tightens the belt on her old pink terry cloth robe, and slipper-scuffs to the bedroom. She snaps on the light, picks up a pen and her journal from her bedside table and returns to her welcoming recliner.

Her hand is steady as she writes: *Another New Year. I can't believe Rudy's been gone for two-and-a-half years. I miss him so. He'd be eighty-five now. Eighty-six next August. Is it really possible I'll be eighty in September? My hourglass is emptying. And there's something I need to do.*

The entry finished, she returns to the bedroom and pokes her current journal into the drawer by the bed, but slips the pen into her housecoat pocket. For a moment she stands motionless beside her bed, aware she's still very wide awake. She senses a restlessness, an urge. A compulsion.

She shakes her head and a stubborn silver strand of hair tumbles forward. With the back of a veined hand she pushes it off her forehead. Then she steps over to the bookcase beside the dresser. The place where she keeps her filled journals. She searches out four of them, starting in late November, 2015, and ending in mid-July, 2016.

She carries the journals to the living room and piles them on the stand beside her chair. Then she bobs into the den. In the dim light from the hall, she picks up a blank notebook from her supply beside the computer.

Back in the living room, she settles into her favourite sitting place. She riffles through her journals in chronological order. Some pages are slightly stuck together and discoloured by tears. Her stomach knots when she sees the page with nothing but a giant X, another torn through by a savage zigzag.

Perusing finished, she sets the books aside on the stand.

After opening her fresh notebook, she pauses, pen poised. *It's now. Or never.*

In the darkness of early morning, her hand cramps and she surrenders her pen. Closes her notebook, many pages now solid with longhand. The first words:

227

Jockie Loomer-Kruger

Until the Day We Die

First Draft

Part One

This is a work of fiction. It draws on stories lived, told, heard, and imagined...

The end

Until the Day We Die

Jockie Loomer-Kruger

Acknowledgements

Writing may be a solitary pursuit, but reaching publication draws on the skills and knowledge of many others.

Catherine Muss, my initial editor, who became a dear and special friend, believed in this story from the beginning, and with a chuckle, put up with many last minute revisions each time I sent her a new draft.

Others read, critiqued, and encouraged: Jane Bell, Debby Spitzig, Geoff Marriott, Helen Montagna, Janet Robinson, Janet Baker and Linda Goonewardene.

My daughter, Heather Taylor, rescued me whenever I stepped into technological quicksand.

Rebekah Wetmore, whose artistic talent I so appreciate, created the cover design that captured the vision in my head.

Until the Day We Die would not be in your hands without Moose House Publications and the insightful editing of Andrew Wetmore. With each edit, I learned something new. And how I appreciated Andrew's touches of humour along the way.

To each of you, a very special hug-wrapped 'thank you' for what you did to make my late-life dream a reality.

Jockie Loomer-Kruger

About the author

Jockie Loomer-Kruger moved back to Nova Scotia in early 2020, following retirement years spent in Saskatchewan and Ontario. Her return to the town she left forty years earlier came just in time to be locked down in her Truro condo.

Throughout the COVID-19 isolation of 2020 she applied herself to polishing the manuscript of her first novel, and sometimes ducking into her art room to create whimsical folk art paintings.

Jockie describes her working life as a potpourri. She has been a nursery school teacher, receptionist, bookkeeper, florist, and antiques shop owner. Her playtime life has included writing for amateur theatre, *The Globe and Mail, Homemakers, Humanist Perspectives, Folklore,* and *50 Plus Magazine;* and now a novel.

She wrote, illustrated, and self-published her first book, *Valley Child—A Memoir* (2016), the year she turned 80, with support from the Region of Waterloo Arts Fund. In the summer of 2020 she donated the book rights and her 33 original folk-art illustrations to the West Hants Historical Society Museum in Windsor, Nova Scotia.

She has two daughters in Nova Scotia; and a son, daughter-in-law and two grandchildren in Ontario.

Website: **www.jockie.ca**

Contact the author: **jockie.novel@gmail.com**

CPSIA information can be obtained
at www.ICGtesting.com
Printed in the USA
BVHW062007070122
625635BV00003B/4